THE REGENCY
LORDS & LADIES
COLLECTION

**Glittering Regency Love Affairs
from your favourite historical authors.**

THE REGENCY LORDS & LADIES COLLECTION

Available from the
Regency Lords & Ladies Large Print Collection

TEN GUINEAS
ON LOVE

Claire Thornton

First published in Great Britain 1992
Large Print Edition 2009
Harlequin Mills & Boon Limited,
Eton House, 18-24 Paradise Road, Richmond, Surrey TW9 1SR

© Alice Thornton 1992
(Originally published in Great Britain in 1996
under the name Alice Thornton).

ISBN: 978 0 263 21043 9

Set in Times Roman 15¼ on 17 pt.
083-0809-81400

Harlequin Mills & Boon policy is to use papers that are natural, renewable and recyclable products and made from wood grown in sustainable forests. The logging and manufacturing process conform to the legal environmental regulations of the country of origin.

Printed and bound in Great Britain
by CPI Antony Rowe, Chippenham, Wiltshire

Chapter One

"Mr Canby! Are you telling me that unless we can find *twenty thousand* pounds by the end of the month we are going to lose our home?" Charity demanded.

"I—er—that is to say—yes, Miss Mayfield," the attorney replied miserably.

For a moment there was silence as Charity gazed at Mr Canby in disbelief and Mr Canby stared dismally at the faded library carpet.

"Why?" said Charity at last.

"Your father used Hazelhurst as security for a loan," Mr Canby explained. "According to the terms of the agreement, he had one year to repay the money, with the total sum due on the first of March 1766—but unfortunately he was killed within two days of signing the agreement."

"Yes, I understand that," said Charity impatiently. She was holding a copy of the document in her hand. "What I don't understand is why he borrowed the money in the first place—and why it is only now, nearly a year later, that you tell us about it."

The attorney began to look rather hunted.

"It…it's entirely my fault," he stammered. "I knew about the agreement from the beginning—I'm sure Mr Mayfield meant to repay…but then he was…and it was at that time that our youngest died…and Mrs Canby so upset—I really feared for her. Everything to do with business went clean out of my head."

His distress was so palpable that when he briefly raised his eyes to Charity's face she found herself nodding reassuringly at him.

Her father had died almost eleven months ago, and at nearly the same time the Canbys had lost their last and youngest child. Mrs Canby had been hysterical with grief—for a while it had been feared that she might never regain her reason—and Mr Canby had been distracted with anxiety on her behalf. It was understandable if he had temporarily neglected his work.

The attorney sighed, grateful for Charity's forbearance, and continued with his explanation.

"The document got lost under other papers and by the time I could attend to things properly I…I'm afraid I'd forgotten it. I only found it again yesterday evening. I came at once. I hope… I'm sorry." He fell once more into dejected silence.

"I see," said Charity. She walked over to the window and stared out at the snow-covered garden.

February snow. By the beginning of March she and her mother would have to leave Hazelhurst. The glare of reflected sunlight hurt her eyes and when she turned back to Mr Canby the room seemed very dark in comparison.

"I still don't understand what can have prompted Papa to make such an agreement," she said. "I didn't even know he knew the Earl…" she paused, glancing down at the document in her hand, searching for the name "…the Earl of Ashbourne," she continued. "What did he want the money for? And how did he think he was going to re-pay it?"

The enormity of the situation was finally coming home to Charity and her voice rose as she asked the last question.

The attorney shuffled his feet and concentrated his attention on the carpet. He'd been hoping to avoid the need to explain that part of the story.

"I think…I believe…"

The clock on the mantel suddenly began to chime the hour, and Mr Canby started with surprise. He looked up at the clock-face, almost as if he expected to find the answer to Charity's question there, and, without quite realising what he was doing, he began to count the chimes.

…Eight, nine, ten. Ten o'clock in the morning, and all was not well.

"Mr Canby!"

"It was a gambling debt," he said desperately.

"A gambling debt. Dear God!" Charity sat down suddenly and put her hands up to her face.

She had been hoping that, although her father had borrowed the money, he hadn't had time to spend it. She'd been hoping that they might be able to recover it and use it to repay the loan—but if it was a gambling debt it was gone forever.

Mr Canby looked down at her anxiously, but her face was hidden from him. All he could see were the wayward dark curls which, despite the prevailing fashion, she invariably wore unpowdered. She was a pretty, vivacious girl, with expressive hands that she used to emphasise everything she said. But today she seemed unnaturally still and her usually merry brown eyes looked strained and sombre when she raised her head and smiled bleakly at Mr Canby.

"That's it, then," she said. "I was hoping...but never mind. We must start making arrangements for the move. Can you...?" She stopped abruptly, an arrested expression in her eyes.

"What about the money Uncle Jacob left me?" she asked suddenly, wondering why she hadn't remembered it at once. "Isn't there some way we could use that to pay the debt?"

"Not until you are thirty," Mr Canby replied. "Mr Kelland's will is very clear on that point."

"And I couldn't borrow, using it as security?" Charity frowned, wishing her uncle hadn't been quite so firmly convinced that wisdom could only be acquired with age.

The attorney pursed his lips and shook his head slowly.

"Possibly, he said, "but, even if you could find a lender who would agree to such terms, I wouldn't advise such a course. A great deal could happen in the next seven years—and I'm sure that Mr Mayfield would not have wanted you to burden yourself with such a debt."

Mr Canby winced a little as he said those last few words—whatever Mr Mayfield's intentions might have been, he had hardly set his daughter a good example—but Charity simply nodded. Her immediate impulse was to do anything she could to save the family estate, but she had no desire to take on an enormous debt that she would be unable to repay for years to come.

"You won't be destitute," Mr Canby pointed out, glad that the situation was not totally black. "There's still your mother's jointure and the quarterly allowance Mr Kelland left to you. You will be able to live quite comfortably—but not here." Mr Canby bit his lip; he didn't think his words of reassurance had helped much.

"No, not here," said Charity.

Then she remembered her duties as a hostess and managed to smile at the attorney.

"I'm sorry, Mr Canby, I haven't offered you any refreshment, and it's a bitter day to be out," she said. "Would you like some tea, or perhaps some brandy? It's a fair ride back to Horsham."

"No, no, thank you, Miss Mayfield," he replied uncomfortably, thinking how like Charity it was to be thinking of his comfort even at such a time. In all her dealings with him, both before and after the death of her father, she had been unfailingly generous and good-natured. She deserved better than this, Mr Canby thought wretchedly.

So did Mrs Mayfield, of course, but Mr Canby had always found her a more difficult woman and he had been secretly rather glad that a minor indisposition had kept her in bed that morning and obliged him to make his explanations directly to Charity. Charity could always be relied upon to listen rationally to what was said to her.

"I'm so sorry!" he burst out suddenly. "If only I'd remembered sooner…"

"Perhaps it was better that you didn't," Charity said quickly. She'd had enough of the attorney's regrets and self-recriminations. All she wanted now was to be left alone so that she could think, but she was too kind-hearted to dismiss Mr Canby without saying anything to assuage his guilt.

"There was nothing we could have done and we've had nearly an extra year here without having to worry about the future," she pointed out. "Now, have you heard from Lord Ashbourne yet?"

"No," Mr Canby replied, gazing at her in some bewilderment. Her brisk assumption of a business-like manner rather confounded him.

"Then I think you'd better contact him," said Charity. "I'd also like you to come back tomorrow when I've had time to consider the situation in more detail. There will be a great many arrangements to make—and I must also tell Mama…"

She paused, and he suddenly saw that her eyes were suspiciously bright. She was very close to tears, though she was doing her best to hide it.

"Of course," he said quietly. "I'll see myself out."

He turned to go, then paused with his hand on the door-handle as he remembered something.

"I meant to tell you—there will be other changes in the neighbourhood soon," he said. "I heard only yesterday that Lord Riversleigh is dead."

"Lord Riversleigh? Good heavens!" said Charity faintly. At any other time the fortunes of her neighbours, even those of one she disliked as much as Lord Riversleigh, would have been of considerable interest to her. Now she hardly cared.

"What did he die of? Apoplexy?" she asked, with rather disconcerting bluntness.

Lord Riversleigh's bad temper and feuds had been a byword for miles around. He'd given every indication of having loathed his one surviving son, and Charity had good reason to know that his treatment of his grandson had been no better.

"His carriage overturned in London," Mr Canby replied, reflecting that no one could accuse Miss Charity of being mealy-mouthed.

"Mr Harry Riversleigh was also with him. I think they were both killed. Of course, I may have been misinformed," he added pedantically, "but I don't think I was. No doubt we'll be seeing Master Edward—I mean, Lord Riversleigh back at the Hall before long. Well, I must be going. Please let me know if there's any way I can be of assistance to you. Good day, Miss Mayfield."

He closed the library door quietly, unconcerned that Charity hardly seemed to be aware that he was leaving and rather pleased with himself that even at such a black moment he had been able to give a new direction to her thoughts. Everyone knew that Miss Charity and young Edward Riversleigh had always been uncommonly friendly.

For a while after Mr Canby had gone Charity continued to be preoccupied by his final piece of news, partly because at that moment she would have welcomed anything that distracted her from her own troubles, but mainly because, as Mr Canby had suspected, she was genuinely interested in what happened to Edward.

In her opinion there hadn't been much to choose between Harry Riversleigh and his father: one had been an elderly tyrant, the other a middle-aged bully; she couldn't pretend to grieve for either of them.

Edward, on the other hand, she most definitely liked, and she was glad that for once he seemed to be having good luck. Harry had never married, and Edward was the child of the late Lord Riversleigh's youngest son. He had been orphaned at an early age and he had been brought up at Riversleigh Hall in an atmosphere of contention, his wishes constantly thwarted by his uncle or his grandfather. In the circumstances, it said a great deal for Edward that he should have grown into a generous and likeable man. Charity thought he deserved his good fortune and she was pleased for him—then she remembered that she wasn't likely to be there to see him enjoy it, and she sighed.

The library seemed cold and she was more aware than ever of the draughts coming in through the cracks in the mullioned windows. The heavy curtains stirred restlessly as a particularly large gust of wind hit the corner of the house, and outside the snow began to drift. If the weather continued so the roads would become impassable. It wasn't a good time to have to leave one's home.

When Charity entered her mother's room Mrs Mayfield was sitting up in bed, a shawl wrapped round her shoulders and a cup of chocolate in her hands. She had taken a chill the previous day and the cold weather had inclined her to stay in bed longer than usual. She smiled when she saw her daughter and patted the edge of her bed invitingly.

"Hello, love. Come and sit down. Tabby tells me we had a visitor this morning—Mr Canby. I'm glad I missed him. Such a well-meaning man, but he does fidget me so. What did he want? You look cold. Good heavens, your hands are like ice. What *have* you been doing? Why don't you ring for some chocolate?"

"I am a little cold," Charity acknowledged, grateful for her mother's habit of never requiring an answer to more than one or two of the questions that invariably formed such a large part of her conversation. "I think the wind must be in the east; it's certainly very draughty in the library."

"I hate winter." Mrs Mayfield shivered and instinctively pulled her shawl more tightly about her, though in fact her room was one of the cosiest in the house. Her dislike of the cold was well known and her maid, Tabitha, always made sure that the fire was blazing in the hearth before she allowed her mistress to venture from her bed.

"Well, perhaps the cold weather will soon be over," said Mrs Mayfield hopefully when Charity, did not immediately reply to her previous comment. "Tabby told me she saw several snowdrops yesterday. Spring must be on its way."

"Yes, Mama." Charity tried to smile. "I saw them as well. I'll pick you some later."

"Thank you, dear. Oh, I *do* hope the weather improves," said Mrs Mayfield, her gentle voice running on without pause. "I'm so looking forward to the Leydons' party, and if the weather is too bad we won't be able to go. Though it will be worse if it rains, of course. Nothing is as bad for the roads as a flood. I still haven't forgotten that dreadful time when I went to London with your father and the coach got stuck above the axles in the mud and there was no inn for *five miles!* I had to wait in the most *uncomfortable* cottage for *hours* before we could continue our journey."

"Papa said it was only forty-five minutes," Charity said mildly.

"It was nearly three hours," said Mrs Mayfield firmly. "You should have known better than to believe what *Papa* had to say on such a matter. You know how he always used to make light of even the most dreadful situations."

"He was an optimist," said Charity. "Mama, there's something I have to tell you."

"Really, dear? Do you know, I've been wondering what I ought to wear to Sir Humphrey's party? Do you think that gown I had made up in Horsham last November would—"

"Mama!" Charity interrupted, suddenly unable to endure her mother's flow of gentle chatter any longer.

"Yes, love?" Mrs Mayfield said in surprise. Then she saw the look on Charity's face and her own expression altered abruptly. "What is it?" she asked.

Charity hesitated, then she gripped her hands tightly together, took a deep breath and began to tell Mrs Mayfield what Mr Canby had told her.

It was late that evening before Charity could even consider going to bed. Mr Canby's news had thrown the whole household into turmoil. Not only Mrs Mayfield but the servants too were anxious about their future, and no sooner had Charity managed to calm her mother than she had had to face worried questions from the housekeeper.

She had done her best to reassure Mrs Wendle, but she was ruefully aware that she hadn't entirely succeeded. She was also resigned to the fact that soon the whole parish would know of their troubles. It wouldn't be long before they received visits from the more sympathetic—or curious—of their neighbours. She could only hope the cold weather would keep them at home for as long as possible.

She sighed, and put another log on the library fire. Everyone else was in bed but now she needed time alone to think, and for some reason she'd always felt more at peace surrounded by the shelves of old books than she did in any other room in the house.

The wind had died down, but she knew that if she pulled back the curtains she would see large white flakes of snow, falling down against the darkness beyond. She tucked up her feet beneath her, rested her chin on her hand, and gazed into the fire as she considered ways and means.

Whatever they did would be up to her. Mrs Mayfield had never been a decisive woman, and ever since the death of her husband she had increasingly allowed Charity to take on the responsibility for managing their affairs. It was a task which Charity relished and, even now, she was aware of a small spark of excitement at the thought of the new challenge she had been set. Somehow she would manage, not only for her mother, but for everyone on the Hazelhurst estate.

It was well past midnight when she finally thought of a way to do it.

She turned the plan over in her mind a couple of times in case there was a flaw, then, with typical energy, she set about executing it.

She'd been sitting in the firelight, but now she lit a candle and put it on the desk while she found the necessary materials to write a letter. She moved the candle once, so that it cast no shadow upon the paper, dipped the pen in the ink, and began to cover the sheet with bold, confident writing.

My dear friend,

Today I heard the news of your unexpected change of fortune and I write at once to congratulate you. I dare say that perhaps I ought to commiserate with you also, but we know each other too well for such *commonplace* utterances to be necessary. I don't suppose there is a single person at Riversleigh Hall, or on the rest of the estate for that matter, who is not thanking heaven that it is you, not Harry, who will be their new master.

I wish that I need do no more than send you my congratulations but, unfortunately, on the same day that I learnt of your advancement I received news which may have disastrous consequences for all of us here at Hazelhurst. However, on reflection I think the coincidence may be fortuitous, and that, now you are Lord Riversleigh, it may be possible for us to be of mutual service to each other.

Just before he died, Papa ran up monstrous gambling debts and now—because, of course, we can't pay them—his entire property is forfeit! We have to leave Hazelhurst within the month! You can't think what a relief it is to be able to tell that to someone who won't moan and wring their hands and say, "But Miss Charity, what are we going to *do?*"

Poor Mrs Wendle; it must have come as a dreadful shock to her—she's been living at Hazelhurst for more than forty years, ever since she first began as a chambermaid. Well, none of that's relevant now, of course.

Charity paused briefly, biting the end of the pen. In the relief of being able to express herself freely she had nearly strayed completely from the point, and it was going to cost Edward enough to receive this letter without her adding unnecessary digressions. She dipped the pen in the ink again and carried on writing.

At first I didn't know what we should do, but, after thinking about it, I believe I might have come up with a solution. One that may be of benefit to both of us—you as well.

Do you remember Mama's brother, Jacob Kelland, who'd been sent to India in disgrace years ago? The one who suddenly turned up here at Hazelhurst about three years ago and demanded to be taken in? He was such a fusspot. He drove Mama to distraction, worrying about the price of candles, and when he started telling Papa how to manage the estate Papa was provoked into saying that India must have ruined his disposition, as well as his health and his fortune! Anyway, he stayed for weeks—we thought we'd never get rid of him—then one morning we got up to find that he'd left in the night without even telling us; it was so peculiar—and not at all polite—but Mama was relieved. Though, I must admit, I quite liked him—he used to make me laugh.

Oh, dear, I've wandered off the point again. The point is that Mama and I found out only last autumn that he hadn't been poor at all. He knew that his health had been undermined by the Indian climate and he suddenly took a quixotic notion into his head to come back to England—posing as a poor man—and see which of his relatives most deserved to inherit his fortune! When he'd made his decision he didn't tell anyone, he just went back to India and carried on getting richer until he died! It's hard to believe he was Mama's brother.

Anyway, for some reason he decided that I was the most trustworthy person to receive his worldly goods. That's how he described me in his will—trustworthy.

Charity paused again, remembering the less than courteous epithets which her uncle had used to describe her parents. She didn't intend to share those with anyone—even Edward. She continued.

I'm afraid I've been gossiping on here, but I'll try to make the rest briefer. Uncle Jacob left me his entire fortune, but I cannot have access to it until I am thirty—or until I am married. Apparently he didn't think I was *that* trustworthy!

Anyway, Mama and I agreed not to tell anyone about it, because I'm happy as we are, and I don't want my *prospects* to be more attractive to the people I meet than I am.

But now it occurs to me that I can save Hazelhurst myself—if only I can find a husband before the end of February!

I know that an early marriage has never been part of your plans. And I suspect that, even now, you are more concerned with pursuing your studies than you are with other, more worldly considerations—but, even so, I think Uncle Jacob's fortune may be able to serve both our interests.

It's no secret that Riversleigh is mortgaged to the hilt and, however conscientiously you may discharge your duties, it will be years before the estate is back on its feet. Such a situation can only be to your disadvantage, particularly as your interests lie elsewhere.

If you were to marry me, Uncle Jacob's fortune

could buy back Hazelhurst, release Riversleigh from the most crippling of its debts, and still provide you with sufficient funds to visit Rome and the other places you have been longing to see.

I dare say that it is very *unladylike* for me to make such a suggestion, but it does seem to me to be an extremely *practical* solution to both our problems, and I do hope that you will agree to it.

Yours hopefully
Charity

She signed the letter boldly and was just about to fold and seal it when she suddenly thought of something and opened the paper up again.

PS The lease on Bellow's farm has now expired and, since Mr Bellow had decided to go and live with his daughter in Middlesex, you will need to look for a new tenant. Your grandfather favoured Cooper, but both Mr Guthrie and I think Jerry Burden would be a much better choice. I hope you will look into this matter *as soon as possible* because it is not profitable to you or Jerry to leave the farm untenanted for long.

She glanced quickly through what she had written, refolded the letter, sealed it and wrote the direction on the outside. Then she sat back with a sigh of satisfaction that she had at least done something towards saving Hazelhurst. Now all she had to do was send the letter off and wait for Edward to reply.

Chapter Two

"Good morning, Mr Guthrie. Isn't it a lovely day?"

"Aye, so it is, Miss Charity," replied Mr Guthrie, the land agent for the Riversleigh estate. "Though I'm told all this melted snow has rendered the roads well nigh impassable halfway to London."

"But the sky is blue, the sun is shining and I've found some snowdrops. Look!" Charity held the flowers up in the bright morning light for the land agent to see. "Who cares about a little mud?" she finished exultantly. It was true that earlier that morning she had been quite worried in case the mail-coach foundered. But out in the sunshine her doubts could not linger, and now she was convinced that it would not be long before Edward would be reading her letter.

It was only two days since Mr Canby had visited, but the weather had broken and Charity had been unable to stay indoors a moment longer. She had gone out into the garden and then, enticed by the crisp fresh air, she had walked down the drive to the gate. It had been while she was standing there that Mr Guthrie had passed by.

The land agent's dour expression softened slightly as he looked down at Charity and the fragile blooms she held in her hand.

"I've always had a fondness for the brave wee flowers, growing in the snow," he said, managing to give the impression that he was rather ashamed to admit to such a weakness; then he swung down stiffly from his horse.

"Does your leg hurt?" Charity asked, concerned to see how awkwardly the land agent was moving.

"No, no. Mebbe the cold weather aggravates it—but nothing to speak of," he said impatiently, his Scottish accent more pronounced than usual.

"So don't *fuss,* woman!" Charity finished for him.

Mr Guthrie looked at her disapprovingly. "You ought to mind that pert tongue of yours," he said. "One day it will get you into trouble."

"It already has—many times," Charity agreed, undaunted by the grim expression on his weather-beaten face. "Would you like some snowdrops?"

Without waiting for a reply, she stood on tiptoe and carefully inserted a small bunch of flowers into Mr Guthrie's buttonhole.

"Thank you," he said gruffly. "Is it true you must

leave Hazelhurst?" he continued, his sharp eyes scanning her face intently as she stepped back to admire her handiwork. "You're looking more cheerful than I had expected."

"There, it's amazing what a difference a buttonhole can make," Charity said. "If you'd only smile a bit more often you'd look quite festive. Yes, it's true. But I hadn't expected the news to get out *quite* so soon."

"You sent Charles to post a letter for you yesterday. I dare say the whole village knows by now," said Mr Guthrie drily.

"So I did; I'd forgotten that," Charity said ruefully. "Never mind, it was bound to come out sooner or later, and I dare say people will lose interest very quickly. I think *your* news is much more dramatic. It must have been a terrible shock to you, Lord Riversleigh and Mr Riversleigh being killed at the same time like that," she added in her forthright manner.

"It was," said the land agent grimly. "There'll be great changes at Riversleigh now, I don't doubt."

"For the better, surely?" said Charity.

She had known Mr Guthrie for a long time and she was well aware that he had shared her dislike for his late master. In fact, she had often wondered why the land agent had remained at Riversleigh, and she had been sure he would be pleased with the unexpected course of events.

"I know Edward's always dreaming of designing

the perfect building," she said, "but he must be an improvement on his grandfather!"

"Aye, but…"

"Miss Charity! Miss Charity! Mrs Wendle says, please can you come at once?" A maid came running down the drive towards them, stumbling over her gown in her haste.

Mr Guthrie's mare shied back and tossed her head nervously, and the land agent seized her bridle and spoke soothingly to her while Charity turned to greet the girl.

"What is it?" she asked.

"It's Mrs Mayfield," Ellen gasped. "She was trying to decide which furniture to take and she got upset! Please come quickly, miss!"

"Of course. Excuse me, Mr Guthrie." Charity smiled briefly but warmly at the land agent, then she picked up her skirts and ran back to the house, with Ellen following behind her.

Mr Guthrie watched until she had disappeared, then he sighed and put his foot in the stirrup and dragged himself into the saddle. He had broken his right leg in a riding accident nearly fifteen years ago and it was aching more than usual today. I must be getting old, he thought; but he'd known Charity since she was a child, and he was going to miss her.

"Miss Charity!"

"I'm here, Charles. What is it?" Charity looked up

as the footman picked his way towards her through the crowded and dusty attic.

It was nearly a week later and Charity had finally persuaded her mother that it would do her good to visit the Leydons, and now she was taking advantage of Mrs Mayfield's absence to sort through the attic, trying to decide if there was anything up there worth taking with them.

"Lord Riversleigh is here to see you, miss!" Charles announced, and, even in the gloom, Charity thought she caught sight of a conspiratorial gleam in his eyes.

Charles had only been working at Hazelhurst for a few months, but he was already devoted to Charity and it had been he who had posted the letter for her. She had asked him not to tell anyone else she was writing to Lord Riversleigh and, as far as she was aware, he had not done so. But no doubt someone must have told him she had always been on very friendly terms with Edward Riversleigh. Never mind; if her plan succeeded he was welcome to share some of the credit.

"He's in the library, miss," said Charles as he followed Charity out of the attic. "That being the only room apart from Mrs Mayfield's where a fire's been lit."

"Thank you, Charles," Charity called over her shoulder. In her haste she was already halfway down the stairs and she didn't pause in her headlong flight until she had burst impetuously through the library door.

"Edward! I'm so pleased you could..." She stopped short.

The tall man standing by the window was not Edward Riversleigh. Edward could never have appeared so casually elegant, nor could he have imposed his presence on a room so completely that his surroundings faded into insignificance. Yet the stranger had done nothing dramatic, he had simply turned at the sound of the opening door and looked at Charity; but, as her eyes met his, she was instantly aware that he possessed an aura of strength and sophistication which seemed quite out of place in the small, comfortably shabby library.

"I...I beg your pardon, sir," she stammered, dazedly wondering how Charles could possibly have mistaken this man for the far from grand Edward. "I was expecting someone else. How... how do you do? May I help you?" she finished rather breathlessly.

"Thank you, you are very kind," the gentleman replied, and even in her confusion Charity could not help noticing that his voice was deep and melodious. "But I am afraid it is I who should apologise to you."

He came towards her as he spoke and as the light

from the window fell on his face she could see that he had grey eyes, a firm chin and a decisive mouth.

He halted before her and bowed courteously over the hand she instinctively offered him.

"You...you *should?*" Charity said, still somewhat confused by his presence, and disconcertingly aware of the firm clasp of his fingers on hers.

"Certainly." The gentleman straightened up and released her hand. His expression was grave, but there was a distant glint of amusement in his grey eyes as he looked at Charity, though she was far too bewildered to notice it.

"I believe I have the honour of addressing Miss Mayfield...Miss Charity Mayfield?" he said, his eyebrow lifting enquiringly as he spoke.

"Yes, but..."

"It's always wise to make certain of these things, don't you think?" he continued smoothly. "My name is Jack Riversleigh."

"Jack Riversleigh?" Charity echoed, staring up at him blankly.

"Richard's son," he explained. "Richard was the late Lord Riversleigh's second son."

"Oh!" Charity gazed, open-mouthed, at her unexpected visitor, still so stunned that it was several minutes before she understood the significance of what he had said.

"You mean *you* come before Edward in the succession?" she said at last."

"I'm afraid so," he agreed.

"But I thought Richard died in disgrace years ago!" Charity burst out, losing some of her awe in her amazement at this remarkable turn of events.

Lord Riversleigh smiled.

"My father died in the most respectable of circumstances seventeen years ago," he said. "I believe it was only the late Lord Riversleigh who held him in such aversion."

"I'm sorry." Charity blushed, painfully aware of what a poor impression she must be making. "I didn't mean to be rude. It's just that…it's all rather surprising. Good grief!" she exclaimed suddenly. "You must have received my letter!"

"Yes, ma'am," Jack Riversleigh said gently. "It was that which prompted my visit today. I thought, in the circumstances, you would prefer to be appraised of your misapprehension in private."

"Oh, how dreadful!" Charity put up her hands to her burning cheeks and closed her eyes, not really listening to what he was saying as she realised with horror that she had proposed marriage to a stranger!

"Come, I think you should sit down," he said, and he guided her unresistingly to a chair. "You've had quite a shock."

"No, no, I'm all right," she said mechanically.

Her thoughts were in such a turmoil of confusion and embarrassment that she hardly knew what to say—or do—but almost instinctively she sought refuge in her role as hostess.

"I'm so sorry, I should have invited you to sit down, my lord," she said with an attempt at polite formality, which she immediately spoiled by bursting out impetuously, "Oh, dear! You must have formed the most *dreadful* impression of me!"

"No." Suddenly, and quite unexpectedly, he laughed. "No, Miss Mayfield, dreadful is not the word I would have used. I apologise for startling you; I should have introduced myself less baldly."

Charity looked at him doubtfully. Then she smiled hesitantly. Now that her first shock was receding she could see that the strength in his face was tempered by humour, and she began to feel slightly more at ease with him. She thought that perhaps it was his fine black coat which had made him seem so grand—and then realised almost immediately that he must be in mourning for his grandfather.

She felt relieved to have discovered the reason for her unexpected lack of composure earlier, and instantly resolved never to be impressed by fine clothes again. Then, just as she was about to make a polite comment on the weather, or the state of the roads, or some other bland, innocuous topic—to indicate her own level of unconcern and sophistication—it suddenly dawned on her that he was finding the situation amusing, and she began to feel flustered all over again.

She raised startled and rather alarmed eyes to his— and then began to feel more comfortable as she realised that, although he was certainly amused, he was equally definitely not gloating over her discomfiture. She even thought she detected a gleam of sympathy in his expression.

She thought ruefully that he might well find it amusing to receive a proposal of marriage from a woman whose existence he had hitherto been completely unaware of and cursed herself for not having addressed the letter more precisely.

"Good," he said when he saw she had recovered at least partially from her initial astonishment. "I was sure you would have too much presence of mind to be overset by my visit. I believe, in fairness to you, I ought to explain how this peculiar situation has arisen—if you're interested?"

"Oh, yes!" said Charity, leaning forward eagerly and momentarily forgetting her embarrassment in her desire to find out just how it had come about that Riversleigh had been inherited by a complete stranger. "Oh, I beg your pardon." She blushed again as she suddenly remembered all her mother's lectures on decorum. In a belated attempt to make amends for her unmannerly interest she sat up straight and folded her hands demurely in her lap. "I mean, thank you, that would be very kind of you."

Jack smiled. He had been slightly concerned by

Charity's earlier evident confusion, but now that she had regained much of her composure his amusement at the situation in which he found himself had revived, though he was careful not to show it too openly. He was also slightly surprised by the lack of interest she had so far shown in the fate of the man she had just proposed to. It did not seem to suggest that her heart was inextricably bound to Edward.

"Well, as I said before," he began, "my father, Richard, was the late Lord Riversleigh's second son, and Edward's father was his third son. But my father left Riversleigh thirty years ago, and when he did so Lord Riversleigh declared that as far as he was concerned he now had only two sons—Richard was dead to him."

"How *inhuman!*" Charity gasped, her eyes fixed on Jack's face, her dark curls dancing with indignation. "I *never* liked him! He behaved most unkindly to Edward for no good reason at all. Was there any reason for him to dislike your papa? Oh, dear! I mean…I mean…" She floundered to a halt, uncomfortably aware that once again she had allowed her tongue to run away with her.

"No," said Jack. "My father refused to be ruled by my grandfather, but he never behaved dishonourably."

"I never suspected he did!" Charity exclaimed indignantly. "Lord Riversleigh disliked Edward for being conscientious in his studies—and if that isn't a crackbrained attitude for a guardian to hold I don't know what is!"

"Quite." Jack's lips twitched, but he maintained an admirable gravity. "Anyway, my father married my mother not long after he left Riversleigh and, no doubt much to Lord Riversleigh's annoyance, I was one of the consequences."

"Did he know you existed?" Charity asked curiously. The workings of the late Lord Riversleigh's mind had always been a mystery to her; she had never understood how he could be so cruel to those who should be closest to him.

"Oh, yes," Jack replied. "I met him once, after my father died. I made it my business to do so—I wanted to know what kind of man he was—but when he discovered who I was he refused to acknowledge me. It didn't greatly concern me. I had no idea that I might eventually succeed him."

"Nor had anyone else," said Charity. "At least... Edward didn't know, did he?"

"No," Jack said. "I believe my grandfather gave orders that my father's name was never to be mentioned again. Over the years people must have forgotten, and even those who did know wouldn't have spoken of the matter."

"Of course not," said Charity. "He could be quite... Poor Edward; I wonder what he'll do now."

In her first amazement she had not considered how

Edward must feel about the whole thing, but now she felt sad that once more he had been unlucky. She stood up and walked over to the window, looking out at the holly tree that stood up against the blue sky beyond.

"You mustn't think I'm not pleased for you, my lord," she said. "But it must have been rather hard on Edward. Not that he wanted the title, but even if he hadn't accepted my propo— I mean, at the very least the revenues of the estate could probably have provided him with a trip to Rome... Where is he?"

She swung round to face Jack as she suddenly realised that, interesting though all this was, she still didn't have the one piece of information which was essential for the success of *her* plans.

"I'm afraid he's already on his way to Italy," Jack said quietly, watching Charity's face carefully as he spoke.

He suspected that this news would be a great disappointment to her and, though he was not above being amused by the situation, he was reluctant to give her tidings which he was afraid would cause her real distress.

"Italy? But how on earth...?"

"As you said, it was something he'd wanted to do for a long time," Jack continued smoothly. "I believe when he had the opportunity the excitement drove all other thoughts from his head. I'm sure he'll be writing to you soon."

"You mean, someone's going to help him in his

efforts to become an architect?" Charity asked incredulously.

"Yes."

"Oh, I'm so glad!" she exclaimed, forgetting her own problems in her relief at Edward's good fortune. "He's worked so hard, and had so little support. He'll enjoy that much more than being Lord Riversleigh!"

"I hope so," said Jack, relieved at Charity's reaction.

"He will," Charity assured him. "Last time I saw him he insisted on reading me extracts from a book he'd just acquired about the ruins of some palace at Spal... Spally..."

"Spalatro," Jack supplied. "I believe you mean the book by Robert Adam on *The Ruins of the Palace of the Emperor Diocletian at Spalatro in Dalmatia.*"

"That's it!" said Charity. "How on earth did you know?"

"I've read it," said Jack apologetically.

"Oh." She looked at him blankly. "Are you an architect too, sir?"

"No, but I've always been interested in a variety of different crafts. It's important not to have too narrow a viewpoint," Jack said, and changed the subject abruptly. "At the risk of being impertinent, may I ask you a question, Miss Mayfield?"

"Of course. What is it?" Charity glanced at him apprehensively, suddenly reminded that he had read her letter and consequently knew far more about her than she might have wished.

"Are you very disappointed by the turn of events?" he asked. "As I'm sure you've realised, I'm afraid I read your letter. I must apologise for that—I don't make a habit of reading other people's correspondence, and I assure you I will treat what I read in confidence—but at first I didn't quite know what to make of it." He paused.

"No, I understand," said Charity; she looked down at her hands, feeling very self-conscious.

"I hope so. When I realised you'd intended it for Edward I would have forwarded it to him unread, but it seemed as if you needed his assistance urgently *because* he was Lord Riversleigh, so I hoped that I might be able to help instead. I'm sorry that I can't. But if you wish I'll do everything in my power to get your message to him as soon as possible."

"Thank you," she said. "But it would be too late. Edward was my first choice, but I dare say I can manage without him. I shall just have to look about me again."

"You mean, you're going to ask someone *else* to marry you?" Jack had been leaning back negligently in his chair, but he sat up straight at this.

"No," said Charity. "Unfortunately Edward is the only man I know who can be relied upon to be sensible about such things. Next time I must try and persuade *them* to propose to *me*."

"Good God!" said Jack. For the first time during the interview he looked startled—he hadn't expected this. "But what about Edward?"

"What about him?" Charity looked puzzled.

"Less than ten days ago you asked him to marry you!" Jack pointed out.

"Yes, but that was when I thought he was available. He's no good to me in Italy!"

"No, I suppose not," said Jack. He had relaxed again, his surprise giving way to amusement. "I gathered from your letter that you had very little time at your disposal, but I hope you will forgive me if I tell you that you seem to have a rather prosaic view of matrimony."

"No, just practical," Charity replied. "One should always be practical, don't you think?"

"An admirable philosophy," Jack agreed. "May I ask if you have anyone in particular in mind? I imagine the supply of eligible bachelors is fairly limited in this part of Sussex—though being an heiress must widen your choice."

"You mean, you can't imagine why anyone should want me without the sweetener of Uncle Jacob's fortune?" Charity demanded, seizing on his last comment.

"No, of course not!" he replied quickly as he saw the flash in her dark eyes. "I was thinking aloud and what I said was very badly phrased. I only meant that for various reasons most heiresses have, or could have, a wider circle of acquaintances than many other ladies. More—perfectly unexceptional—doors are open to you. That must be useful if you're looking for a husband."

"Possibly," said Charity cautiously. "Lord Riversleigh, may I ask a great favour of you? Until now, nobody apart from Mama and me—and our lawyer, of course—has known about Uncle Jacob's fortune. I didn't want them to. I still don't."

"Yes, I see," said Jack slowly. "You mentioned something about that in your letter; I should have remembered. Don't be alarmed; I'll keep your secret."

"Thank you." She smiled with relief. "As you said, there aren't a great many suitable men in the neighbourhood, but at least I know them, and I needn't worry about their motives if one of them…" She paused, an arrested expression in her eyes. "Yes, yes, definitely," she said after a moment as if she was speaking to herself—which she was. Then she suddenly recollected herself.

"Good heavens! How remiss of me. I haven't even offered you any refreshment. Would you like some tea, my lord? Or some wine?" she asked brightly.

"Thank you." Jack watched her pull the bell, and then allowed her to steer the conversation on to more mundane matters until after Charles had arrived with the tray and then departed, desperate with curiosity to know more of what was happening in the library.

"Is it really essential that you be married?" Jack asked when they were alone again. "I've no wish to appear impertinent, but our acquaintance began in such an unusual way that I trust you won't be offended if I seem a little outspoken."

Charity looked at him suspiciously, but his expression was perfectly grave and it was impossible to accuse him of laughing at her.

"No, it's not essential," she said at last. "But, since you've read my letter, you know why I need a husband."

"To retain your home," he said. "I can understand why you would wish to do that." He looked appreciatively round the library as he spoke. "It's a fine old house. When was it built?"

"Just before the Civil War," Charity replied. "There were Mayfields living here for at least a century before that, but the old house was in a sad state of decay by the beginning of Charles I's reign, and Thomas Mayfield had this one built. That's Thomas there."

She pointed at a portrait hanging on the chimney breast. It was quite a dark, almost a gloomy picture, certainly not by the hand of a master. But somehow it seemed to capture something of the spirit of the man it depicted. He was not a handsome man, but he looked both amiable and sensible—and his gaze was as direct as Charity's.

"Unfortunately he didn't have long to enjoy the house," Charity continued. "He died a few years later, fighting for the Royalist cause, but his baby son inherited it and it's remained in the family ever since."

She sighed, and some of the animation died out of her face. She loved her home, and now that she had recovered from her initial astonishment at Jack Riversleigh's unexpected arrival she was feeling sadly deflated. She hadn't realised until now how much she had been counting on Edward.

"I'm sorry," said Jack. "Is there no other way to save it?"

"No." Charity shook her head.

"I see. It did occur to me that you would have to leave your home anyway, if you were married. Doesn't that rather defeat your purpose?" Jack asked delicately.

"Yes, I know," Charity replied impatiently. "But Mama would be able to continue here, and the rest of the household. It's been their home for so long… Oh, well," she continued more briskly, "I shouldn't be burdening you with our problems, my lord. At least…" She paused, a speculative expression in her eyes as they rested on his face.

"Are you married, sir?" she asked at last.

Jack blinked and then gave a shout of laughter. "No, Miss Mayfield, nor do I have any immediate plans to be. Thank you."

"Are you sure?" said Charity. "After all, the same considerations apply to you as did to Edward. Riversleigh is still mortgaged; it will still be difficult for you to pull it out of debt."

"Miss Mayfield, you don't know me," Jack said more soberly. "Don't think I'm not flattered, but I hope you don't intend to fling yourself at every man you meet until the end of February. That's a sure way to come to grief—particularly if you intend to offer them a fortune at the same time!"

"No, of course not," said Charity impatiently. "You may think I'm a hoyden, but I assure you I'm not entirely lacking in sense. If you had agreed to marry me you would have kept the bargain—wouldn't you?"

"Do you think every man would?" Jack asked, without answering her question.

"No. But I shan't ask one who won't."

"I hope you don't," he said quietly, and stood up. "I must be going; I have already stayed far too long. Thank you for your hospitality. I trust your schemes will meet with success."

"So do I." Charity held out her hand and felt a curious moment of regret as his lips lightly brushed her fingers.

"Who is your next target?" he asked. "You've decided already, haven't you?"

She looked at him consideringly. "I don't think I'll tell you that," she said at last. "You might warn him."

He laughed. "You do me an injustice," he said. "I

look forward with interest to our next meeting. Your servant, Miss Mayfield."

When he was gone the library seemed oddly empty without his presence to fill it. Charity sat in the window-seat and gazed with unfocused eyes at the holly tree. All her plans had been completely overturned and now she would have to begin again, with ten days already wasted.

She was only roused when she heard her mother's voice in the hall and realised Mrs Mayfield had returned from the Leydons'. No doubt she had already heard that Lord Riversleigh had visited. Charity suddenly woke up to the fact that she was going to have to tell her mother that Edward *wasn't* the new Lord Riversleigh, and to explain why *Jack* Riversleigh had come to call!

She gasped and quickly tried to think of an excuse. And by the time the door opened and Mrs Mayfield came into the library she was able to smile at her mother quite calmly, ready for any question.

Chapter Three

The morning after Jack Riversleigh's unexpected visit Charity went out early for a walk. Mrs Mayfield was still in bed and Charity needed some peace away from the house to think. Her mind seemed to be divided: part of her was busy planning for their departure; part of her was hoping they'd never have to leave.

Mr Canby had visited again to tell her that Lord Ashbourne's agent would soon be arriving to discuss the transfer, and Charity was trying to get everything in order before he did so. Mr Canby was doing what he could to help, and Mr Guthrie had offered his services also, but there were a great many things which only Charity *could* do.

Yet all the time she was adding up the household and farm accounts, or overseeing the packing of boxes, a voice in her head kept telling her that none of this was necessary, that everything would turn out fine in the end.

She shook her head irritably in an effort to clear it and walked briskly down the lane. There had been no rain since the last of the snow and, despite Mrs Mayfield's fears and Mr Guthrie's comments, the roads had remained surprisingly good. Charity had only to pick her way round the odd puddle and to avoid those boggy patches which never dried out except during exceptionally fine summers.

She still thought her plan of getting married was a good one, and Lord Riversleigh had been correct when he had suspected that she already had someone in mind.

Owen Leydon was much of an age with Edward Riversleigh and she had known him, like Edward, all her life. He would not have been her first choice—indeed, he hadn't been—but she thought he would suit her purposes very well. The only difficulty was that she would have to adopt more circuitous means to achieve her end. With Edward you could be as blunt as you liked and he wouldn't take offence—but she had always had to coax Owen round to her viewpoint. In fact, there had been occasions when his stubbornness had driven her to distraction, but this time she was determined to be subtle.

The hedges on both sides of the lane were thick and well tended and, because she couldn't see much over the top of them, she was glad when she reached a gate. There was no stock in the field and the gate had been left open, so she walked through it and stood looking out across the rolling farmland—Hazelhurst land. The sun was shining and it was surprisingly warm. It was the kind of morning when Charity found that it was impossible to stay indoors.

She took a deep breath and looked about her. To the right the field was edged by a hazel coppice, and in the centre a huge old oak tree raised its branches to the sky. She had climbed that tree as a child, and every year since she could remember she had come nutting here in autumn. She wondered if Lord Ashbourne liked hazelnuts, but, even if he did, he was unlikely to pick his own.

She would miss this when she left Hazelhurst. She would miss the easy access to the countryside, and the freedom she had always enjoyed there—but it wasn't just memories she would be leaving behind her. She had worked hard and accomplished a great deal in the past few years and now, just as she felt she was really beginning to get somewhere, she had to hand over everything to a stranger.

Hazelhurst was a small estate, consisting only of the home farm and two tenant farms, but in the last few years, even before her father's death, Charity had started to increase its efficiency. It wasn't easy: the heavy Sussex Wealden clay didn't lend itself to all the improvements possible in Norfolk or even further south on the Sussex Downs or coastal regions; and the impatience of her father and the old-fashioned notions of one of the tenants hadn't helped.

But Charity had persisted. She had watched and waited and made tactful suggestions whenever the opportunity arose, coaxing change—never forcing it—and at last she was beginning to see the reward for her patience in the increased yields from all three farms. Only days ago she had been optimistic about the future, busy making plans for further improvements—and now she was to lose it all.

Soon she would be sitting meekly in a shabby drawing-room in a provincial town, with nothing more exciting to think about than her embroidery or the gossip of her neighbours.

I'll go mad, she thought. But, of course, if her plans succeeded she would be married to Owen and living at Leydon House. For a moment her courage failed her—was that really the best solution? The memory of her conversation with Lord Riversleigh rose unbidden in her mind and once again she experienced an unaccountable sense of regret. But then she thought of Mrs Mayfield and Mrs Wendle and all the other people for whom Hazelhurst was home, and her resolve to marry Owen returned. To be sure, her household didn't know she was planning their salvation, but, all the same, she couldn't let them down.

There were catkins in the hedge and she picked some, meaning to take them back for Mrs Mayfield.

In the distance she could hear the sound of hounds in full cry and she was dimly aware that the hunt was out, but it was not until the fox ran straight past her and out through the gate that she realised how close it was. She swung round and saw the first of the hounds racing towards her across the field.

Later she couldn't explain what she did next, but at the time she was only aware of a sudden uncharacteristic anger at the dogs. Perhaps she felt a momentary affinity with the fox because she felt it was being driven from its home in much the same way that she was being driven from hers.

Whether that was the case or not, with Charity thinking inevitably led to action. She dropped the bunch of catkins, heaved the heavy gate up on its hinges and staggered round to close it, letting it fall back in place just as the first of the huntsmen came over the opposite hedge, hard on the heels of the hounds. At the same moment the enormity of what she had done occurred to her—and she realised that she had shut herself in on the wrong side of the gate.

She wasn't frightened of the hounds, but the dogs would be followed by men, and even Charity's courage failed her at the thought of what Sir Humphrey Leydon would have to say about what she'd done!

She began to edge her way along the hedge, hoping that in the heat of the chase no one would notice her.

The hounds had already reached the gate and checked. They couldn't get through it, or below it—it was too low to the ground and the bars were too closely spaced. They whined and spread out on either side of it, forcing their way through gaps in the thick hedge. The first of them were through, but they checked again: they had temporarily lost the scent.

Charity kept walking along the hedge and, to her relief, it seemed that nobody had noticed her, or knew what she had done. She spotted Sir Humphrey and some red-faced tenant farmers and a thin-faced man she didn't recognise, but none of them saw her. They were anxious for the gate to be opened, for the chance to continue the chase.

There was a fuss and some delay. It was a heavy gate, not easily opened from the back of a horse, and one of the whippers-in had to dismount. Then the last of the hounds went through, followed by the riders, and Charity was alone again, listening to the sounds of the retreating hunt.

"Charity! What the *devil* did you do that for? How *dare* you ruin my father's hunt?"

Charity stopped and turned round slowly.

Owen Leydon was riding up behind her—and he was furious.

"I don't know what you mean," she said weakly; she couldn't afford to argue with Owen now!

"I saw you close the gate. How *dare* you do such

a thing?" Owen was almost shaking with rage at what he considered to be her unpardonable interference; and his anger was undoubtedly made worse because until she'd closed the gate they'd been enjoying one of the best chases of the season.

"Oh." She realised he must have been the first rider over the hedge, and she could hardly deny his accusation.

"I…I don't know what came over me," she said, trying to propitiate him, but unfortunately only increasing his anger by her procrastination. "I think I must have been startled when I suddenly saw all those hounds bearing down on me!"

"Nonsense!" Owen might have been conciliated if Charity had made an immediate and frank apology, but he had known her far too long to be convinced by what he considered a very feeble excuse. "I don't believe you. You're no more frightened of the hounds than I am. You were deliberately trying to sabotage the hunt! What were you trying to do? Make my father look like a fool? Don't you know we have an important visitor from London staying with us?"

"Indeed I don't know. How should I?" Any intention Charity might have had to apologise disintegrated completely at this unfounded accusation. "Why *should* I want to ruin your stupid hunt?"

"I don't know," Owen said disagreeably, the heat of his fury having died down into sullen animosity.

"I've never understood the crazy notions you take in your head. But I do know a more contrary, obstinate, self-willed girl can't exist!"

"I beg your pardon?" By now Charity was so rigid with indignation that she hardly cared what she said. "But this is Hazelhurst land you're riding across— and cutting up with all your pounding hoofs—and if I want to close the gate on my own land I have every right to do so!"

"Not when the hounds are running! Well, all I can say is that it's fortunate my father doesn't know what you did. Good day, Miss Mayfield," Owen ended, and wheeled about to follow the hunt without waiting for Charity to reply.

She stepped back to avoid the mud thrown up from the horse's hoofs and tripped over a rut in the ground, falling heavily.

It hurt; but instead of calling out she sat up and rubbed her elbow ruefully, watching Owen disappear through the gate, unaware of her accident.

"And a perfect opportunity missed," said an amused voice behind her.

She looked up quickly to see Lord Riversleigh dismounting from a fine bay gelding.

"Are you hurt, Miss Mayfield?" He pulled the reins over the horse's head and led him over to her.

"No, of course not!" Charity exclaimed, feeling rather annoyed at being discovered in such an undignified position by someone who seemed so very point-device. Nevertheless, she accepted the hand he offered her and allowed him to pull her to her feet.

"Thank you. What are you doing here? What do you mean, 'a perfect opportunity'?" she asked, running one question straight on from the other.

"And I'm delighted to meet *you* again, Miss Mayfield. Very fine weather we're having for the time of year, don't you think?" Jack said, looking at her in some amusement. She was so unselfconsciously outspoken that he found the impulse to tease her irresistible.

Charity blinked at him, then she laughed and held out her hand. "I'm sorry, I've never been very good at polite conversation. How do you do?"

"Very well, thank you." He took her hand and kissed it gracefully, and she felt her fingers tingle at the touch of his lips.

"As to your first question, I was out riding when I heard the sound of the hunt and I thought I'd watch it pass," he explained as he straightened up. "And as to your second...am I by any chance correct in suspecting that that's the young man who is destined to take Edward's place in your plans?"

"What if he is?" Charity asked cautiously. She was trying, ineffectually, to brush the mud and pieces of dead twig from her skirts, and feeling at a decided disadvantage.

"Then I stand by my first opinion: you did indeed miss a perfect opportunity," Jack declared.

"I don't understand," Charity said. She was still feeling ruffled from her encounter with Owen and she wasn't at all sure she cared for the amused expression in Lord Riversleigh's grey eyes. He was so entirely different from the other men she knew that she couldn't predict his reactions at all.

"You should have cried out when you fell," he explained gravely. "A few tears, perhaps a little raillery against his brutish conduct in causing you to fall, and he would have been your devoted servant. You could probably have had the whole thing settled in a trice."

Charity gasped. "How could you think me so ungentlemanly?" she demanded. "It wasn't Owen's fault I fell over. I should scorn to use such devious methods!"

Jack shook his head in mock sadness, an appreciative gleam in his eyes as they rested on the riot of dark curls which framed a face both unselfconsciously pretty and very feminine.

"Then I fear that if you cannot bring yourself to be ungentlemanly in the pursuit of a husband you are destined to remain a spinster, Miss Mayfield," he said.

"I am not!" Charity declared, outraged. "I wager you ten guineas I'm married by the end of the month."

Lord Riversleigh laughed. "Come, allow me to escort you home," he said, and offered her the support of his arm.

She stepped away from him and put her hands behind her back.

"Are you refusing my wager, sir?"

"Well, it's certainly not my habit to make bets on such a subject." Jack looked at her in some exasperation. "Are you coming down to the gate or are you going to try to force your way through the hedge?"

Charity stopped backing away—it was perfectly true that the sharp hawthorn twigs were beginning to dig into her—and looked at him challengingly. "I think you're afraid I'll win," she said scornfully.

There was a moment's silence. Then, "Very well, Miss Mayfield," Lord Riversleigh replied. "I accept your wager. If I lose I'll buy you a wedding present—unless you'd prefer cash."

"Thank you," Charity said regally. "But perhaps you'd better not make the wager after all. I'm afraid you'll soon be sadly out of pocket."

"I hope so, Miss Mayfield," said Jack politely. "I would hate to see you dwindle into an old maid."

For a moment they stared at each other, then Charity laughed and took his proffered arm.

"I wouldn't like it either," she confided. "It wouldn't suit my plans at all. How are you settling in at the Hall? Do you feel at home?"

"I wouldn't say that it much resembles my notion of a home," said Jack precisely as they made their way over the uneven ground towards the gate. "Too much decaying grandeur for my taste. You must realise, I'm a simple man, Miss Mayfield. On the other hand, the people have been very welcoming."

"I expect they're curious," said Charity, without mentioning that his notions of simplicity didn't quite tally with hers. "Besides, *anyone* would be a better master than Lord Riversleigh was, or Harry would have been," she continued.

"It's not what I've been brought up to," said Jack, "but I shall do my best not to disappoint them." And Charity heard an unaccustomed note of seriousness in his voice as he spoke.

"There's no need to come any further with me," she said as they reached the gate. "If you're going back to the Hall our paths lie in opposite directions. Are you really going to do your best for Riversleigh?"

"Certainly." He looked down at her. "I did not ask for the responsibility, but I have no intention of shirking it."

"You could milk the estate for all it's worth and live the high life in London, just like your grandfather," Charity said. "But I hope you won't. Lord Riversleigh was a bad landlord—sometimes I think Mr Guthrie despaired of him."

"Yes, I trust I shall do better than my grandfather," said Jack. He gathered up the reins and swung easily into the saddle.

"Good morning, Miss Mayfield; I hope all your

plans meet with success," he said, but as he glanced down at her upturned face it occurred to him that it might be a pity if she was too successful. His impression of Owen Leydon was necessarily imperfect, but he was afraid that Charity's more unusual and delightful qualities would be wasted on the young man.

"I look forward to our next meeting," he said. "I shall be anxious to hear of your progress with your friend—or shall I say victim?" He smiled at her wickedly and touched his heels to the bay's sides before Charity could think of a suitable response.

She watched him go, fulminating at his impertinence. Then her mood changed abruptly and she sighed. Her conversations with Lord Riversleigh seemed destined to follow unusual channels, but at least he had never exasperated her with his stupidity. How different he was from Owen—or even Edward, who had never been more than half aware of the world around him. But Edward was on his way to Rome, and Owen was the only hope of saving Hazelhurst.

She turned and began to walk home, hoping that she could get back into the house without anyone seeing her, because if they did she'd no doubt be drawn into a tedious explanation about how she had come to be covered in mud. She seemed to be spending all her time at the moment explaining awkward circumstances—and she was annoyed with herself for having lost her temper first with Owen and then a second time with Lord Riversleigh. How could he have provoked her into making such a foolish wager? And now she had to find some way of ingratiating herself with Owen again.

"Well, m'lord?" Mr Guthrie asked, his eyes on Lord Riversleigh's face.

"Not well at all," said Jack. He sat back and looked at the land agent, a book of accounts open on the desk before him. "Even from my cursory glance at the accounts I can see that things are in a bad way and, from my understanding, the whole of Riversleigh is in a run-down or dilapidated state."

"Aye, m'lord," said Mr Guthrie drily.

"Very well." Jack tapped his fingers thoughtfully on the desk once or twice before continuing. "Now, as you know, my experience hitherto has been entirely confined to the City, and, whatever success I might have had there, I am a complete novice at estate management. On the other hand, I see no reason why I shouldn't learn—and my father always spoke very highly of *your* capabilities, so..." suddenly he smiled "...I don't see any reason why between us we can't bring Riversleigh about."

"It won't be easy," the land agent warned. "It needs money to be put into it, not taken out—there'll be no easy profits here."

"Do I look like your idea of a complaisant banker, Guthrie?" Jack asked gently.

"No, m'lord." The land agent looked at him thoughtfully. "I'm bound to say you lack sufficient girth to be convincing in the role."

"Thank you." Lord Riversleigh inclined his head ironically. "I'll need to study the books at greater leisure, of course. And I'd like you to show me over the estate as soon as possible. I have a lot to learn."

"Whenever it's convenient." Mr Guthrie stood up, wincing a little as he took his weight on his bad leg. "There is one matter that should be dealt with urgently, m'lord."

"What is it?"

"You're in need of a tenant for one of your farms. The present lease has expired, and Bellow doesn't want to renew it."

"I see." Jack remembered the reference to Bellow in Charity's letter to Edward; he also remembered her advice as to his choice of tenant, but he didn't mention that the matter was already familiar to him. Instead he asked, "Do you have anyone in mind?"

"Yes, sir. Jerry Burden. He's the eldest son of one of the Mayfields' tenants. He's young, but he's learned a lot from his father, and Sam Burden is one of the best farmers in the area. I think he would be a good choice. Of course..." Mr Guthrie hesitated "...I should tell you that your grandfather disagreed with me," he said at last, somewhat reluctantly. "He favoured Nat Cooper."

"But you didn't," said Jack. "Well, my knowledge of farming may be limited, but I believe I'm a fair judge of men. You say this young man lives on the Mayfield estate? I'll ride over tomorrow and meet him."

"I could have him come to the hall," Mr Guthrie offered.

"No, don't do that; I'd rather meet him on his home ground when he's *not* expecting me."

"Do you wish me to accompany you?"

"Thank you, no. I'll find my own way," Jack said as he stood up. If the luck favoured him—and Jack had a way of influencing his own luck—he might meet Charity again; and he had no particular desire for the land agent to be present at such a meeting.

He had been quite sincere when he had told Charity that he had no immediate plans for marriage, but it was also true that he had found her an extremely stimulating and entertaining companion. He was certainly looking forward to further encounters with her and, though he had no real expectation that her scheme to inveigle Owen into proposing would be successful, their wager gave him an excellent excuse to seek her out. All in all, his stay in Sussex promised to be far more pleasurable than he had anticipated.

He dismissed that train of thought from his mind and said to Guthrie, "I won't need you in the morning, but if you have no other pressing business to attend to I'd like to see the rest of Riversleigh tomorrow afternoon."

"Very well, m'lord." Mr Guthrie bowed stiffly and went out. To all appearances, his new master was a vast improvement on the old, and the land agent had always liked Richard Riversleigh, but Guthrie was not in the habit of making hasty decisions and he would reserve judgement for a little longer.

"Mr Leydon, ma'am," Charles announced.

"Owen! Good heavens! Whatever can he want?" Mrs Mayfield exclaimed. "How very peculiar. Yes, of course, show him in, Charles."

"Mrs Mayfield." Owen bowed punctiliously in her direction and then turned with a hint of awkwardness in his manner to Charity.

"Good evening, Owen," she said cautiously, hoping he wasn't going to say anything embarrassing in front of her mother. She'd told Mrs Mayfield she'd tripped in the lane; she didn't want any more lectures on her unladylike behaviour.

"Charity." He stood in the middle of the room, looking uncomfortable. "I came… I wanted… That's a very pretty cap you're wearing, ma'am," he finished desperately, addressing himself to Mrs Mayfield as his courage failed him.

"Thank you," she smiled, delighted at the compliment. "Won't you sit down? I'll ask Charles to bring us some wine. How dark it is already. These short winter days pass so quickly, don't they? Ring the bell, Charity."

"Yes, Mama." Charity stood up, grateful for an opportunity to hide her face.

"And how is dear Lady Leydon?" Mrs Mayfield said, continuing to address herself to Owen. "To be sure, I only visited her yesterday. She seemed in very good health."

"Yes," said Owen baldly. Then he realised that Mrs Mayfield was looking at him and he stumbled into speech again. "That is to say, I believe she is very well. Lord Travers came to visit us yesterday, and I think she's been looking forward to his arrival."

"Of course; she told me he was coming," Mrs Mayfield said. "I hope I shall have the opportunity of meeting him. But no doubt I shall on the fourteenth."

"The fourteenth?" said Owen, looking as if he hadn't got a clue what she was talking about.

"The day of your party," Mrs Mayfield said reprovingly.

"Oh, the party; yes, of course." Owen took a steadying gulp of his wine. "I'm looking forward to it. I hope…I hope you'll be able to come, Charity." He looked at her, his expression half appealing and half belligerent.

"Of course she'll be there," said Mrs Mayfield,

then she sighed. "Oh, dear, I don't suppose we'll be going to many more parties.

"Of course we will, Mama," Charity said bracingly, but the thought had depressed Mrs Mayfield and she suddenly fell silent. Unfortunately her silence daunted Owen almost as much as her earlier loquacity, and he suddenly jumped to his feet, declaring that he was expected at home.

"Let me fetch your coat," said Charity, taking pity on his obvious desire to speak to her alone. Besides, she wanted the opportunity to further her own plans.

"Thank you," he said. But once they were in the hall he picked up a candle from the small table and pulled her into the front parlour, which was otherwise unlit and unheated.

"Charity, I had to come," he burst into speech. "I meant…I wanted to tell you I didn't mean what I said this morning. I ought to have my tongue cut out! But when I get angry I can't help myself. I hope you'll forgive me." He looked at her miserably, holding the candle at an angle.

"Owen! Of course I do!" Charity exclaimed, genuinely touched by his generosity. She took the candle away from him as she spoke and made a mental note that she must get Ellen to scrape the melted wax from the carpet tomorrow. "Besides, it was all my fault. I behaved abominably."

"No, you didn't," he said, not necessarily because

he believed it, but rather because he hated them to be at odds with one another, and Sir Humphrey had always told him to make allowances for the peculiar fancies of the weaker sex. "I said some terrible things in the heat of the moment… I'm sure your motives were excellent—but what on earth made you shut the gate? You must have known it would spoil the sport!" he finished, forgetting some of his good intentions.

Charity was just about to make a sharp retort when she remembered that not only the future of Hazelhurst but also the fate of her ten guineas were riding on the outcome of this interview. So, with a remarkable piece of self-discipline, she hung her head and confessed that she'd felt sorry for the fox.

"Sorry for the fox!" Owen exclaimed, looking at her as if she were mad. "How very singular. But you always did take some odd notions into your head. Well, I'm glad that's settled. I'll be off now. We're taking the hounds out again tomorrow. Father was mortified that we couldn't show Lord Travers better sport today."

"Oh," said Charity, "I see. The fox got away, then, did it?"

"Yes. Now, where's my coat?" Owen followed Charity back into the hall.

"It's here. Are you sure you wouldn't like to stay any longer?" Charity smiled meltingly at him. Unfortunately Owen was too busy struggling into his greatcoat to notice.

"And next time you hear the hounds running, make sure you don't interfere with them," he said severely as he buttoned it up.

"Yes, Owen," she said meekly. "Owen!" She had a sudden inspiration. "Won't you come and see me tomorrow? I have so much to arrange before we move and I would really value your advice."

"Oh, yes…yes, certainly," he said, puffing up. "Yes, I'll come tomorrow without fail."

He would have to give up his sport, but the idea that his advice was invaluable flattered his pride, and he was really very good-natured. He didn't like to think of Charity struggling alone with all the problems of moving house.

"I'm so glad," she said gratefully. But as she closed the front door after him she was trying to think of which particular piece of unimportant business she could get Owen to help her with. She had a much higher opinion of his good will than she did of his good sense.

Chapter Four

Charity woke up suddenly at two o'clock in the morning and lay quietly in the darkness, wondering what had roused her. Her room was directly above the library and, as she lay listening, she thought she heard a noise in the room below.

She sighed. She'd had the windows opened that day to air the room and she supposed that Ellen had neglected to shut them. It wasn't the first time that such a thing had happened, and once she had gone downstairs to find that the wind-blown curtains had knocked over one of Mrs Mayfield's favourite vases.

She wondered whether it was worth getting up and then decided that it probably was. If she didn't she was bound to find all her papers blown about by morning. She slid out of bed and put on her robe, not bothering to light a candle because she knew the way so well—and because it was always such a bothersome business to strike a spark from the steel and flint. She could probably be downstairs and back in bed again before she got the tinder to catch light.

She padded silently downstairs, feeling her way with one hand on the banister, and opened the library door. After the darkness of the hall the room seemed quite light because the curtains were drawn back and the moon was nearly full. She saw with some irritation that the window was indeed open, and went over to close it.

At that moment she heard a startled exclamation from the shadows and realised, unbelievably, that she wasn't alone. There was a dark figure standing by the bookshelves.

"Who's there?" she said sharply. "Charles, is that you?"

The next minute she was pushed violently aside. She fell heavily against the oak table, bruising her hip and sending a chair crashing to the floor. She pushed herself up, intending to grab the poker from the fireplace, and briefly saw a dark shape in the window, silhouetted against the moonlight. Then she was alone.

She sat down suddenly, annoyed to find that her legs felt weak with reaction. Her hip was aching and she rubbed it absently. The next minute the library door burst open and her heart leapt nervously—then she heard Charles's voice demanding to know what was going on, and she sank back in relief.

"Miss Charity, is that you?" he asked, confused. "Is something the matter?"

"Not any more," she said. "We had an intruder, but he's gone now. Please close the window and then light some candles."

"An intruder!" he exclaimed, without moving.

"Charles! The window!"

"I'm sorry, miss. I'll close it at once." Charles hurried across the room and drew it shut. "Did he hurt you, Miss Charity?" he asked anxiously.

"Not really. I think I frightened him as much as he frightened me," Charity said; she was beginning to feel more like herself.

"Whatever did you want to go and tackle him on your own for?" Charles wondered.

"I didn't know anyone was in here. I thought Ellen had forgotten to close the window," Charity explained. "Could you light the candles, please?"

"I'll fetch a tinder-box." Charles turned round and cannoned straight into the housekeeper, who let out a small scream.

"Goodness! Is that you, Mrs Wendle?" Charity asked weakly. "I hope you weren't disturbed by all the noise."

Before the housekeeper could reply both women were electrified by a scream from the hall.

"Good grief! What's happened now?" Charity leapt up and hurried to the door.

"It's Ellen, miss," said Charles's voice apologetically from the hall. "She's fainted. I bumped into her in the darkness. I must have frightened her."

"I see." Charity took a deep breath. "Mrs Wendle, would you please go and tell Mama that everything is all right while I try and revive Ellen? And for heaven's sake provide us with some light, Charles!"

"Yes, miss. But should I lay Ellen down on the floor?"

"No, no. Bring her in here and put her on the sofa." Charity crossed to the parlour and held the door open for Charles to carry Ellen through.

"Now," she said, "if you would just fetch some candles. And I think perhaps you'd better get dressed as well." The footman was wearing nothing but his nightshirt.

"Oh, yes, miss, of course." Charles blushed in the darkness and hurried away.

Charity let out her breath in a long sigh and turned her attention to Ellen.

It was not until long after dawn, when Mrs Mayfield was eating breakfast in the comforting presence of Mrs Wendle, that Charity finally had a moment's respite. She sighed with relief and slipped quietly out of the house and into the garden, grateful for the chance to be alone. She couldn't remember ever having had such a dreadful night. Her encounter with the intruder had been the least part of it.

Not only had Ellen had hysterics when she had recovered from her faint, but Mrs Mayfield too had become extremely nervous when she had discovered that they'd almost been burgled. She'd insisted that Charles check every room and by the time he had done this, and checked that every door and window was securely fastened, everyone had been far too jumpy to go back to bed.

Charity was exhausted. Charles was certainly willing, but the unexpected events of the night seemed to have fuddled his wits so much that she'd had to continually remind him of what to do next; and everyone else had been suffering from an extreme agitation of the nerves. It was only with the daylight that they'd all begun to feel somewhat reassured.

Charity leant against an old apple tree and closed her eyes, feeling the sun on her face. The wind was quite strong, but in the shelter of the garden it was remarkably warm and she wondered how much longer the fine weather would last.

"Miss Mayfield!"

She jumped visibly, putting her hand up to her throat as she felt a sickening jolt of surprise.

"I'm sorry, I didn't mean to startle you." Lord Riversleigh was standing just behind her, his approach having been muffled by the short grass. He frowned, an expression of concern on his face as he saw the alarm in Charity's startled eyes. "Is something wrong?"

"No. I just didn't hear you coming," Charity said.

She was both relieved and unexpectedly pleased to see who it was; yet she felt a slight, unfamiliar flutter, almost of nervousness, as she looked up at him. Then she remembered how their last meeting had begun and in an effort of liveliness she held out her hand politely.

"Good morning, my lord. Isn't it mild for the time of year?"

"Very." He took her hand and held it for a moment, looking down into her face. "What's the matter?" he asked abruptly.

"Nothing really." She drew her hand away and tried to laugh. "Were you coming to see us? I'm sure my mother would like to meet you."

"Not exactly, although I would, of course, be delighted to meet Mrs Mayfield. In fact, I was riding past on my way to visit Jerry Burden when I saw you in the garden. So I thought I'd stop to let you know how assiduously I was following your advice."

"What?" Charity stared at him blankly for a minute. "Oh! You mean in my letter to Edward."

"Of course." Jack looked at her searchingly. He could see the signs of weariness and past alarm in her face, and he felt a sudden surge of admiration for her. She was facing the difficult situation in which she found herself with such good-humoured courage that it was easy to underestimate how badly she must be hurt by the imminent loss of her home.

"Miss Mayfield, are you sure you're quite yourself?" he asked. "Is there anything I can do?"

"You mean, you've been talking to me for a whole five minutes and I haven't said anything outrageous yet," Charity said, pulling herself together and smiling ruefully.

"I would have said, rather, that you seem a little subdued," he replied. "Is it something to do with leaving Hazelhurst? Perhaps I can help. I'm not unacquainted with matters of business."

"No. Thank you. But it's very kind of you to offer," Charity replied gratefully, but without offering to explain her uncharacteristic behaviour. Despite her occasionally disastrous outspokenness, she nevertheless possessed a good deal of reserve and she had always been reluctant to share her problems with others.

"I'm glad you're going to see Jerry," she said. "You certainly don't waste any time, my lord."

Jack smiled. "As I recall, you wanted the matter dealt with 'as soon as possible'," he said. "I'm simply complying with your wishes."

"Oh, dear." Charity blushed. "I'd never have written so if I'd known you weren't Edward. Things used to slip his memory, you know."

"I didn't know, but I can well imagine they might,"

Jack replied, "and also that you'd have had no hesitation in reminding him if they did! I'm glad you approve of my promptness. And now I must be on my way. I'm afraid I've already intruded upon you long enough. Please convey my compliments to Mrs Mayfield." He stepped back and bowed with the careless grace which characterised all his movements.

Charity felt a flicker of disappointment. She enjoyed talking to Lord Riversleigh, and after the alarms of the previous night she found his presence remarkably reassuring. She didn't want him to leave, and it occurred to her that it might, after all, be a relief to discuss what had happened with someone who could be relied upon to take her meaning without tedious explanations—and who would certainly *not* have the vapours.

"We had an intruder last night," she said abruptly, without any form of preamble. "I heard a noise downstairs and thought Ellen must have left a window open, so I went down to close it and surprised a burglar. He escaped through the window. No harm was done."

"Were you hurt?" Jack came back to her, a gleam of concern in his grey eyes which Charity found almost disconcerting. She wasn't used to people being worried about her.

"No." she looked away, annoyed to find she was blushing. "I think I frightened him more than he frightened me. But in his haste to get away he pushed me aside and I knocked over a chair," which woke up the household. Poor Mama was very upset."

"Very understandably so, I imagine," Jack said. Without conscious thought he had taken Charity's hand in his, and now he held it in a comforting clasp. "Are you sure he didn't hurt you?"

"No, indeed he didn't," she assured him.

He had braced his free hand against the branch over her head and he was standing so close to her that she had to tip her head back to meet his gaze. He seemed very strong, and she was intensely aware of how much taller than her he was. The half-formed thought even flitted across her mind that it might be rather nice to be able to cast her problems on to somebody else's broad shoulders. Most people were so used to the way she always dealt with every problem that arose that they tended to take it for granted that she could manage.

So she could, she reminded herself. Nevertheless, it was very pleasant to stand quietly beside him, and she was quite content for him to break the lengthening silence.

The early-morning sun was behind her head and, though she didn't realise it, it lit up her hair until it almost seemed as if she wore a halo. She looked so gallant and vulnerable as she smiled up into his eyes that Jack felt a strong desire to take her into his arms, and he suddenly realised that he was becoming more involved than he had intended. His hold on her hand tightened briefly—but only briefly. He knew that, despite her slightly misleading outspokenness, she had in many respects led a very cloistered life. It showed in so many ways, including the way in which she smiled up at him with such open trust—and it was not his practice to play games with innocent young women.

For an instant Charity had felt an unaccustomed fluttering breathlessness as she had gazed up at Jack. But then he released her hand, although he continued to lean against the apple tree, and she realised he was speaking to her. With an effort she tried to concentrate on what he was saying.

"Would you recognise the intruder again?" he asked.

"I don't think so," she replied, with commendable composure. "I never saw his face. At first he was standing in the shadows, then he was silhouetted in the window. I never saw him properly at all. And he didn't take anything—I checked this morning—so even if he was caught there wouldn't be any way of identifying him. I don't think there's any point in pursuing him," Charity concluded. "That's what you were trying to find out, isn't it?"

"Yes." Jack smiled faintly. "You have a remarkable trick of taking disaster in your stride," he observed. "Has anything ever overset you for long, Miss Mayfield?"

"Once or twice," Charity replied, unexpectedly serious; she was remembering her grief at the death of her father, a grief that time had still not entirely mended. Then her expression lightened and she reverted to her more characteristic manner.

"One must be *practical* about these things, after all," she said, and took the opportunity to move slightly away from him.

"A very sensible attitude to take," Jack agreed, turning so that he was still facing her.

"Now you're laughing at me," Charity said amiably, feeling more relaxed now that she had the open space of the garden, rather than the apple tree, behind her. "Never mind; would you like to come in and meet Mama?" she asked. "She's very anxious to find out what… I mean, I'm sure she'd be delighted to make your acquaintance."

"I imagine I must be an object of curiosity to quite a lot of people," Jack agreed. "I'll be very happy to meet Mrs Mayfield, and perhaps even divert her mind from the alarms of last night. But what did I ought to do about my horse?" He pointed to where the handsome bay gelding he had been riding the previous day was tied to the post of the kitchen garden gate.

"Well! I don't know how you can reprove *me* for

impropriety when you can say things like *that!*" Charity said after a moment. "Though it's perfectly true I did think you might give Mama something else to think about. Bring him through and we'll take him to the stables."

"Across the kitchen garden?" Jack asked.

"Well, he's not going to do it much harm if you lead him round the edge," Charity said. "Besides, it'll soon be Lord Ashbourne's garden—and I don't suppose he cares much one way or another."

"I don't suppose he does," Jack agreed gravely, untying the reins from the gatepost. He clicked his tongue and the bay walked willingly towards him. "Lead the way, Miss Mayfield."

"Lord Riversleigh! How wonderful to meet you! Do sit down. Charity, get Charles to bring in some tea." Mrs Mayfield was indeed delighted with her unexpected visitor, the more so because she was comfortably aware that she must be one of the first people in the neighbourhood to meet him.

"I'm afraid you find us in rather a turmoil," she continued brightly. "We had a burglar last night and we're all still in something of a flutter."

"Yes, Miss Mayfield told me," Jack said. "I hope it's not an inconvenient moment for me to call. I was riding past when I saw Miss Mayfield in the garden, and when I stopped to speak to her she invited me in."

"And I'm so glad she did!" Mrs Mayfield exclaimed. "I've been longing to thank you in person for the kind message you brought us from Edward. So thoughtful of him, and of you."

"Not at all, ma'am," said Jack immediately, without a flicker of surprise.

"Mama was very touched that in the midst of all his preparations Edward remembered us and commissioned you especially to bring us his good wishes," Charity explained hastily, wishing she'd thought to tell Lord Riversleigh the excuse she'd given her mother for his visit two days earlier.

"And for your own kindness in bringing us the message so quickly," Mrs Mayfield assured him.

"I beg you won't mention it," Jack said smoothly. "Edward spoke very highly of you and he particularly desired that you should receive good news of him."

"Yes. Well, I'm sure he'll have a wonderful time in Rome," said Charity, anxious to change the subject. She could imagine all too clearly how horrified Mrs Mayfield would be if she ever found out Charity had proposed to a stranger!

"Will you be staying up at the Hall long, Lord Riversleigh?" she continued.

"I'm not entirely sure. Thank you." Jack leant forward and accepted the cup of tea she was offering him. "I have affairs in town which cannot be neglected for too long, but there is also a great deal of work to be done here."

"Your home is in London?" Mrs Mayfield pounced on this snippet of information eagerly. She was fascinated by the deliciously mysterious way in which the unknown heir had suddenly appeared.

"Yes, ma'am." Jack sipped his tea. He gave the impression of being a man who, while perfectly willing to answer questions, had no intention of volunteering gratuitous information about himself. Charity thought he was quietly amused by her mother's good-natured curiosity. Whether that was the case or not, Mrs Mayfield rose handsomely to the challenge and within half an hour, without once appearing vulgarly inquisitive, she had discovered a number of interesting facts about her visitor.

Charity listened in amazement. It suddenly occurred to her that she had been remarkably incurious about Jack Riversleigh. Yet she guessed he must be nearly thirty years old, and somehow she had gained the impression that he had made his mark on whatever world he had inhabited during those years. Perhaps her lack of curiosity had been caused by the peculiar nature of their first meeting—or perhaps it was because of a subconscious awareness that if she allowed herself to be too curious about him he might begin to intrude uncomfortably upon her thoughts. She had stern and important schemes afoot and she couldn't allow herself to be distracted.

Mrs Mayfield was far more interested in Jack's family than in any other aspect of his life and, as a result of her efforts, she learned that he had two sisters, Elizabeth and Fanny; that Elizabeth was married and that Fanny, who was only twenty-one, lived with his mother. She also learned that he wasn't married, a fact that Charity had already discovered on their first meeting, though she'd lost interest in it after he'd refused to take Edward's place in her schemes.

"Well, I dare say you will find things quite different, now you are Lord Riversleigh," said Mrs Mayfield comfortably. "I'm sure your mother and sisters must be very pleased. You will be able to launch Miss Riversleigh into society in some style now."

"I think Fanny will probably launch herself," Jack murmured irrepressibly.

"The Riversleigh town house will be an excellent setting for her introduction to the highest ranks of society," Mrs Mayfield continued, not really attending. "I beg your pardon, my lord, did you say something?"

"Nothing of importance," he assured her, and stood up. "Thank you for your hospitality, but I believe I must be going now. I'm on my way to visit the son of one of your tenants, to discuss a lease."

"Oh?" Mrs Mayfield looked blank. She'd never

bothered to pay much attention to the management of the estate.

"Jerry Burden, Mama," Charity explained.

"Oh, Jerry!" Mrs Mayfield said, relieved. "Yes, Jerry is a fine young man. I'm sure he'll answer your purposes excellently. I wonder…?" She paused; she'd obviously had an idea. "Do you know the way, my lord? Perhaps Charity ought to show you. She's been cooped up indoors for days now, planning this wretched move of ours. I'm sure the fresh air would do her good."

"Oh, no!" said Charity instinctively. "I've far too much to do this morning. I'm sure Lord Riversleigh can find his own way; it's not at all difficult."

"But you said you were going to see Mrs Burden today, anyway," Mrs Mayfield pointed out.

She'd had a sudden, delightful vision of her daughter as Lady Riversleigh and both their futures assured. To be sure, everyone knew Riversleigh was heavily mortgaged, but living in debt at Riversleigh had to be better than living in lodgings in Horsham. Besides, even in the short time she had known Jack Riversleigh, she'd decided that she liked him a great deal better than Owen Leydon, and Charity didn't know many other men. Mrs Mayfield, in fact, had her own scheme for ensuring the future happiness of herself and her daughter—and paying off the debt on Hazelhurst wasn't part of it.

"Very well." Charity capitulated suddenly. "Can you wait while I get ready, my lord?"

"Certainly, Miss Mayfield." Jack sat down again and smiled at Mrs Mayfield.

"I'm so glad she's going out riding with you," Mrs Mayfield confided when they were alone. "She's had so much to worry her with all the arrangements for the move, and then last night—it was Charity who found the burglar, you know!"

"Yes, ma'am," said Jack gently.

"You don't think he'll come back, do you?" Mrs Mayfield twisted her handkerchief nervously in her hands. "Charity says he won't, but I can't help worrying…"

"No, ma'am," Jack said, his deep voice very reassuring. "I'm sure he won't be back. But if you're nervous, have a couple of your manservants sleep downstairs for a few days."

"That's a good idea." Mrs Mayfield seemed relieved. "I'll suggest it to Charity."

"Thank you for not telling Mama why you really came to see me that first day!" Charity said as she rode beside Lord Riversleigh on a placid grey mare, her groom a discreet distance behind them.

"You didn't think I would, did you?" he sounded amused.

"I didn't know," she confessed. "I suppose not, but

I meant to warn you anyway, just in case. I forgot."
She seemed annoyed with herself.

"You have a great deal on your mind," he said
soothingly. "Even you can't expect to remember
everything."

"I don't see why not," Charity said. "Are you really
going to give Jerry the lease?"

"How can I tell until I meet him?" Jack replied.
"What I *would* like to know, however, is why both
you and Guthrie appear so set against Cooper."

"I don't like him," Charity admitted frankly. "But,
apart from that, I really think Jerry would make a
better tenant. Cooper already leases two farms, and
he just wants the opportunity to increase his profits
and his consequence. He's more experienced than
Jerry and he'd be a safe choice—that's why your
grandfather favoured him—but I think Jerry would
be a better investment. He's very young, but he's
learnt a lot from his father, and he's not only hard-
working and enthusiastic but he's also desperate for
a chance to prove himself. I think if you gave him that
chance it would be very profitable for both of you."

"I see," said Jack slowly. "You seem to have a remarkable head for business, Miss Mayfield."

"It seemed like common sense to me," Charity
said, rather surprised.

"Possibly, but if that's the case it's amazing how
few people possess it," Jack replied, smiling slightly.

"Have you had much to do with the management of Hazelhurst?"

"I've always been interested, and Papa wasn't…" Charity caught herself up just in time before she criticised her father to Lord Riversleigh. She knew Mr Mayfield hadn't always been very consistent in the management of his affairs, but she was far too loyal to say so.

"I've always been interested in it," she amended her reply, "and since my father died it's been entirely in my hands—apart from Sam Burden's help, of course. I don't know what we'd have done without Sam—he oversees the home farm for us. But you mustn't think there's anything grand about Hazelhurst," she added hastily, in case he'd gained the wrong impression. "It's not like Riversleigh, or even Sir Humphrey's estate. We only have two tenants and then the home farm. It's not difficult to manage. May I ask you a question, my lord?"

"Of course." Jack hadn't missed her fleeting reference to Mr Mayfield, though he was far too polite to remark upon it.

"What is your business?"

Jack smiled, apparently not at all offended by her blunt question.

"I'm a banker."

"A *banker!* Good gracious!" Charity exclaimed, rather startled. "I must say, you don't look like one."

"No, Guthrie didn't think I was stout enough, either," Jack remarked humorously. "Perhaps I ought to do something to rectify the matter."

"That's not what I meant at all!" said Charity firmly, although there was a slight, tell-tale blush to her cheeks. "But however did you get to be a banker? Somehow it seems such an unlikely occupation for *Lord Riversleigh's* grandson."

"It does, doesn't it?" Jack grinned, thinking of all the money Lord Riversleigh had borrowed during his lifetime. "But it isn't at all an unlikely occupation for Joseph Pembroke's grandson. Besides, strangely enough, it was my father who had most to do with developing that side of the business."

"Joseph Pembroke was your mother's father?" Charity said, trying to get Jack's family tree untangled in her mind. "Was *he* a banker, then?"

"Eventually," Jack replied. "He was originally apprenticed as a goldsmith, but the two professions have always had very close links, so it was a fairly natural development—particularly after he'd met my father. By all accounts, Father was fascinated by the business and played a large part in developing it, even though he'd had no previous experience."

"He must have been a very different kind of man from *his* father or his brother Harry," Charity said. "They only seemed to take pleasure in destroying things."

Jack smiled. "He was," he said.

"When you said that your grandfather was a gold-smith," said Charity, going back to the other point that interested her, "do you mean that he could actually make things in gold?"

"Oh, yes," Jack replied, looking amused. "Though in fact, despite the name, most goldsmiths usually work in silver. But, of course, once grandfather became more involved in banking he had less time to devote to the workshop."

"You mean, he gave up his craft?" Charity exclaimed, surprising Jack with her vehemence. "How could he? Surely it must be more rewarding to create a beautiful object than it is to…to…?"

"Deal in filthy lucre?" Jack supplied when she seemed at a loss. "Perhaps I should have said that my grandfather didn't entirely abandon his craft. He and my father did become preoccupied with banking, but his other partner was, and still is, very much a working goldsmith—and an important part of the business."

He didn't sound annoyed, but Charity blushed painfully as she realised that once again she had been more outspoken than courtesy demanded.

"I'm sorry, my lord," she said. "I didn't mean to offend you. It's just that I have so little talent myself that it seems almost criminal to me when people who do have a skill waste it."

"Are you thinking of Edward?" Jack asked, beginning to understand her reaction.

"I suppose so," Charity replied slowly. "But not because he deliberately wasted his talent—quite the contrary. In fact, I think it's probably because I watched him struggling against so many obstacles that I feel so strongly on the subject."

For a moment she gazed over the winter landscape almost as if she was remembering something. Then she roused herself and laughed.

"There were times when I almost envied him," she confessed. "Painting, sketching, carving—it all came so easily to him. As I said, I've no talent for that kind of thing at all, and perhaps that was partly why I liked him. Nearly everyone else used to get annoyed with him because he seemed so vague, half foolish even. But I saw him when he was sketching, and heard him talk about the things he really cared about—and he was a different person then, so quick and decisive."

She smiled reminiscently.

"Do you miss him very much?" Jack asked abruptly, responding to the almost wistful note in Charity's voice. "I'm sure, if you wish it, it would be possible to contact him—even recall him to England."

Yet, even as he spoke, he was aware of a reluctance to carry out his own suggestion, and he suddenly realised that the unfamiliar—and hitherto unnamed—sensation he was experiencing was jealousy. The knowledge shook him. He had thought he knew himself better than that and he damned himself silently for his folly—nevertheless, he was relieved when he heard Charity's surprised rejection of his offer.

"Oh, no!" she exclaimed. "I do miss him; he was like the older brother I never had—and he used to side with me against Owen. But I'd never deny him this opportunity. Besides, I only asked him to marry me when I thought we could be of mutual assistance to each other—and now he's already on the way to Rome he doesn't need my help."

She turned her head and smiled at Jack.

"But I do thank you," she said. "It was very kind of you to offer to help."

"It would have been my pleasure," Jack replied formally, but the more familiar gleam of humour had returned to his eyes. He found Charity's unusual out-spokenness very entertaining—and her unthinking reference to Owen very revealing. He was less inclined than ever to believe that she really intended to marry him.

Charity laughed.

"You do the grand manner very well," she said. "It wouldn't have been a pleasure at all—but that only makes your offer all the more generous. Are you acquainted with Lord Ashbourne?"

"Lord Ashbourne?" Jack repeated, wondering if

he'd missed part of the conversation. He still wasn't used to Charity's tendency to change the subject in almost mid-sentence.

"He's the man who lent Papa the money," Charity explained. "Didn't I mention it in my letter?"

"Not as far as I remember," Jack replied slowly. "What was it you wanted to know?"

"Only if you'd ever met him," Charity said. "It didn't occur to me before, but when you told us this morning that you live in London I wondered if you knew him. I believe he also spends a great deal of time there."

She smiled ruefully.

"Mama and I have never met him, and I can't help being slightly curious about the man who will soon own our home," she admitted.

"Of course," said Jack. "It must seem very odd. But I'm afraid…" He paused, looking absently ahead. "No, I'm afraid that I can't be of much help to you," he continued at last. "I have occasionally encountered the Earl, but he moves in the most fashionable of circles and my home has always been in the City. The two worlds are not always…compatible."

"I just wondered, but it's not important," said Charity quickly.

It had suddenly occurred to her that perhaps the reason the Earl and Jack had encountered each other was because Lord Ashbourne had ordered some silver from Jack. If that was the case the two men were hardly likely to be on intimate terms—especially if the Earl hadn't yet paid his bill. And Charity knew that the aristocracy were notorious for procrastinating over their debts to tradesmen!

"We live in such a small community here that we all know each other," she continued, trying to steer the conversation on to a less potentially embarrassing subject. "I'm afraid I tend to imagine that the same is true of London, but of course it isn't—it's so much bigger."

"With so many more inhabitants," Jack agreed humorously. He didn't know exactly what Charity was thinking, though he could make a fair guess.

Charity looked at him doubtfully. She thought he seemed amused, but she couldn't understand why and she wasn't sure what to say next. She glanced ahead and then pointed towards some roof-tops just becoming visible over the brow of the hill.

"Look, we're nearly there," she said.

Chapter Five

"Well, you've met Jerry now. Are you going to give him the lease?" Charity asked as they rode back across the field to Hazelhurst.

"Yes, I think so," Jack replied. "I'd say you summed him up very accurately earlier."

"I'm so glad!" Charity exclaimed. "What a relief it will be to Mrs Burden. She's very anxious about the changes Lord Ashbourne might want to make when he takes over. The Burdens have a twenty-one-year lease, you know, but it has only four years left to run. Of course, I always intended to renew it, but now... Still, at least they won't have to worry about Jerry any more."

"Yes, it's a difficult time for everyone," Jack said quietly, not that he had ever doubted it, but his conversation with Sam and Jerry Burden had confirmed it very forcefully.

He and Charity had met the Burdens just outside

their house and, after introducing them to each other, Charity had left the three men alone together while she went in to see Mrs Burden. It was only after the business part of their discussion had been concluded that Sam had invited Lord Riversleigh into the house.

For Jack it had been an enlightening meeting in more ways than one. Not only had he come to the conclusion that Guthrie and Charity were right in their assessment of the younger Burden's capabilities, but he had also learnt far more about Charity. He had always suspected that beneath her somewhat scatter-brained exterior she had a great deal of common sense, but he had not hitherto realised just how much she had had to do with management of Hazelhurst. Both Sam and Jerry clearly held her in great respect, not only because of who she was, but also because of her hard work and diligence in doing everything she could to improve the estate.

Jack was no fool and, despite the fact that nothing had openly been said, he had guessed that Mr Mayfield had been an indifferent landlord. From various sources he had gained the impression that Charity's father had been a man of grand visions and generous impulses, but that he had always lacked the stamina or patience to see his plans through to their completion. During his lifetime Mr Mayfield had probably never realised how much Charity had contributed to the smooth running of his affairs—and since his death she had dealt with everything.

"You must find it very galling, having to give up Hazelhurst after all the work you've put into it," Jack said quietly, putting his thoughts into words.

Galling! It's more than…" Charity broke off sharply, biting her lip in vexation. "Let's race!" she exclaimed. "I haven't had a good gallop for days. To the oak in the next field." She touched her heel to the mare's side as she spoke and suddenly the sleepy air left the grey horse. She sprang forward like a charger.

Lord Riversleigh was taken by surprise and the bay skittered nervously sideways—then Jack had him under control and was urging him on.

The grey mare was running like a steeplechaser, anxious for the first jump, and for a moment Jack thought she was bolting. Sudden fear for Charity filled him and he leant forward, urging the bay on in an effort to overtake her—but the grey mare hated to be passed, and when she heard the thunder of hoofs behind her she put back her ears and lengthened her stride.

They were approaching a thick hawthorn hedge, not an impossible obstacle, but challenging, and from their outward journey Jack remembered that the drop on the other side was longer than on the take-off.

He was still convinced that the mare had run away with Charity and he forced the bay on, intending to turn the grey before she took the jump. Then the horses were abreast and, as he glanced sideways at Charity, he saw that she had the mare under complete control. He felt a surge of anger at the alarm she had caused him; then he concentrated on the jump. Both horses thundered on towards the hedge—there was a heart-stopping silence as they took off at almost the same moment, and then they both landed safely.

At that point Jack stopped worrying about Charity and turned his attention to winning the race. The bay was willing, and Jack a clever horseman, but the grey mare wouldn't give up and both horses went past the oak tree together.

In the distance, the groom trotted sedately on, heading for the gate. He was grinning to himself, thinking what a fright Miss Charity must have given his lordship—*he* couldn't know that she was the best horsewoman in Sussex. Gregory was partial, of course, but then most people who worked for Charity were.

Charity slowed the mare to a walk and leant forward, patting her neck.

Jack drew alongside her, his first impulse to give vent to his anger at the alarm she had caused him. Then he remembered the expression on her face just before she'd set the grey mare running and changed his mind.

"That is a remarkably deceptive animal, Miss Mayfield!" he exclaimed.

Charity laughed; her cheeks were flushed and her eyes were bright with excitement.

"She looks as if she's so tired that she's in danger of tripping over her own feet, doesn't she?" she said. "But she runs like an angel, and when she hears the huntsman's horn she goes away like a demon. She was Papa's horse and everyone told him he was a fool to buy her, but the first time he rode her she went at a jump so hard that she threw him and finished the hunt on her own, up with the leaders to the end. Then she came quietly back to the stable for her hot mash like a true veteran. Sir Humphrey was most impressed. He's tried to buy her several times, but Papa wouldn't sell. How did you know?"

"Miss Mayfield?" The bay was fidgeting, excited by the race, and Jack soothed him.

"Even Guthrie doesn't really understand," Charity continued, sitting easily as the mare stretched out her neck and shook her head. "He thinks it's sad that we must lose our home—but that's all. He told me the other day that he thinks it's a good thing that I won't have to worry about the estate any more—as if it ought to come as a relief to me! As if I ought to be *glad* to hand over everything I've worked for to someone else! Someone who won't even *care!*"

She turned her head away as she finished speaking, but the anguish in her voice was unmistakable, and painful to hear.

"I knew how you felt, because I know how I'd feel if the same thing happened to me," Jack said quietly.

Her distress wrenched at his heart and he wanted to take her in his arms to comfort her; but he knew that, at that moment, her thoughts were far away from him, and he was reluctant to do, or say, anything which might upset her even more.

For a second or two longer Charity continued to gaze away across the fields, then she turned and looked at him—and saw in his eyes that he really did understand. She felt the tears threaten and instinctively put up her hand to cover her eyes. Until that moment she'd received a great deal of sympathy—but no one had really understood how she felt. She'd never expected that they would.

"Miss Mayfield?" Jack said gently.

"Sometimes I feel so angry," she said, without looking at him, and dashed the tears from her cheeks. "I shouldn't. It's not right to feel so angry."

"I'd be angry—very angry. There's no reason to feel guilty. It's a measure of how much you care," Jack said.

"Perhaps. But it's not… Well, never mind, there's no point in talking about it. Shall we go on, my lord?"

"In a minute." Jack leant forward and took hold of the grey mare's bridle, drawing her to a halt. "What were you about to say?"

"Nothing important." Charity tried unsuccessfully to laugh. "I'm sure we should be going, my lord. You must have a great many things to do."

"Nothing that won't wait." Jack released the

mare's bridle, but he didn't encourage the bay to walk on. "I'm not trying to force your confidence, but I'm usually considered a good listener—and I'm not easily shocked."

"Do you think I'm going to say something shocking?" Charity tried to smile, but there wasn't much humour in her expression.

"No." Jack's voice was deeper than ever, slow and curiously reassuring.

"I'm angry with Papa!" she bursts out, and felt a sudden, overwhelming relief that she'd finally told someone what she was really thinking. She knew that most of the neighbourhood were probably harbouring critical thoughts about her father, but until that moment she had never done anything but defend him. Even to herself she'd tried to make excuses for what he'd done.

"I'm angry with Papa," she said again, more temperately, "and then I'm angry with myself. Because I *know* what he was like. How can I be angry with him for being himself? And he's not even here to defend himself."

"No. But he should be, shouldn't he?" said Jack. "It wasn't fair to leave you in such a fix."

Charity looked at him, shaken by how accurately he had guessed her feelings.

"How did you know?" she whispered.

Jack smiled wryly. "It seemed like a natural

reaction," he said. "You're too hard on yourself. How did he die?"

"He was shot by a highwayman. By all accounts it was the most farcical situation. Typical of Papa." Charity tried to laugh, but Jack knew she wasn't far from tears. "He was on his way home when he came across a coach being held up by three high-waymen. Being Papa, he couldn't ignore it, so he decided to intervene. Apparently he charged down on them, shouting like a madman and waving his pistol. I can almost see him doing it." She smiled affectionately. She had happy as well as sad memories of her father.

"He was trying to take them by surprise, of course," she continued, "and he did. At first it looked as if everything was going to turn out all right—but one of the highwaymen couldn't control his horse at all. They said afterwards that he'd never meant to fire, that his pistol had gone off by accident—but Papa was in the way."

"He must have been a brave man," said Jack.

"For getting shot!" Charity flashed, and there was hostility in the glance she threw at Jack. She was afraid he was mocking her.

"No," said Jack equably. "For trying to help. The odds were against him, were they not?"

"Yes." Charity looked down. "Poor Papa; some-how they always were. I think we should go back now, my lord." She shortened her reins and chirruped to the mare.

Jack brought the bay round and they began to walk slowly back to Hazelhurst.

For a moment neither of them spoke; then, without looking at Jack, Charity said, "Thank you. I'm sure I shouldn't have said some of the things I have, and I hope you will forget that I did, but...well, thank you." She glanced at him briefly as she finished speaking, then looked away again.

"I was honoured by your confidence," Jack replied quietly, and he meant it. "As to the rest...my memory is at your disposal."

Charity looked at him gravely for a moment, then she smiled, as warmly and as openly as a daisy might unfurl its petals in the morning sun.

Jack looked down at her, unable to take his eyes from her face. Ever since he had met her Charity had been trying to manipulate events in her favour—even now she was busy trying to inveigle Owen Leydon into marrying her—yet Jack could not remember ever having met such an honest woman. It was a quality he prized highly. He knew how difficult it could be to speak the truth, or to say what one really felt, without fear of ridicule or censure. A friend with whom one could be oneself, without pretence, was a friend worth knowing—and a woman with whom one could be oneself...

Charity saw the warmth in his eyes and turned her head away. She felt embarrassed and vaguely uncomfortable, yet at the same time reassured. She could not remember ever having spoken so openly to anyone before and she felt very vulnerable, yet it never occurred to her that she couldn't trust Jack with her secrets. She knew he could be relied on not to hurt or betray her; she didn't even wonder how she knew. And he had helped her, not because he had offered trite words of sympathy, but because he had understood her mixed feelings towards her father. He had not been shocked or horrified, and that meant a great deal to her.

On the other hand, she was afraid that he might pursue the subject, and she didn't want that. She had already opened herself up far more than she had intended and she needed time to adjust, and to regain her equilibrium. She began, with a hint of awkwardness in her manner, to discuss his plans for Riversleigh, and felt a sudden surge of relief when he answered in kind. But it was only when she saw Owen in the distance that she finally lost her self-consciousness and was once more completely herself.

"There's Owen!" she exclaimed. "I quite forgot, he's coming to see me today."

Yet, despite the fact that this was what she had wanted, she felt a tinge of regret as she realised that now she would have to cut short her conversation with Lord Riversleigh. Then she told herself severely that she had more important concerns to think about than her own pleasure. She had made her decision to save Hazelhurst and it was not Jack but Owen who was going to help her do it. She should be pleased to see Owen.

"You're back on speaking terms, then?" Jack said, a hint of amusement in his voice—he still didn't take her matrimonial plans entirely seriously.

"Of course we are!" Charity pulled herself together, chiding herself for having let her mind wander. "He came to see me yesterday evening just to apologise. I was very relieved; it saved a great deal of time."

"So you're going ahead with your scheme?" Jack asked.

"Well, of course!" She sounded surprised that he should have doubted it. "I never give up something once I've started! I wasn't immediately sure how to proceed, but I had a brilliant idea last night, and now I'm afraid your ten guineas are in great jeopardy."

"Are they, indeed? And may I ask what your brilliant idea is?" Jack said. "Have you decided to tell him about your inheritance, after all?"

"Certainly not," said Charity firmly. "The money wouldn't make any difference to Owen."

Even as she spoke she wondered if she was right, but she pushed the thought aside as unworthy of both Owen and herself.

"It might even have the opposite effect," she said. "He can be *very* stubborn. No, my idea was completely different, but I'm not sure I ought to tell you." She looked at him doubtfully. "You might try to make me lose the bet."

"Miss Mayfield!" Jack said, outraged. "Are you suggesting I might *cheat?*" But even as he spoke he realised that that was precisely what he intended to do—though he wasn't yet prepared to admit as much to his companion.

For a moment Charity was taken aback—the haughty indignation in Jack's voice was so real that she was suddenly reminded of how grand he had seemed on their first meeting—then she saw the twinkle in his eye and relaxed.

"Please accept my apologies..." she began formally, then interrupted herself almost immediately. "Oh, good heavens! He's almost upon us! You must know I asked him to give me his advice with all the arrangements I have to make. He was immensely flattered, and I have great hopes for our meeting this afternoon."

"And do you wish for his advice?" Jack asked mildly.

"Of course not," Charity replied. "But that's not important. He'll *think* I need his advice, and that's what counts."

"You don't think that's rather a poor basis for a lifelong partnership?" Jack asked.

"I don't see why. As long as he leaves the management of everything to me, I dare say we'll do splendidly," Charity said firmly.

"Poor fellow," said Jack provocatively. "Perhaps I ought to warn him of the dreadful fate in store for him."

"Don't you dare!" Charity exclaimed hotly. "It would be...it would be..."

"Ungentlemanly?" Jack suggested helpfully as she cast around for a word strong enough to condemn such underhand conduct.

"Worse than that," she began darkly, but Owen was already within earshot and she had to turn her attention to him.

Owen had sacrificed a day's sport to ride over to help Charity. Consequently he felt rather aggrieved to find her jaunting about the countryside with a total stranger as if she hadn't a care in the world. His manner was decidedly stiff as he greeted Charity and her escort and, when he found out who Jack was, he became quite hostile.

"Lord Riversleigh, eh?" he said, looking at Jack suspiciously. "I don't believe I've ever had the pleasure of meeting you before, my lord. Will you be staying in Sussex long?"

"I'm not entirely sure," Jack replied, amused rather than offended by Owen's ungraciousness. He found it impossible to imagine Charity united in blissful wedlock with this hot-headed young man.

"But I certainly have unfinished business that will keep me here until the end of the month," he continued.

"Unfinished business?"

"A contract," Jack explained, a slight chill in his polite voice, "the terms of which cannot be fulfilled until the end of February."

He heard Charity gasp as she realised he was talking about their wager, but he gave no indication of his amusement as he continued smoothly, "I won't bore you with the details. Are you much interested in business, Mr Leydon?" He raised his eyebrows, a faint, and not altogether encouraging, smile on his lips.

Owen looked into the cool grey eyes and suddenly felt rather hot. He knew that somehow he had been put at a disadvantage and he was afraid that his annoyance with the stranger had led him beyond the bounds of courtesy.

"No, no, not at all," he stammered. He was angry with himself, and angrier still with Jack, but most of all he was angry with Charity. He thought that he had been made to look a fool, and he was sure it was her fault.

"We've been over to see the Burdens," Charity explained. "Lord Riversleigh is going to lease Bellow's farm to Jerry, and I went with him to show him the way."

"I see," said Owen stiffly; he looked very put out.

"I thought you wanted *me* to come and see you today, but if you've changed your mind…"

"No, no, indeed I haven't," Charity said hastily. "I'm so glad you've come. There's something I particularly need to ask you.

"Lord Riversleigh," she turned to Jack, "thank you for giving Jerry the lease; I'm sure you won't regret doing so. And thank you for escorting me so far of the way home. I don't think I need to trespass on your time any further—I'm sure Owen will be happy to see me the rest of the way."

"The pleasure has been all mine, Miss Mayfield," Jack replied politely, accepting his dismissal gracefully. His expression was grave, but she thought she saw amusement in his eyes and she acknowledged it with a slightly rueful look in her own.

"Mr Leydon." Jack took his leave of Owen. Then he turned the bay and considerately urged him into a steady canter. He thought Owen, and therefore Charity, would probably be glad to see the back of him as quickly as possible. It was very difficult to have a good argument when the cause of it was still within earshot—and the more Charity and Owen argued, the better.

"I thought you were going to be busy today," said Owen belligerently as he watched Jack disappear from view. "Couldn't Gregory have shown that fellow where the Burdens live just as well? There was no need for you to make a spectacle of yourself, riding about the fields with a total stranger!"

"I *am* busy," Charity retorted, "but I had to see Mrs Burden anyway. She's very anxious about all the changes that are going to happen. Besides, 'that fellow' is not a total stranger, he's Lord Riversleigh, and a perfectly respectable gentleman."

"Respectable gentleman!" Owen exclaimed. "I heard he's nothing but the grandson of a common tradesman. He may possess the title, but he certainly doesn't have any breeding. Father was saying only last night that it's not surprising the old Lord should have disowned his son if he married so far beneath him. He must be turning in his grave at the thought of such an upstart stepping into his shoes!"

"If that's what Sir Humphrey thinks then he must be a narrow, bigoted fool!" Charity declared, her eyes sparkling with indignation. "I'd rather see an honest *coal-heaver's* son as Lord of Riversleigh than the mean-spirited, bullying, apology for a man who would otherwise have inherited it. *Harry's* birth might have been unimpeachable, but the only man I've ever respected less was his father!"

"Well, I know the late Lord wasn't exactly…" Owen was beginning, somewhat taken aback by Charity's vehemence and precluded by his innate honesty from defending the late Riversleigh, when he suddenly remembered what she'd said about Sir Humphrey.

"How dare you speak about my father so? At least he's not a worthless wastrel who gambled away his family's inheritance, and left his wife and children to be turned out of their home!" Owen stopped, appalled at what he had just said.

Charity stared at him, her face deathly pale. She was too shocked even to be angry, and she didn't say a word.

"Charity, I'm sorry! I never meant to say that...you just made me so angry. Charity! Don't look like that!"

In his agitation Owen leant over and gripped Charity's arm, shaking it in an effort to get through to her.

The grey mare didn't like being crowded so close, and snorted. Then she tossed up her head and sidled away.

"No. You didn't mean to say it, but it was what you were thinking," Charity said, her voice cold and even. "And who shall blame you? It must be what everyone in the country is thinking. But don't ever say so in my presence again, Owen."

"No, I promise. I'll go now," said Owen humbly. This cold, calm Charity was new to him, and much more disturbing than the old hot-tempered Charity who flared up at the slightest annoyance.

He began to ride away, and Charity watched him go.

The groom watched with interest. Miss Charity was certainly having a busy ride. First the conversation under the oak tree with Lord Riversleigh, now a full-scale quarrel with Mr Owen. Gregory hadn't been able to hear what had been said under the oak tree, but he knew what the argument with Owen had been about and he felt sorry for Charity. She might be too free with her tongue, and she certainly shouldn't have said what she did about Sir Humphrey, but Owen had had no business to come back at her like that. Any fool could guess how badly she felt about what Mr Mayfield had done—she didn't need her face rubbed in it. Gregory was glad to see Owen riding away. He was disappointed when he heard Charity call after him.

"Owen! Owen, wait a minute. It was my fault. If I hadn't abused Sir Humphrey you'd never have said it. I know that."

Owen came back to her. "That's no excuse," he said. "Just because you provoked me I should never…"

"Let's forget we ever had this conversation, shall we?" Charity asked, and held out her hand, smiling at him, though she couldn't quite hide the hurt in her eyes. "We've been friends for far too long to be on bad terms now." Strangely enough, she wasn't thinking about her plans to save Hazelhurst; she just didn't like being seriously at odds with someone she had played and bickered with since childhood.

Owen looked at her as if seeing her for the first time—perhaps he was. He'd known her for so long that he never really thought about her, or what she thought or felt. He'd taken her for granted. But now he was seeing a side of her he'd never even suspected, and he thought he liked it.

"You're a remarkable girl," he said slowly. "Lyddy wouldn't have forgiven me." Lydia was his sister.

"I'm not Lyddy." Charity smiled wryly. Lydia was the darling of the Leydon household, pampered and spoiled since birth. She was perfectly good-natured, but Charity had never had much in common with her.

"Come back to the house and I'll find you something to eat," Charity offered.

"Well, I must admit, I am *devilish* hungry," Owen confessed. "It seems such a long time since I last ate."

"It's *always* a long time since you last ate." Charity laughed. "Even if it was only five minutes ago!"

"No, that's not fair!" Owen declared. But from his new perspective he was thinking how well Charity knew him. He remembered all the times she had anticipated his wishes in the past, and how bravely she had bandaged up his leg with her petticoats when they had both been thirteen and he had fallen out of a tree and cut himself on a sharp stone. Perhaps his mother was right; perhaps it was time to start thinking about finding a wife.

Chapter Six

"My dear Mrs Mayfield, I came at once when Owen told me what had happened here last night. It must have been very distressing for you, but, Owen tells me, no harm done."

Sir Humphrey stepped briskly up to Mrs Mayfield as he spoke. He was a large, vigorous man in his middle fifties, and his devotion to both his sport and his wine could be clearly seen in his face and figure.

He was also the local magistrate, and he pursued his duties with a kind of casual diligence that served his neighbourhood remarkably well. Like most Sussex gentlemen, he paid no duty on the smuggled brandy in his cellar, and he knew as well as the next man when to look the other way, but for all that, his parish was remarkably well-governed. Charity particularly respected him for his ability to temper justice with compassion—though he always denied that he did any such thing. He was a man who knew his own worth and who valued his place in his community—but change made him nervous.

"Sir Humphrey, how kind of you to come!" Mrs Mayfield exclaimed. "I really wouldn't have had you put yourself to so much trouble."

"Nonsense, no trouble at all," Sir Humphrey declared, taking the seat Mrs Mayfield offered him. "Did you get a look at the scoundrel, m'dear?" he added, turning to Charity.

"I'm afraid not, Sir Humphrey," Charity replied. "It was dark and I was taken by surprise. I'm afraid I wouldn't be able to recognise him again."

"Pity," Sir Humphrey grunted. "I don't like to think of him getting away with this, but, if he didn't take anything and you can't recognise him, there's not much I can do."

"Oh, no, we quite understand," Charity assured him.

"I'm so looking forward to your party tomorrow night," Mrs Mayfield said. "It will be our last before we leave here. I shall be so glad of an opportunity to see everyone before we go."

"Hmph, yes." Sir Humphrey cleared his throat, looking uncomfortable. "It's a bad business, Mrs Mayfield. I don't say anything as to the cause of your leaving, but Lady Leydon and I shall be sorry to see you go. There've been Mayfields at Hazelhurst so long that it won't seem the same without you. If there's anything we can do, don't hesitate to ask."

"Thank you, it's so kind of you. Everyone has been very kind to us this last year." Mrs Mayfield smiled at Sir Humphrey. She hadn't caught his fleeting reference to her husband and, even if she had, she was spared some of Charity's distress because she divided the blame for what had happened between the Earl and Mr Canby.

Mrs Mayfield had conceived a violent dislike of the unknown Lord Ashbourne, but she saved her greatest ire for the unfortunate attorney. She blamed his negligence for their uncomfortable situation and, in the first few days after they had heard they must leave Hazelhurst, she had tried Charity's patience high by demanding they take action against him. Fortunately she had been diverted from the subject by the preparations for the move, and she hadn't returned to it.

"Owen particularly," Mrs Mayfield continued. "He was here only this afternoon, helping Charity with some of the arrangements. It's so complicated—I can't understand all these legal documents at all."

"Owen, helping! Well, well, I'm pleased to hear it. Not that he's got any experience. You should have asked me, Charity. I would have been glad to help." Sir Humphrey sounded slightly put out that Charity hadn't applied to *him* for assistance.

"You were my first thought," Charity assured him hastily. "And I know your advice would be invaluable. But I know how busy your magisterial duties keep you, sir, and how little time you have for your own affairs. I didn't want to trespass on your good will if I could get help from someone else, and, Owen being your son…"

"Well, you're a thoughtful young woman," said Sir Humphrey, puffing up with gratification in a way that reminded Charity irresistibly of Owen. There was a distinct likeness between father and son.

"But I'm here now, so if there's anything you'd like to ask me…"

"Thank you!" Charity tried to assume an expression of eager pleasure while her heart sank within her. "Oh…" she seemed to hesitate "…only if you're sure you have the time."

"All the time in the world for you, m'dear," Sir Humphrey assured her.

Despite the fact that she occasionally shocked him to his conventional core, the magistrate had always liked Charity. He thought she was a spunky little thing, and the day she'd tried to jump clear across the lily pond for a dare and climbed out covered in green weed and mud he'd laughed until tears had poured out of his eyes. Not that he necessarily regarded her wisdom as highly as he did her courage.

Charity saw the reminiscent gleam in his eyes and hurried into speech before he could comment once again on her childhood misdemeanours. That was the problem with being surrounded by people who'd seen you grow up—most of them still thought of you as the child you'd been ten years ago.

"If you'd like to come down to the library, Sir Humphrey," she said. "I have all the papers there."

"I'd be delighted, m'dear." Sir Humphrey stood up and bowed to Mrs Mayfield. "Excuse us, ma'am."

"Of course, so kind of you to help." Mrs Mayfield smiled brightly.

An hour later, feeling quite shattered, Charity led Sir Humphrey back upstairs again. She had not enjoyed the last sixty minutes and she hoped she wouldn't have to repeat them. It was not that Sir Humphrey's advice was bad—in fact, it was very good, just as she had known it would be. But he couldn't help commenting on her father's system— or lack of it—and regretting that there was no man to see to things properly.

Charity was grateful for his help, but she didn't like opening up her family affairs to the disapprobation of her neighbours, and she didn't intend to let it happen again. But she knew it was her fault: she shouldn't have used her need for advice as an excuse to get Owen to visit her. She should have guessed what would happen next.

"Well, I hope I've been of assistance," Sir Humphrey said as he sat down opposite Mrs Mayfield again. "Your late husband seems to have had a very peculiar way of doing things, ma'am. Not but the more recent records are in far better order. Still, it will be a relief to you, no doubt, when everything is sorted out and you're safely established in Horsham."

"I shall be glad to be settled again," Mrs Mayfield admitted. "Oh, Sir Humphrey! I met the new Lord Riversleigh this morning!" she exclaimed, changing the subject completely.

"What did you make of him?" Sir Humphrey asked cautiously.

"I thought he was a charming man. Not at all like his grandfather!" Mrs Mayfield declared.

"No, by all accounts. I hear his *maternal* grandfather was a common tradesman! And apparently the new Lord is no better than… Well, there's no need to go into that! But it's a pity that such a fine old title should be brought to this!" And Sir Humphrey shook his head disapprovingly.

Charity bit her lip in an effort to avoid saying something rude. She knew that Sir Humphrey didn't like change and hated any hint of social climbing, but she couldn't understand why both he and Owen should be so badly disposed towards a man they hadn't even met.

"Who told you about Lord Riversleigh, Sir Humphrey?" she asked, trying to keep her voice friendly.

"Lord Travers. He's staying with us at the moment.

Splendid fellow, marvellous horseman. He knows all about the new Lord," Sir Humphrey explained.

"Does he? What did he say?" Charity asked.

"Oh, he told us how the grandfather—Pembroke, I believe his name was—started as a common apprentice. He'd no family or position; dare say he couldn't even read or write. No doubt a good enough man in his way, but rough, very rough. Not the kind of blood any man would want in the family," Sir Humphrey concluded, refraining from repeating some of the warmer stories Lord Travers had told him. He didn't think they were suitable for female ears.

"Lord Travers said that?" Charity said, resisting the urge to make a more heated reply.

She was beginning to feel extremely indignant on Jack's behalf, but it was clear that the slurs on his character and antecedents had not originated with the magistrate. Sir Humphrey was only repeating what he had been told, and it would do no good to be angry with him.

"Did Lord Travers say what the apprentice grandfather became, sir Humphrey?" she asked.

"No, I don't think so." Sir Humphrey frowned in an effort of memory. "No doubt he completed his apprenticeship and set up as a tradesman somewhere—if he could raise the capital. I wouldn't want any son of mine marrying a tradesman's daughter. Though by all accounts that must have been the least of Richard's crimes."

"Perhaps," said Charity slowly.

It seemed to her that there was a definite hint of vindictiveness in what Lord Travers had told Sir Humphrey. Apart from anything else, goldsmith-ing had always been one of the few trades in which it *was* possible for gentlemen to interest them-selves. That was why so many French Huguenot refugees had links with the craft. Yet, despite his loquacity, Lord Travers didn't seem to have men-tioned to the magistrate which trade Joseph Pembroke had been apprenticed in—or how he had developed his business. What other facts had Lord Travers misrepresented?

"Sir Humphrey!" she said suddenly. "Until a few days ago I'd always thought that Richard died more than thirty years ago. You've lived here all your life. Did *you* know Richard wasn't dead? Or, at least, that he didn't die until only seventeen years ago?"

"No-o-o." Sir Humphrey looked at her with a puzzled expression. "Now I come to think of it, I didn't. But I wasn't here at the time. My father had packed me off to France to finish my education—and a dreadful place it was too."

For a moment he was distracted from the subject in hand by his recollections of his time abroad. Like many Georgian gentlemen, Sir Humphrey had little love for the French and, when in his cups, he was quite likely to shout "Hurrah for the roast beef of good old England".

"Yes, but what do you remember about Richard?" Charity reminded him.

"Oh, Richard," said Sir Humphrey, cut off before he could begin a diatribe against all foreigners. "Not a lot. When I got back he was gone, name never to be mentioned again in Lord Riversleigh's presence. I wasn't much interested and it's a long time ago."

"But did you think he was dead, or did you think he'd done something terrible?" Charity persisted.

Sir Humphrey thought about it. "Both!" he said suddenly. "I mean, I thought he was dead, but I was sure he'd disgraced the family. Not a savoury topic for discussing in the drawing-room. I dare say that this was why his name was never to be mentioned again."

"But what was it he did that was so disgraceful?" Charity asked, impatience finally creeping into her voice.

She was becoming increasingly annoyed by lack of substance in the magistrate's account. It seemed outrageous to her that Jack, his father and grandfather should all be condemned for sins or crimes which she was sure they hadn't committed, and which no one even seemed able to name.

"Damned if I know, m'dear," Sir Humphrey confessed. "In fact now I come to think of it, young Richard always seemed devilish strait-laced to me. It just goes to show how you can be deceived in a man. Travers was telling me only last night…well, well, I beg your pardon, Mrs Mayfield, that's hardly a suitable story for your ears. But if this fellow is anything like his father I should be on your guard in his presence, that's all I can say."

"I think I would have had more reason to be on my guard in the old Lord's presence than I have in this one's!" said Mrs Mayfield unexpectedly. "It seems most unjust to blame a man for the sins of his father. *Edward* never gave us any cause to doubt him, and his father was hardly a saint. Why should his cousin Jack be any different?"

"Well said, Mama!" Charity exclaimed impetuously, and Mrs Mayfield blushed.

"You agree with Lady Leydon, then, that I should call on him and invite him to our party?" Sir Humphrey asked.

"Certainly I do," said Mrs Mayfield firmly. "It wouldn't be right to condemn him without even having met him. And *I* found him charming."

"If that's your view, ma'am, I shall call upon him tomorrow morning," Sir Humphrey declared, despite his continuing personal misgivings. He took his leave of them soon after that, but he left Charity at least with a number of unanswered questions.

* * *

"Good morning, Mr Guthrie. How are you today?" Charity asked as the land agent rode by.

She was sitting on the same gate which had caused all the trouble on the day of the hunt, and the land agent had been too engrossed in his thoughts to notice she was there until she spoke.

"Miss Charity! Don't you know better than to go startling a man like that?" he reproved her. "I've been worse. How about yourself?"

"I've been worse too," Charity replied. "How do you like your new master? Isn't it a good thing he gave Jerry the lease?"

"A very good thing. And how did you know that?" Mr Guthrie looked at her suspiciously.

"I showed him the way to the Burdens'," Charity explained.

"Did you, indeed? I didn't think you'd met the man."

"Mr Guthrie! Haven't you been listening to the local gossip recently?" Charity looked shocked. "I've met him twice." She conveniently forgot the occasion when he had witnessed her quarrel with Owen over the gate.

"First he came to visit us with a message from Edward, only Mama was out," she continued un-blushingly. "Then he was riding by on the way to the Burdens' and noticed me in the garden. Naturally I invited him in to meet Mama. He seems to be a great improvement on Harry."

She twirled the hazel twig she held in her hands as she spoke. With the blue sky behind her, and her hood thrown back carelessly from her dark curls, she looked the picture of innocence, but Mr Guthrie was not deceived.

"That's your opinion, is it?" he said drily.

"Certainly." Charity smiled at him ravishingly. Then she threw the twig away and jumped down from the gate. Mr Guthrie sighed ostentatiously and dismounted painfully.

"I'm too old for all this climbing on and off horses," he complained.

"I never asked you to get down," Charity pointed out.

"Mebbe not, but I'll get a crick in my neck if I try and talk to you from up there."

"How did you know I wanted to talk to you?" Charity asked, just as if she hadn't been sitting on the gate for the last forty-five minutes, waiting for the land agent to pass by. Mr Guthrie didn't deign to reply, and after a moment Charity laughed.

"I did want to ask you something," she admitted. "You were here when Richard left. Why did Lord Riversleigh disown him? Did he do something dreadful?"

"I couldn't say. I was never admitted into his lordship's confidence," the land agent replied, his manner colder than usual when speaking to Charity.

"But you do *know,*" said Charity, undaunted.

"After knowing the late Lord Riversleigh, and having met the new one, I can't believe it was anything to Richard's discredit, but that's what everyone will think—unless they know the truth."

"I dare say that's what they'll think anyway," Guthrie replied. "And why are you so concerned?"

"I don't know," said Charity, rather disconcerted to find herself blushing. "But I don't think it's fair if people think badly of a man for something his father didn't even do," she added hastily as she met the land agent's shrewd gaze.

"No." Guthrie looked down at Charity thoughtfully. "No, you wouldn't." He hesitated, and then seemed to make up his mind. "You're quite right, of course," he said. "Richard never did anything wrong. There was no scandal. That's the pity of it, the grievous pity. He wasn't like Harry. He fathered no bastards and ran up no debts he couldn't pay. He didn't cheat…" The land agent caught himself up.

"Cheat!" Charity exclaimed. "Did Harry cheat?"

"That's another story, and nothing to do with Richard. Don't you go repeating it." Guthrie looked annoyed with himself. "Where was I?"

"There was no scandal," Charity prompted him.

"No," said Guthrie. "But Richard never could get on with his father. He was a man who couldn't abide to see things done badly, and he hated cruelty. I mind the time I was talking in West Street with him when we saw a horse struggling to pull a cart it couldn't shift because the wheels were locked. The idiot carter hadn't even bothered to get down and look. You should have heard what Richard said to the man." Guthrie smiled reminiscently.

"So what happened?" Charity asked.

"Well, he didn't like his father's methods. He wanted improvements carried out at Riversleigh. He was a great believer in finding a better way of doing a job. Lord Riversleigh hated it—so did Harry. I think it was Harry who started that last quarrel; he always liked making trouble for Richard. I can't even remember what it was about—nothing important. But it was the last straw; Richard left that day and never returned. Lord Riversleigh gave orders that his name was never to be mentioned again. He was dead. I think Richard was glad to go. He'd given up any idea of trying his schemes at Riversleigh, and there was nothing else for him there—except his mother."

"His mother!" Charity exclaimed. "What did she have to say about all this?"

"Very little. She was a quiet little woman, very much afraid of her husband. But she was brave enough to go with me in secret to see Richard in London. He couldn't come to her, you see. He'd sworn never to set foot on Riversleigh land again."

"Good heavens!" said Charity. "What a terrible thing! Poor Lady Riversleigh. How could she bear it?"

"I don't think she could," said Guthrie sombrely. "She died two years later. I've always believed it was grief that killed her."

"Why did you stay?" Charity demanded suddenly. "Why did you work for that…that monster?"

"For Lady Riversleigh's sake at first. She trusted me to take her to Richard, d'y'see? And later… habit." The land agent shrugged.

Charity looked at him steadily for a moment. "Habit?" she said at last.

"Aye. And there was my wife: she came from these parts, she didn't want to leave. Besides…there were others who couldn't leave and I'd a foolish notion I ought to do my best for them." Guthrie looked half ashamed of his confession.

Charity smiled suddenly. "You're a good man," she said. "I'm glad I know you." She stood on tiptoe and kissed him on the cheek before he knew what she was about.

He flushed and mumbled with embarrassment.

"Did Richard meet his wife *after* he left Riversleigh?" Charity asked.

"Indeed he did. *She* never caused the breach with his father. It would be a wicked thing to suggest!" the land agent declared hotly, and from his immediate response Charity suspected he wasn't as unacquainted with the rumours as he might like her to imagine.

"I met her a couple of times. She was a lovely

girl," he continued. "Half-French she was, and none the worse for it. Her grandfather on her mother's side was a Huguenot who'd come to England to escape persecution in his own land. She'd be much older now, of course. But I always thought Richard had done well for himself. Blood and birth don't count for everything, not by a long way."

"I never thought they did," Charity replied quietly. "Did Harry know Richard was married?"

"Oh, yes." Guthrie smiled grimly. "That's why he never married himself. It was his revenge on the old Lord. Lord Riversleigh dreaded the thought that Richard might one day inherit and Harry tormented him with it. He told me once that he'd wed the day the old man was finally in his grave—but not before."

"What a hideous pair!" Charity exclaimed. "Why did Harry hate his father so much?"

"That's a different story, and not one you need to know," Guthrie said. He gathered up the reins and prepared to climb up on his horse again. "As for the present Lord, I don't think you need worry about him. By all I can see, he's well able to take care of himself. I don't think a few unfounded rumours are going to upset him."

"You are pleased he's come, aren't you?" Charity said.

"Aye." Mr Guthrie settled himself more comfortably in the saddle. "Aye, I reckon it'll be a grand thing for Riversleigh. Mind, it's early days yet," he added with his customary caution. "Anything could happen. I'll be saying good day to you, Miss Charity. I have a great deal to do this morning."

"Of course, I didn't mean to hold you up," she smiled up at him. "Mr Guthrie, if anyone mentions the matter to you again, will you put them right?"

"Are you asking me to indulge in idle gossip?" the land agent asked austerely.

"No," she said quietly. "But so few people remember what really happened—even Sir Humphrey believes the rumours that Richard was disgraced. Don't you think his friends, those who remember him, have a duty to defend him?"

For a moment Guthrie stared down at her, then he said slowly, "Sometimes you're a very *daunting* young woman. Don't you think you've troubles enough of your own without taking up cudgels in defence of a stranger and a long-dead man?"

"Perhaps." She smiled wistfully, almost sadly. "But I'd like to think someone might do the same for me, or my family—if it was necessary."

"We do, my dear," said the land agent, speaking gruffly because he knew what people were saying about Mr Mayfield and he was distressed for Charity and her mother.

He couldn't tell her that he'd already defended them vigorously, because that would only confirm her obvious suspicions that her family was the subject of unkind gossip. But he could tell her that he'd defended Richard and perhaps, in the circumstances, that would do just as well.

"If you must know," he said, sounding as if he were speaking against his will, because that was what she'd expect, "if you must know, I've spoken out already against the lies I've heard about Richard. But the real scandal-mongers lie outside my circle. I can't confront them."

"No, I know," Charity replied, thinking how it was Lord Travers who had played such a part in prejudicing Sir Humphrey against Jack Riversleigh and his father. "I'm sorry, Mr Guthrie," she continued. "I should have known you wouldn't stay silent."

The land agent smiled grimly to show he'd accepted her apology, and clicked his tongue at his horse.

"Well, if you've no further orders for me I'll be on my way," he said. "And mind you don't go startling any more travellers out of their wits this morning!"

Charity laughed and went back to the house, where she found Mr Canby and Lord Ashbourne's agent waiting for her in the library. She spent the rest of the morning making arrangements.

Chapter Seven

"I was so sorry to hear you must leave Hazelhurst," Mrs Carmichael said, patting Charity's hand comfortingly as they sat together on Lady Leydon's sofa. "It must have come as a terrible shock to you."

"It was a trifle…unexpected," Charity agreed steadily, and drew her hand away.

She wanted to say that it hadn't been a shock at all, that she and her mother had known all along that they were leaving Hazelhurst—but it would have been too obvious that she was lying. It was bad enough knowing that everyone was gossiping about her family, without giving them the added opportunity to talk pityingly about her futile attempts to cover up what had happened.

"You must have been so distressed," Mrs Carmichael continued. "I assure you, I felt for you and Mrs Mayfield when I heard the news. It's not even as if you have any other relatives to turn to; at least…

doesn't Mrs Mayfield have a brother? I believe he came to visit you a few years ago. But perhaps he's back in India." She paused interrogatively.

"He did go back to India," Charity agreed calmly. "But I'm afraid he's dead now. In any case, we have received so much help from our friends, particularly Sir Humphrey, that we hardly feel our lack of relatives."

She glanced around the crowded room as she spoke. She recognised nearly everybody at the supper-party; indeed, she had known many of them all her life. Normally she would have expected nothing but enjoyment from the evening, but tonight she was afraid that there were too many people present who, like Mrs Carmichael, would make it their business to pry into her affairs.

Charity knew that some of the questions she would be asked that evening would be prompted by genuine concern for her mother and herself, but she had no illusions about Mrs Carmichael's motives—and no hesitation at all in retaliating in kind.

"How is Mr Carmichael?" she asked innocently, before Mrs Carmichael could frame another question. "Is he not with you tonight? I was looking forward to seeing *all* our old friends before we leave the county."

"I'm afraid he's not well," said Mrs Carmichael. She seemed slightly disconcerted by the turn of the conversation. "Are you leaving the district? I'd heard you were moving to Horsham."

"I'm so sorry to hear that," said Charity, addressing herself to the first part of her companion's reply and ignoring the second. "When I met Mr Carmichael in the Carfax in Horsham a couple of weeks ago he seemed to be in excellent spirits. I do hope it's nothing serious?" She looked at Mrs Carmichael earnestly.

"No, no," Mrs Carmichael replied hastily. "A trifling indisposition—no more than that. I'm sure he'll be recovered by tomorrow, but it wouldn't have been wise for him to risk coming out in the cold night air."

"No, of course not. But I'm so glad that it's not serious," Charity said brightly. "You must know that Mr Carmichael has always been a great favourite of mine, he's such a friendly, genial man. He was *so* charming the last time we met, and very complimentary about my new hat. He became quite incoherent in his praise."

She smiled blandly, though she felt a small bubble of amusement rising within her as she remembered *exactly* what the intoxicated Mr Carmichael had said. She didn't blame him in the least for his excesses; she thought she too might take comfort in the brandy bottle if she were married to Mrs Carmichael.

"Thank you," said Mrs Carmichael, her smile as insincere as her reply. "He'll be delighted to know he made such a favourable impression on you; be sure I'll let him know what you said. But I believe you were telling me where you'll be moving to."

"Was I?" Charity frowned slightly; she was feeling a brief pang of sympathy for the hapless Mr Carmichael. "I'd quite forgotten. How scatter-brained I am, to be sure. We're going to London, Mama and I—did I not tell you? Now that we can leave Hazelhurst there's nothing to keep us in Sussex any longer—we are free to live where we please. Ah, excuse me." She stood up as she spoke. "I think Lady Leydon wants me. It's been so nice to see you again." She smiled politely and moved away before Mrs Carmichael could reply.

Well! said Mrs Carmichael to herself. Then, London? Who'd have thought it? She looked around for someone to whom she could pass on this interesting snippet of information.

Charity made her way quietly to Lady Leydon's side, smiling at her old friends and acquaintances as she passed between them, and occasionally pausing to exchange a few words. From her demeanour it would have been impossible to guess that she wasn't completely at ease, and only the faint shadows beneath her eyes hinted that she still hadn't caught up on the sleep she'd lost two nights previously.

The room was very hot, and brilliantly lit. There was an ornate chandelier hanging from the ceiling, a fierce fire blazing in the hearth and numerous candelabra standing on every free surface. There were even candles on the mantelpiece, their flickering flames reflected in the huge gilt-framed mirror that hung on the chimney breast.

Lady Leydon was standing beneath the mirror, fanning herself, and surveying her crowded room with satisfaction. She had never dared to hope that so many people would come to an out of season, out of town party, and she was savouring her triumph. It hadn't occurred to her that she owed a great deal of her party's success to the widespread curiosity about the new Lord Riversleigh. A curiosity which had only been increased by the rumours most people had heard about him, and by Sir Humphrey's ill-concealed doubts about the wisdom of inviting him.

Not that anyone had seriously believed that Jack wouldn't be present that evening, of course, and most people were anxious to meet him as soon as possible. Unfortunately he hadn't arrived yet and, as Charity threaded her way across the crowded floor towards Lady Leydon, she was aware of an atmosphere of thwarted curiosity. Life was imitating art, and the audience were getting restless as they waited for the principal actor in the latest local melodrama to appear.

Charity found it very distasteful, perhaps because she herself was experiencing at first hand what it was like to be an object of curiosity, and on at least one occasion she had been hard pressed to find a polite reply to a speculative remark made by one of her old friends.

She glanced around, noticing that her mother was deep in conversation with Lady Dalrymple, a dowager who lived to the north of Horsham. Then she reached Lady Leydon's side and smiled at her hostess.

"Ah, Charity!" Lady Leydon exclaimed with simple pleasure. "I wanted particularly to introduce you to Lord Travers. Lord Travers, this is my dear Miss Mayfield. Her family have always been our closest neighbours."

"Enchanted, Miss Mayfield!" Lord Travers bowed over Charity's hand with a flourish, but when he straightened up and smiled at her she thought the look in his eyes contained more appraisal than warmth.

It was as if he was assessing how useful she was to him, and had already decided that she would be of no use at all. She didn't like it, but it would have been discourteous to walk away so soon after they had been introduced, especially with Lady Leydon smiling so warmly at her, so she concentrated on attending to what Lord Travers was saying in such confidential tones.

Jack was late, but as soon as he arrived he knew he was the focus of everyone's attention. He also knew that a great deal of the interest was far from kindly, but he refused to allow it to disturb him.

Charity was standing near the wall, talking to Owen, when she first saw Lord Riversleigh. As usual he was dressed in black as a mark of respect for his grandfather, but she was immediately convinced that he was the most elegant man in the room. He was certainly the tallest, and he bowed over Lady Leydon's hand with the lazy grace which typified all his movements. His hostess was clearly delighted with him, and immediately took the opportunity to introduce him to her daughter, Lydia.

Charity watched surreptitiously, quite forgetting that Owen was standing beside her and paying no attention at all to what he was saying to her. She was too far away to hear what Lady Leydon was saying, but for a moment she was surprised that her hostess should respond so favourably to Jack—surprised, that was, because Lord Travers's conversation had been composed almost entirely of delicate but extremely damaging slanders against Lord Riversleigh.

From his description one would have supposed Jack not only to be a hardened rake, but also a man of dubious integrity in all matters of honour.

Charity had done her best to deny the stories, but Lord Travers had adopted a worldly air which was almost impossible for her to counteract. It was also very difficult for Charity to say too much without laying herself open to unwelcome questions.

On the whole, therefore, it was understandable

that she should be momentarily startled by Lady Leydon's apparent willingness to introduce Lord Riversleigh to her daughter.

Then Charity realised that she was being foolish: one had only to meet Lord Riversleigh to realise at once that Lord Travers's insinuations could not possibly be true. Of course Lady Leydon had discounted the stories. She gave a faint sigh of relief and relaxed slightly, and it was only then that she discovered that in her first agitation she had gripped her fan so tightly that she had snapped one of its fragile sticks.

It was perhaps fortunate for her continued good opinion of her hostess that she didn't realise that Lady Leydon hadn't really been paying much attention to Lord Travers, and that most of what he had said had passed completely over her head. Lady Leydon, in fact, had been far more influenced in her opinions by what she had discovered from Lady Dalrymple—and Lady Dalrymple had made it very plain that Jack was an extremely wealthy man.

"So he's here, then," said Owen darkly, his eyes also on Lord Riversleigh. Unlike his mother, he continued to be more influenced by what he'd been told by another man, rather than by an old woman's foolish gossiping. "After what Lord Travers has told us I'm surprised he dares to show his face in public."

"And I'm surprised at you, Owen Leydon!"

Charity rounded on him. "I hadn't spent more than two minutes with Lord Travers before realising he was a spiteful scandalmonger. He's making all the stories up! They have no basis in reality. He's a small-minded man; he'd hate to make a fool of himself in front of others. No doubt he did something stupid in Lord Riversleigh's presence and this is his notion of revenge!"

"How can you say such a thing about our guest?" Owen demanded. "Lord Travers..." He suddenly realised he had allowed his voice to rise, and broke off, continuing more quietly, but no less furiously, "Lord Travers is a *gentleman,* and a friend of my father, and you have as good as accused him of lying!"

"Not 'as good as', Owen," Charity corrected him, her eyes sparkling dangerously. "You know me better than that. I say he *is* lying. It would be interesting to know the real reason."

They were standing a little aside from the rest of the guests and no one had overheard what they'd said, but it was apparent to everyone that they were arguing. Mrs Carmichael was not the only one who began to edge closer in an attempt to find out what was going on.

"Not Lord Travers, Lord Riversleigh!" said Owen furiously. "What lies has *he* told you? How did *he* cozen his way into your favour? They say he has a way with the ladies. I think more must have

happened on your ride together than you admit to!"
He stopped, aghast at what he had said, and alarmed
at the look in Charity's eyes.

Owen wasn't the only one to see Charity's expression change. Everyone knew Owen Leydon and
Charity Mayfield had been arguing with each other
ever sine they had been children, and no one, not
even Lady Leydon, took very much notice of their
bickering. But this was different, and for the second
time in two days Owen knew he had gone too far.

Charity didn't say anything; for a moment she just
stared at him, her eyes dark in her pale face—then
she walked away. She didn't exclaim and she didn't
flounce, she acted as if she were quite alone in the
room, and in the sudden silence the people simply
parted before her. Even the musicians Sir Humphrey
had engaged to add lustre to the occasion were aware
that something was wrong, and paused briefly and
discordantly in the middle of a tune.

Anger got Charity safely to her mother's side, then
she realised what she had done and she nearly faltered,
but pride took over, and she managed to smile at Mrs
Mayfield, almost as if nothing had happened.

"Charity! Whatever did Owen say?" Mrs Mayfield
asked anxiously.

"Nothing, Mama, don't worry. Would you like
some lemonade?" Charity suddenly decided she
couldn't bear to be questioned at that moment, and

she seized at the first excuse she could think of to take her away from her mother's side.

"Yes, but…" Mrs Mayfield began. The hum of conversation had returned, and Lady Leydon had gestured urgently for the musicians to continue playing, but both Charity and Owen were receiving several surreptitious glances, and Charity knew that she had given the gossips something else to talk about.

"I'll get you some lemonade," she said, more curtly than usual, and stood up.

She was intercepted before she could reach the sideboard, or find a footman to serve her.

"Charity, I couldn't help noticing… I do hope Owen didn't offend you," Lady Leydon murmured anxiously.

"No. Please don't concern yourself." Lady Leydon was the last person Charity wanted to speak to, but she forced herself to relax and smile pleasantly to her hostess. "It was just a silly misunderstanding. I'm sorry if I distressed you; I didn't mean to disrupt the party."

"Owen can be too outspoken at times," Lady Leydon said. "I'm sure you know he doesn't mean anything by it. Please don't be annoyed."

"I'm not, really I'm not," Charity assured her, thinking that it was typical of Lady Leydon to be apologising for Owen without really knowing whether or not he was at fault. She was a quiet, nervous woman, often disconcerted by the more forthright, forceful characters of her husband and son.

"I was just going to fetch Mama some of your excellent lemonade," said Charity. "I believe you must have some secret ingredient which makes it so much more delicious than other people's. I always used to think so when I was a child."

"Thank you!" Lady Leydon exclaimed, glad that the conversation had moved on to a more innocuous topic. "You're quite right—however did you guess? It was my mother's recipe; she always insisted that one should put in half a teaspoon of..." She led Charity away, still talking about the best way of making lemonade.

"Do you know where Mr Edward Riversleigh is?" Mrs Carmichael asked. "It seems strange that he hasn't come back to Sussex. But perhaps the experience would be too painful for him—so soon after his grandfather's death," she finished with spurious innocence.

"I believe he's in Rome," Jack said calmly.

"Rome!" Mrs Carmichael exclaimed, genuinely surprised. "Whatever made him go there?" She looked at Lord Riversleigh suspiciously.

"His interest in the architecture," said Jack with rather chilly politeness. "He told me that he has always had a great desire to see it at first hand. I think he was looking forward to the opportunity."

"Oh," said Mrs Carmichael. She was clearly not convinced. She undoubtedly suspected that Edward had gone away to nurse his grievances in private; or, even worse, that Jack had engineered Edward's absence deliberately in an attempt to remove a possible rival.

Jack sighed inwardly. He could make a fairly accurate guess at Mrs Carmichael's thoughts and he was annoyed—he disliked having his motives mis-construed—but he had no intention of justifying or explaining himself to her or anyone else. In any case, he had known that his unexpected arrival in Sussex would give rise to rumour and possibly suspicion, and he had thought that it would only be a matter of time before both died down.

What he hadn't expected was to discover that his own character, and those of his parents and his maternal grandfather, had been determinedly black-ened. Jack still didn't know exactly what was being said—nobody repeated the stories to his face—but when he saw Lord Travers he knew who was behind the rumours.

He also knew that there were a number of people at the Leydons' that night who, out of consideration for his title or his wealth, were quite prepared to forgive him for his own supposed misdemeanours, for the trifling anomaly that his mother had been a trades-man's daughter, and even for the fact that his father had been anything from a cardsharp to a murderer—Lord Travers's stories were becoming increasingly lurid.

"Ah, Charity!" Mrs Carmichael reached out and caught Charity by the arm as she was trying to pass by with two glasses of lemonade. "Have you met Lord Riversleigh?"

"Yes, thank you." Charity extended her arms slightly so that the lemonade that had spilled when Mrs Carmichael jogged her arm didn't drip too badly on to her dress. "How do you do, my lord?"

"Excellently, thank you. May I hold that glass for you?" Jack said.

He took the glass from Charity, offered her a spotless linen handkerchief, and took the other glass while she wiped her hands.

"Oh, I'm sorry, I didn't know you were carrying anything," said Mrs Carmichael with an unconvincing show of concern. "I hope your dress isn't spoiled."

"No, not at all. But I'm afraid Lord Riversleigh's handkerchief is. Thank you, sir." Charity smiled at Jack.

"Lord Riversleigh tells me that *Mr* Riversleigh has gone to *Rome!*" Mrs Carmichael said, because it was to pass on that piece of news that she had stopped Charity in the first place, and she *never* allowed herself to be distracted from her purpose. Besides, everyone knew that Charity and Edward Riversleigh had been on very good terms.

"I know," Charity said immediately. "Mama and I received a letter from him only yesterday. He's enjoying himself immensely. He's always wanted to go there, you know." She smiled warmly at Mrs Carmichael. "But without Lord Riversleigh's generosity it would never have been possible. I believe he's written to you, also, my lord," she continued, turning to Jack. "But in case that letter goes astray he particularly asked us to tell you how very grateful he is to you. To be honest, I think he's rather relieved at the way things have turned out. He's finally got the chance to do what he's always wanted to do. Excuse me, but I promised Mama I'd fetch her some lemonade." She smiled impartially at Jack and Mrs Carmichael and went in search of Mrs Mayfield.

"A charming girl," said Mrs Carmichael, briefly distracted from her attempts to find out more about Edward Riversleigh by her desire to talk about Charity. "But very headstrong. I'm afraid she takes after her father. I dare say you saw that argument she had with Owen Leydon earlier. I wouldn't want any daughter of mine to behave so forwardly in public. Mind you, I shouldn't say this, of course, but Owen could try the patience of a saint. But I expect Helena Mayfield was disappointed; I'm sure she'd like to see Charity settled comfortably. You've heard about their troubles, of course?" But it was a rhetorical question, and Mrs Carmichael didn't wait for Jack to reply. "It will be a sad day for us all when they leave

Hazelhurst," she carried on. "Have you met Lord Ashbourne, my lord? What's he like?"

"I have met him, but I'm afraid I'm not one of his intimates. Excuse me, ma'am," said Jack, and turned away abruptly before he was tempted to reply more forthrightly than he considered wise or desirable.

"Letter, Miss Mayfield?" Lord Riversleigh asked. It was the first time he had had an opportunity to speak to Charity alone, and the evening was already well advanced.

She was standing near a window, unobtrusively pushing the curtain back slightly so that she could feel the cool air on her face. Using her other hand, she was fanning herself with her damaged fan with as much vigour as she considered compatible with decorum.

She blinked at Jack, briefly at a loss, yet suddenly feeling happier than she had done all evening. Then she smiled, that rare, open smile that seemed to distinguish her from almost anyone else Jack had ever met.

"Well, there might have been a letter," she said. "And if there had been that's exactly what Edward would have said, so I'm not going to feel guilty."

"But what possible reason could you have for thinking that Edward has any particular cause to be grateful to me?" Jack asked, something not quite a smile in his eyes.

"You told me the first day we met that he'd found

a patron," Charity pointed out, returning his smile so delightfully that he felt his heart turn over. "I wondered at the time, but I had other things on my mind, so I didn't pursue it. But if you haven't made him, at the very least, a handsome allowance I shall be greatly surprised."

"I'd hate to disappoint you," Jack murmured. He was amused, but gratified by Charity's perception, and by the accuracy of her guess. In fact, Edward Riversleigh now had more financial security than he'd ever had before in his life, and arguably more than he would have had if he had actually inherited Riversleigh. He was very happy with the way things had turned out, though at first he had been somewhat bewildered by Jack's generosity.

"Are you always so quick to defend others?" Lord Riversleigh continued more seriously.

"That depends," Charity said vaguely, her mind on other things. "How much money did you lend Lord Travers?"

Jack gazed down at her in surprise. His anger had been growing throughout the evening, though he had concealed it very well. He wasn't a fool and, and though no one had said anything openly to him, it hadn't taken him long to get the gist of Lord Travers's slanders.

The slurs against his own character annoyed him, but the lies that were being circulated about his father outraged him—partly because they were so unfair, and partly because the breach between the late Lord Riversleigh and his second son made them too easy to believe.

He had been on the brink of challenging Lord Travers several times, but his inherent good sense had warned him that that was not the answer. A duel might well turn a difficult situation into a full-blown scandal. Besides, he had other, better ways of dealing with the man.

He had also known that not everyone would take the stories at face value, but so far no one had given any indication that they disbelieved Lord Travers, and he certainly hadn't expected anyone to see so clearly what lay behind his vindictiveness.

"I'm sorry," said Charity when Jack didn't say anything. "I'm afraid I spoke without thinking again. Please forget it."

"No, no, don't apologise." Jack suddenly realised he had been staring at her in silence for several seconds. "I was surprised, that's all. I hadn't thought anyone would guess."

"You did lend him money, then?"

"The bank did."

"I thought so," Charity said, pleased that her supposition had proved correct. "He looks the kind of extravagant man who'd get himself into debt. I told Owen I was sure he was taking revenge for his own stupidity on y…others," she amended hastily.

"You told Owen?" Jack echoed, an unreadable expression in his eyes. "Was *that* what your argument was about?"

"I think I ought to find Mama," said Charity. She suddenly seemed flustered. She closed her fan with a snap and tried to move away from the window. "It's getting late. We should be leaving soon."

"Miss Mayfield." Jack reached out to rest a detaining hand lightly on her arm.

Neither of them was prepared for the sudden surge of emotion which leapt between them as he touched her, and Charity almost gasped. She stared up into his face with wide, startled eyes, and it was only with an effort that Jack remembered what he had been intending to say.

"I know what's being said about my father, and since Travers is the Leydons' guest I'm sure Owen believes it. Did you defend me?" he asked in a calm voice which belied his inner feelings.

For a second he wondered if she'd heard what he'd said. Her gaze was fixed on his face, her lips slightly parted as if she was trying to understand…but then she looked down at her fan, half opening and closing it with hands that trembled slightly.

"I told Owen that Lord Travers must be lying," she said at last, her voice sounding muffled in her own ears, and her eyes still fixed on her fan. "I think he was annoyed because I'd insulted a guest in his house."

"I see," said Jack slowly. "Thank you." He looked down at her as if he were seeing her for the first time, quite forgetful of their surroundings.

"I am grateful to you, Charity; your good opinion means a great deal to me. But I would hate to think I'd been the cause of a breach between old friends. Please don't make things more difficult for yourself on my account."

"No, don't worry," said Charity, looking up at him once more.

He had used her name, but she had hardly noticed, she was so intensely aware of his unwavering gaze and of the depth of feeling in his voice. She wanted to look away—but somehow she couldn't. Without knowing what she did she began to lean slightly towards him, and for a moment Jack was lost in the dark, luminous eyes. He lifted his hand to draw her closer to him—and suddenly remembered they were standing in a crowded room.

The realisation jolted him badly. Never before had he so nearly lost all sense of his surroundings. He stepped back abruptly, struggling to master his frustration at the self-imposed interruption, and searching for some way to steer the conversation back into safer channels.

For Charity there was a sense of confusion—and of something lost, or not quite found. One minute Jack was so close that he seemed to fill all her senses—the next he had moved away and was asking her politely whether she and her mother had made a final decision about where they were going to move to.

The change was so sudden that for a moment she felt quite bewildered, unable to comprehend what he had said, or frame a coherent reply. But then, once more, she could hear the voices and laughter of the other guests, and remembered where she was.

"Mama suggested that perhaps we ought to move to London," she said at last.

"London!" Jack exclaimed. "I'd thought you were planning to take lodgings in Horsham."

"We were," Charity agreed, beginning to feel more like herself again. "But I think perhaps Mama is right. There's nothing really to keep us in Sussex any more—and I believe that *she* might be happier in London. She likes to be surrounded by people and bustle. She hates it in the winter in Hazelhurst when the weather is bad and she doesn't see anyone."

"Yes, I see," said Jack. "And will you also be happier in London?"

"I…" Charity glanced up at him briefly and, as she saw the expression in his eyes, she began to feel her pulse quicken once more "…I hope so. Mama thinks…Mama suggests that I ask your advice. On where to live, I mean. It's so long since she was…and I only had one Season…" Her voice trailed away as she seemed to lose the sense of her explanation.

"I would be delighted to advise you," Jack replied in a hearty tone which was at a complete variance with the way he normally spoke—and with the way he felt.

He knew that he couldn't allow the refined torture of this very public conversation to continue much longer. He could sense the awakening responsiveness in Charity, and he knew that his own sudden retreat had confused her, but there was nothing he could do or say when at any moment he expected them to be interrupted by Owen, or Mrs Carmichael, or one of the other guests.

"May I fetch you some lemonade?" he asked abruptly; he didn't want to leave her but for her sake it would be better if they had some time apart to regain their composure.

"Lemonade?" Charity echoed, bewildered by the sudden change. "Oh, I… Yes, I am a trifle warm. Thank you." She started to fan herself again, watching as Jack threaded his way across the room.

Something had happened, something was different, but she wasn't quite sure…

"Charity, Charity!" The persistent repetition of her name recalled her attention and she turned reluctantly to find Owen standing beside her.

"I wanted to speak to you," he said, his manner a curious mixture of belligerence and sheepishness.

Chapter Eight

"Oh." Charity looked at Owen blankly. For a moment she had almost forgotten their quarrel. Then she remembered, and instantly decided that he must have sought her out to continue it—or to demand an apology. The idea of any prolonged conversation with him at that moment was so dreadful that she immediately decided her best course of action was to apologise straight away—anything to get rid of him.

"I'm sorry," she said, holding out her hand in a very fair imitation of her usual friendly manner. "It was unforgivable of me to make such a scene at your mother's party."

"No, no, it was all my fault," said Owen, taking her hand. He didn't think it had been, but Charity's ready apology disarmed him, and gave him a welcome opportunity to be magnanimous.

"I should have been more considerate," he said. "I know you're having a very difficult time at the moment. It's not surprising if you're feeling over-wrought. I dare say there is so much on your mind that half the time you hardly know *what* you're saying. I should have made allowances. You look tired; come and sit down."

He drew her hand possessively through his arm as he spoke and led her to a sofa which had been pushed back against a wall. By now the party had turned into an impromptu dance, and the room seemed noisier and more crowded than ever. Charity felt quite dizzy as she watched the swirling dresses.

She wanted to send Owen away, but for some reason her wits seemed to have deserted her and she couldn't think how to do it. He was sitting beside her, but his voice sounded like a distant echo and she seemed unable to concentrate on what he was saying. On the other side of the room she could see that Jack had been waylaid by Lady Leydon and her daughter.

"Do you think it will be convenient for me to call on Mrs Mayfield tomorrow?" Owen asked earnestly.

"What? Oh, I dare say," Charity replied, leaning sideways slightly to get a better view and only half attending. Jack was laughing; what *could* Lydia be saying that was so amusing?

"Good. In the circumstances it seems best. Of course, if you had any close male relatives it would be different. Do you think Mrs Mayfield will be pleased to receive me?" Owen was looking flushed, and his earlier self-assurance seemed to have left him. He tugged at his neckcloth as he spoke.

"We're always pleased to see you," Charity said with automatic and uncomprehending politeness—she still wasn't listening properly. "And it's very kind of you to want to help, but I wouldn't like you to miss out on your hunting."

"Hunting!" He stared at her in disbelief. "Oh, I see. It's very kind of you to be so thoughtful, but in the circumstances I don't object."

"Oh, good," she said vaguely, starting to get up. "I think I'll just go…"

"Damn it all, Charity!" Owen seized her arm and wouldn't let her rise. "Don't you want to marry me?"

"What?" For a moment she gazed at his flushed face in disbelief, then it suddenly dawned on her what he must have been saying. "Oh, Owen, I'm sorry. I wasn't listening."

"No," said Owen, breathing heavily. "You've had a very trying time recently. I dare say it's all been too much for you. You'll feel better when you've had a good night's sleep. I'll escort you home."

"Yes… No! Wait a minute!" Charity exclaimed with an unexpected return to something like her normal manner. "Half an hour ago I didn't think we were on speaking terms; what on earth made you decide to ask me to marry you now?"

"I *was* very angry," Owen admitted, torn between

gratification at this opportunity to explain his actions and exasperation at her lack of proper decorum. "But I shouldn't have been. I've been thinking, and I've realised that after the sheltered life you've led it's not reasonable to expect you to fully understand the ways of the world. I should have made allowances, but I'll be more tolerant in future, I promise." He squeezed her hand reassuringly. He seemed to have regained his confidence.

"Thank you," said Charity, gazing at him rather helplessly. She had suddenly realised that she didn't know what to do. For days she had been manoeuvring to bring this moment about, but now it had arrived all she felt was a sense of anticlimax and an overwhelming desire to laugh. Marriage to Owen!

Then she remembered Hazelhurst, the Burdens and everyone else who depended on her. She couldn't let them down.

"You've made me very happy," she said resolutely, holding out her hand to Owen. "Mama will be delighted to receive you tomorrow. Do come as early as you can."

It had suddenly occurred to her that in order to get Owen's ring on her finger before the end of the month she was going to have to work very fast indeed.

"Yes, well, I think I'd better take you back to your mother now," he said; he still didn't feel entirely comfortable with the way things were turning out.

"It's getting late—no doubt you'll be wanting to go home soon."

"Yes, I expect we will," Charity agreed, and allowed Owen to pull her to her feet.

Although she didn't realise it, he found her apparent docility very soothing, and his half-acknowledged doubts began to fade. He had had a very difficult few hours trying to reconcile his earlier decision to marry her with their sudden, disturbing quarrel. But in the end he had been able to resolve his inner conflict by concluding that Charity's actions had been prompted by an uncharacteristic nervous agitation.

It had been a great relief to him when he had realised that Charity's waywardness was caused partly by her upbringing, and partly by the lack of adequate male guidance in her life, because it was therefore curable.

As he shepherded her back to Mrs Mayfield he was even thinking complacently of what an excellent wife she would make—with a little gentle instruction from him.

"That reminds me," he said abruptly. "I know that your principles are too firm for you to be led easily astray, but I think, in future, it would be a good idea if you didn't have any more to do with Lord Riversleigh. I wasn't at all pleased to see you speaking to him just now, but I suppose if he accosted you you might find it difficult to excuse yourself."

"How d—?" Charity cut short her angry response just in time. An argument with Owen now would be fatal, but at the same time she realised she wasn't prepared to let him think he'd have the ruling of her in this marriage. Compromise was one thing, but her opinions and wishes were important and he must understand that.

"No, Owen," she said, making an effort to speak in a reasonable voice. "I know you only have my best interests at heart, but I am not a fool and I cannot allow you to dictate who I speak to—or what I think. I'm sorry."

"But when we are married you will naturally be guided by me." Owen frowned. "It would be improper for you to flout my authority." He was thinking of his mother, who, to his certain knowledge, had never once disagreed with his father on any matter of significance.

"Of course I will be *guided* by you," said Charity. "But I could never let you form my opinions for me."

Owen looked at her, a hint of irritation in his expression. Then he remembered that she was over-tired and agitated, and decided to make allowances for her.

"You're very tired," he said. "I'll have your carriage called for."

Charity looked at him in exasperation. It seemed that Owen being tolerant could be even more annoying than Owen being dictatorial, but just now she didn't have the energy to argue.

From the other side of the room Jack watched them join Mrs Mayfield. He had finally extricated himself from Lady Leydon and Lydia and he had been about to return to Charity, but he had no wish to provoke another scene, and after a moment's indecision he decided to wait and continue their interrupted conversation in less public surroundings.

"Your luck seems to be quite out tonight, Travers," Sir Humphrey commented genially as he collected up the cards. "Shall we play another hand?"

"By all means," Lord Travers agreed shortly. "I'm out of practice, but I shan't be beaten again, I assure you." A faint crease in his forehead indicated that he was most unhappy at losing so heavily to a provincial squire, and he had every intention of drubbing Sir Humphrey soundly in the next game.

Sir Humphrey looked thoughtful as he shuffled the cards before dealing them again. He had been the perfect host all evening and now he was indulging himself with the pastime that, next to hunting, he enjoyed most. But he was becoming aware that, despite his surface urbanity, Lord Travers deeply resented losing. Most men hated being beaten, but Sir Humphrey thought there was something decidedly unsporting in Lord Travers's manner, and he was beginning to revise his opinion of his guest.

That didn't necessarily mean, however, that he was

also revising his opinion of Jack Riversleigh. Sir Humphrey was still inclined to think that there could be no smoke without fire, and if Jack took after his paternal grandfather, the late Lord Riversleigh, then Lord Travers's innuendoes were more than justified.

Lord Travers picked up his cards and sorted them with brisk, irritable movements. He was annoyed to find that he had a very poor hand, and his annoyance showed in his face as he looked up at the man who had come to stand beside him at the card table.

Jack acknowledged Sir Humphrey courteously, but he spoke to Lord Travers.

"My lord." He nodded briefly in greeting. "It was an unexpected pleasure to see you here tonight. After our last meeting I was under the impression that you would be spending some time in Buckinghamshire. I trust you're in your customary good health."

His voice was cool and unemotional and there was no warmth in his grey eyes as they rested on Lord Travers's face.

"Damn it, Riversleigh! I don't see what concern it is of yours if I chose to come into Sussex," Lord Travers burst out.

Sir Humphrey frowned; he was watching the encounter closely and there seemed to him to be something rather off-key about Lord Travers's response.

"No concern of mine at all," Jack agreed. He rested his hand lightly on the green baize surface of the card table and looked down at Lord Travers. "But—I think you will agree—the same cannot be said for all your...activities." He smiled as he spoke, but the expression in his eyes was singularly cold.

"I don't know what you're talking about," Lord Travers blustered.

He was at a decided disadvantage. He had to crane his head back to meet Jack's gaze, and he could neither stand up nor push his chair back, because the card table was right in the corner of the room.

"Then perhaps you should try searching your memory," Jack said. He was speaking very quietly, yet his words had the sting and impact of a whiplash.

The colour drained out of Lord Travers's face. He looked afraid—and, indeed, he was afraid.

He was remembering—too late—a half-forgotten incident which had occurred nearly three years ago when a young, arrogant nobleman had set out to demonstrate his superiority over the goldsmith-banker's grandson. Lord Penwood had forced a quarrel on Jack Riversleigh, confident of his ability to defeat him with any weapon Jack chose. But it had been young Lord Penwood who had been wounded—even though he was generally considered to be a very fine swordsman—and he had later admitted, with commendable honesty, that it was only because of Jack's forbearance that he was alive at all.

Since then the two men had become friends, but,

as Lord Travers stared into Jack's eyes, he knew that there was no possibility of such an outcome of the present occasion.

His eyes were locked with Jack's, he seemed unable to look away, and when he opened his mouth to speak he found he couldn't.

He ran his tongue nervously over his dry lips.

"I am speaking of certain *business* matters, my lord," Jack said at last. "I think—I really think—it is time we arranged a meeting. Shall we say tomorrow morning? Nine o'clock at Riversleigh?"

It took a moment for Lord Travers to comprehend what Jack had said. When he did his first reaction was one of overwhelming relief, which left him feeling weak and stupid. Then he remembered how much money he owed, and how far behind he was with the repayments, and he was filled with cold, dark foreboding.

Jack hadn't moved; he was still standing before Lord Travers, one eyebrow lifted, clearly waiting for a reply.

Lord Travers tried to speak, found that he couldn't and cleared his throat; then he tried again.

"Nine o'clock, at Riversleigh, I think you said," he croaked. He tired to smile, to put on a bold face, but he failed miserably. "It will be my pleasure, my lord."

Jack smiled sardonically; he was clearly not convinced. "I hope so," he said, and turned to take his leave of the dumbfounded Sir Humphrey.

* * *

Mrs Mayfield and Charity were taking their leave of Lady Leydon when Jack strolled up to join them, and as soon as he realised they were leaving he offered to escort them home—Hazelhurst lay almost directly between Leydon House and Riversleigh. Mrs Mayfield, still nursing her own matchmaking schemes for Charity, had no hesitation in warmly accepting his offer.

Charity herself had mixed feelings. When she had glanced up and seen Jack approaching she had experienced an instant upswell of happiness. But now, instead of looking forward to telling him that she had all but won their wager, she found herself strangely reluctant to mention the matter to him at all. In fact, for some inexplicable reason she felt more like bursting into tears than celebrating her forthcoming victory. She suddenly felt very tired and she longed for the peace and quiet of Hazelhurst.

Both Jack and Mrs Mayfield were aware of her mood, though neither of them fully understood the cause of it, and they both did their best to expedite their departure. Then they struck a hitch.

Owen hadn't been present when Jack had offered to escort the Mayfield ladies home, and when he found out he looked patently horrified, staring at Lord Riversleigh with such a mixture of hostility and suspicion before offering *his* services as escort that Mrs Mayfield began to feel uncharacteristically annoyed.

"It's very thoughtful of you, Owen," she said tartly, "but there is really no need for you to put yourself to so much trouble. As Lord Riversleigh has said, he must pass by Hazelhurst on his way home anyway, and I'm sure he doesn't mind accompanying us—not that I think we really need an escort for such a short journey."

"It's no trouble," Owen said obstinately. "As for his lordship, it would be much quicker for him to go across the fields by way of Bellow's farm. The moon is full—there would be no difficulty in doing so."

"Possibly not," Jack agreed pleasantly, "but I'm still far too new to the district to be confident of my ability to pick my way across unfamiliar fields, even by moonlight. No, I think I must stick to the roads. But I'm sure, if you really think it necessary, Mrs Mayfield would be glad of your escort also," he finished diplomatically but untruthfully.

He could tell that Mrs Mayfield didn't really welcome the idea of Owen's presence—he didn't himself—but he could also see from the set of the young man's jaw that it would take a great deal to persuade him not to come. If Jack had been convinced of the necessity for doing so he might have made the attempt, but he had never been one to pursue an argument for argument's sake and, judging by Charity's expression, all she wanted was to get home as quickly as possible. He wondered what had caused her change of mood and hoped that he had not in any way been the cause of it.

In the end, despite Owen's hostility and Mrs Mayfield's lack of enthusiasm, the entire party set out together. As a compromise, it didn't really please anyone, but at least it satisfied Charity's increasingly obvious desire to go home.

The last farewells were said, the ladies were handed into the coach, the door was shut and the whole equipage rumbled off, with Owen and Lord Riversleigh riding alongside. Owen was stiff and very formal, Jack relaxed and faintly amused.

They didn't have far to go, and it wasn't long before the carriage passed through the main gates of Hazelhurst and began to trundle up the short driveway. Jack and Owen were riding a little way ahead, Owen determined at least to be the one to hand Charity down from the coach.

Jack glanced around appreciatively. The moonlight suited the beautiful old house, and he realised again what a wrench it would be for Charity to leave it. There had been Mayfields at Hazelhurst for so long. This house had been built by one of them nearly one hundred and thirty years before, and the family had been living in the same place for much longer than that.

So far that evening his thoughts had mainly been preoccupied with Charity, but now he decided that he would do everything in his power to save the home she loved. He knew it would mean an encounter with Lord Ashbourne, and he was aware of a flicker of anticipation at the prospect because, despite his somewhat misleading words to Charity, he and the Earl were old opponents.

At that point he was roused from his thoughts by the sudden realisation that, although the curtains were drawn, the library window was slightly ajar. Was that carelessness on the part of the servants, or…?

The front door opened and two men ran out, their feet crunching on the gravel as they raced towards the shrubbery.

Instantly Jack touched his heels to the side of his horse and the bay sprang forward, riding down the men.

"Leydon!" Jack shouted over his shoulder, because for a moment Owen had been too startled to do anything. But almost before Jack had called Owen had urged his horse into a gallop, his huntsman's instincts coming rapidly to the fore.

The man nearest Jack veered away, and Jack followed him. The other kept running straight to the shrubbery, with Owen hard on his heels.

The coachman hauled on the reins and the carriage juddered to a stop. The coachman had seen the men leave the house, and he didn't know whether his ladies would be safer in the carriage or under their own roof. If there were still intruders *inside* the house they would be better outside. He reached for the blunderbuss he always carried but never before had had occasion to use.

"Martin, what is it?" Charity put her head out of the window.

"Stay in the carriage please, miss," he said, his voice a mixture of excitement and apprehension.

Charity looked ahead. She was just in time to see Jack draw level with the running man. As he did so he sprang from the back of the speeding horse, and she felt a moment of sickening fear as both men went down.

Then Jack stood up, dragging his shaken captive to his feet and over to the carriage.

Charity realised she'd stopped breathing, and drew in a shaky breath. Then she remembered Owen— where was he?

"Charity! Charity!" Mrs Mayfield was tugging at her arm. "What's happening? Charity!"

"I don't know, Mama," Charity said briefly. "But I don't think it's anything to get alarmed about."

Jack searched his captive quickly, then he forced the man down on to his knees beside the carriage and ordered him to put his hands on his head.

"Watch him," he said briefly to the coachman, and turned back to the house, taking a pistol from his greatcoat pocket as he did so.

"Stay here, Mama," said Charity. Her earlier weariness forgotten, she opened the carriage door and jumped down on to the drive. Then she picked up her skirts and ran to Jack."

"Go back to the carriage," he said sharply. "I don't think there'll be anyone else in the house, but I can't be sure."

"It's my house," said Charity. "I won't get in the way."

She was slightly breathless, but quite calm, and very determined.

"Very well," said Jack after only the briefest hesitation. "But keep behind me."

He pushed open the front door and stepped into the house. The library door was open and a band of light fell across the floor of the otherwise darkened hall. There was a lantern on the library table, and several of the candles had been lit. It was only because the curtains had been drawn that the light hadn't shown from outside.

There was nobody in the hall, and Jack strode forward to pick up the lantern. Charity followed him into the library, but she didn't get much further than the door. She took one glance around and stopped dead, lifting her hands to her face.

The library was a shambles. All the desk drawers had been broken into and their contents upended on the floor, chairs had been overturned, and books pulled from the shelves.

"Oh, my God!" Charity whispered. "What were they looking for?"

"I don't know," Jack said briefly. "But this is clearly the room they were interested in. I'm sure there won't be anybody else in the house."

Nevertheless, he took the lantern and quickly checked the other rooms before returning to Charity.

She hadn't moved; she was still standing where he had left her, staring with horror at the chaos all around her.

"Here." Jack picked up one of the lighted candles and put it gently into Charity's hand. "Go and light some of the candles in the parlour, and I'll bring your mother in. She won't want to see this." Then he smiled at her reassuringly. "It's not as bad as it looks."

"No." Charity roused herself and walked mechanically out of the library, closing the door gently behind her.

Chapter Nine

When Jack got outside he found the coachman still covering the captured burglar with his blunderbuss, and Mrs Mayfield on the verge of hysterics inside the carriage. She'd tried to ask the coachman what was happening, but he'd been so overcome with the responsibility for guarding his prisoner that he had growled at her to get back inside the carriage and keep quiet.

Consequently Jack found her cowering inside the coach, almost afraid to move.

She jumped convulsively, and gave a muffled scream as Jack's head and shoulders, silhouetted by the moonlight, appeared at the window.

"Don't be alarmed, ma'am, it's only me," he said, his deep voice instantly recognisable. "You can come into the house now." He opened the coach door, let down the steps and helped her out.

"Is Charity all right?" she asked anxiously.

"Yes, ma'am," he replied reassuringly. "The situation seemed more alarming than it was. You're quite safe."

He offered her the support of his arm and escorted her into the house. He'd deliberately gone to the door on the opposite side of the carriage to where the prisoner still knelt, and Mrs Mayfield didn't see him. Jack paused briefly at the door of the parlour, pleased to see that in the short time he'd been gone Charity had already made the room seem comfortably welcoming; then Mrs Mayfield saw her daughter and ran towards her.

Charity was feeling more normal. She had pulled herself together when Jack had gone out to get Mrs Mayfield and not only had she lit most of the candles, but she'd also kindled the fire in the hearth and sent Charles to fetch some brandy.

The servants had been told not to wait up for their mistresses' return from the party, and until they'd heard all the commotion outside they had not realised they had had housebreakers.

Charles, who'd appeared with his breeches and his coat hastily pulled on over his nightshirt, was somewhat inclined to exclaim at the peculiar goings on. But Charity had cut him short and sent him away to find some brandy. She thought it might calm her mother's nerves.

"Oh, Charity! What's happening?" Mrs Mayfield cried, throwing out her arms to her daughter.

"Nothing dreadful, Mama," Charity said reassuringly. For some reason which she didn't full understand, she felt quite calm. There had been a moment when she had first seen the damage that had been done when she'd felt really distressed, but somehow the sight of Jack's tall figure behind her mother seemed immensely comforting.

"Come and sit down by the fire," she said soothingly to Mrs Mayfield. "Charles is going to bring you some brandy. There's nothing to worry about, is there, my lord?" As she spoke she gently persuaded Mrs Mayfield to sit down, and held her mother's cold hands reassuringly in hers.

"Nothing at all," he replied calmly. "I'm afraid you've had intruders again, Mrs Mayfield. But I've checked thoroughly and there's no one here now. You're quite safe."

"Oh, thank you." Mrs Mayfield sighed with relief. As Jack had suspected, the fear of strangers in her house was of more immediate concern to her than the possibility that anything might have been stolen. "I'm sure if you say so it must be true, my lord. Thank goodness you were here. I don't know what we'd have done without you."

"I think Miss Mayfield would probably have managed," he said, a half-smile in his eyes as he looked down at Charity.

She was feeling torn between admiration and exasperation at the ease and speed with which he had allayed Mrs Mayfield's fears. Two nights ago, when the intruders had first appeared, Charity had had to dedicate several hours to achieving the same effect.

"Charles is your manservant, I take it," Jack said, without acknowledging that he'd seen or understood Charity's look. "When he comes back, could you send him out to me, Miss Mayfield? Excuse me, ma'am."

He went back outside and surveyed the moonlit scene before him. The coachman was still grimly guarding the prisoner, and Jack's horse was standing with the reins hanging, near the edge of the shrubbery. Owen was nowhere to be seen.

Jack whistled quietly, and his horse pricked up his ears and began to walk sedately towards him, nuzzling him in the hope of a reward. Jack spoke quietly to him and picked up the reins, tying them to one of the thick stems of ivy that climbed the outside wall of the house. Then he went over to the carriage.

"Well done," he said to the coachman. "You've done excellently. You can leave the prisoner to me now. Take the carriage round to the stables and then come back for my horse."

"Yes, sir." The coachman laid down his blunderbuss with relief and swelled with pride at Jack's words. He hadn't seen much of the new lord, but he'd already come to the conclusion that Jack's praise was worth having. He immediately decided to give Jack's horse the best possible care.

"All right, you can stand up now," Jack said to his prisoner as the coach rumbled away. "But don't try anything. I have a pistol, and if I have to I'll use it. Do you understand?"

"Y-y-y-y-yes," said the man, speaking for the first time, just as Charles arrived.

"Is that him, my lord?" Charles asked darkly, his hands doubled into fists. "Only let me show him what he gets for breaking into a ladies' establishment." He took a determined step towards the man as he spoke.

"Later, perhaps," said Jack coolly. "I want to ask him some questions first. If he doesn't answer to my satisfaction, I may well allow you to teach him better manners." His words were intended for the prisoner's benefit—not Charles's. Fear might induce the man to speak more quickly, and more truthfully, than might otherwise have been the case.

There were sounds of movement coming from the shrubbery, and Jack turned towards them, his pistol once more in his hand, though he suspected it was nothing more alarming than Owen's return.

His supposition proved quite correct. Owen emerged into the moonlight, minus his hat and muttering under his breath. He was leading a strange horse, but he'd lost his quarry and he wasn't in a good mood. He looked down at Jack balefully.

"He got away," he said, somewhat obviously. "They had horses tied up on the other side of the shrubbery. I followed him as far as I could, but I lost him behind the three-acre woods. It would have been a different story if I'd had my hounds with me." He eyed Jack belligerently, as if blaming him for this omission.

"I'm sure it would," said Jack mildly. "And at least you've brought the second horse back. Now we can be certain there were only two of them. Let Charles take the horses round to the stables and we can go into the house and question this fellow." He indicated his prisoner.

Owen hesitated. He could find no real fault with the plan, but he never liked being told what to do at the best of times, and when it was Jack Riversleigh making the suggestion Owen was inclined to disagree on principle.

"What do we need to question him for?" he demanded. "We know what he was doing. We caught him in the act."

"True, but there are one or two unusual circumstances that need explaining," Jack replied. "Of course, if you're not interested in being present when I question him…" He left the words hanging and, after a rather significant pause, Owen jumped down from his horse and handed the reins to Charles.

"My father should be present," he said. "He'd know the best way of going about this."

"I'm sure he would," Jack agreed. "But it's very late, and I don't think there's any need to trouble Sir Humphrey tonight. You can fetch him in the morning. In the meantime, I don't think we'll do any harm if we question the prisoner now. We'll take him into the library."

It was very cold in Charity's bedroom and, by the time she'd undressed and put on her nightgown, she was shivering slightly. She slid quickly into bed and pulled the covers up under her chin, thinking about the events of the evening.

Jack had managed everything so smoothly that there had been very little disruption to the household, but Charity could hardly repress a shudder when she thought of what might have happened. It would have been bad enough to have come home to find they'd been burgled, but it would have been worse if they'd actually disturbed the housebreakers at their work!

Jack had questioned the man he had caught, but the prisoner seemed to be somewhat slow-witted, and that, combined with the fact that he had a very bad stammer, had made it very difficult to make sense of anything he said.

Owen had quickly come to the conclusion that the whole exercise was a waste of time, and had left Jack to get on with it alone while he went to see Charity. He'd intended to reassure her, but neither

Charity nor Mrs Mayfield had seemed to need much reassurance, and Mrs Mayfield had completely exasperated him by her obvious confidence in Lord Riversleigh's ability to manage the whole affair.

Owen's temper was even more uncertain than usual because his failure to catch the second intruder had piqued his pride. He had seemed to feel the need to justify his failure, and he'd explained several times that he had been at a great disadvantage because he'd had to chase *his* man through the shrubbery. Things would have been different if his quarry had stuck to the open drive, as Lord Riversleigh's had done.

Charity had agreed mendaciously with everything Owen said, though inwardly she continued unshaken in the opinion that a few shrubs wouldn't have made any difference to *Jack's* chances of success.

But Owen had slowly talked himself into a better mood; and when Jack finally joined them in the parlour he had been able to greet him with a reasonable level of politeness, though certainly not warmly.

With Mrs Mayfield's permission, Jack had suggested that they lock the burglar in the cellar for the rest of the night, with Charles to guard him, and in the morning Owen should fetch his father to arrange for the disposal of the man. In the meantime, though he didn't anticipate there would be any further disturbances, he suggested that both he and Owen remain at Hazelhurst for the night.

Mrs Mayfield had greeted his suggestion with delighted relief and immediately asked Charity to organise rooms for their unexpected guests. Owen was less delighted by the notion that Jack would be staying under the same roof as Charity, but consoled himself with the thought that his own presence would surely prevent the notorious Lord Riversleigh from doing anything improper.

These knotty problems having been solved, it hadn't been long before the entire household, with the exception of Charles, had retired for what was left of the night.

Charity smiled to herself in the dark. She was aware of a profound sense of relief that, for once, she wasn't solely responsible for the well-being of everyone at Hazelhurst. The idea that there was someone she could rely on was an unusual but far from unwelcome sensation.

She turned over and prepared to go to sleep. Then she remembered the library. There were still books and papers strewn all over the floor, and tomorrow she had another meeting with Lord Ashbourne's agent. She sighed. She could always offer the excuse that they'd been burgled, but for her own sake she wanted matters settled as quickly as possible.

Besides, Sir Humphrey would want to know if anything had been taken, and how could she tell if she hadn't checked? She pushed back the bedclothes and sat up, wondering why Jack hadn't suggested she check to see if anything was missing. Then she decided that he probably hadn't wanted to distress her any further that evening.

She put on her slippers and robe, wrapped a shawl around her shoulders for good measure, and tiptoed quietly downstairs. She didn't want to disturb anyone else.

There was a light shining beneath the library door and she supposed they must have forgotten to put out the candles, but when she opened it she saw Jack sitting in a chair before the fire, a glass of brandy in his hand.

He turned his head quickly as the door opened and stood up when he saw Charity.

"Is something wrong?" he asked.

"No, no. I just came down to…" She looked past him and her eyes widened. "You've tidied up already!" she exclaimed.

She never doubted that it had been Jack who'd collected up all the papers and put them in neat piles on the desk.

"Only very roughly," he said apologetically. "I think I've put most things in a reasonably logical order, though I can't guarantee you'll be able to find everything first time. But I thought you might find it less distressing if you didn't have to scramble on the floor for everything tomorrow. It's not pleasant having your belongings mishandled in such a way."

"No." It was true. Charity had been dreading sorting out the mess—that was partly why she had got up in the night to do it, rather than waiting until the next day. She felt her eyes fill with unexpected tears.

"Thank you," she whispered.

"Come and sit by the fire," Jack suggested. He knew he probably ought to persuade her to go back to bed, but he suspected she needed to talk about what had happened—at least, that was what he told himself. But the truth was, he was too pleased to see her to send her away.

"Thank you." Charity sat down, hugging her shawl about her. "I still don't understand what they wanted," she said, glancing around. "I mean, as far as I can tell, nothing has been taken—and what were they looking for in the *library?* There weren't any valuable papers in the desk—only farm and household accounts!"

"No," said Jack. "That's the puzzle that's been keeping me awake. Your book-keeping is excellent, by the way. I'd have no hesitation in offering you employment—should you ever want it." He grinned at her.

"You really mean it!" Charity exclaimed, quite startled by his praise.

"Of course." The smile warmed his eyes. "I never joke about such *serious* matters."

"Now you're laughing at me," Charity said uncertainly.

"No."

He was teasing her, but there was nothing insincere about the expression in his steady grey eyes, and Charity suddenly felt quite breathless. She looked away, feeling the colour rising in her cheeks.

"May I offer you some of your own excellent brandy, Miss Mayfield?" Jack asked with humorous formality. "There doesn't seem to be much else in the way of refreshment."

"Yes, please," said Charity, rather glad that he'd changed the subject. "I don't drink it as a general rule, but it is good, isn't it? It comes directly from France."

"I thought perhaps it did," said Jack, sounding amused. "I don't suppose you happen to know what kind of arrangements my grandfather had with the smugglers, do you?"

"Gentlemen," Charity corrected him, smiling. "In Sussex they're known as the gentlemen. Mr Guthrie will take care of it for you."

"Will he, indeed? A man of many parts, I perceive." Jack offered Charity a glass of brandy.

"Oh, he doesn't do any smuggling himself," Charity assured him, taking the glass. "But he knows *everyone.* He's lived here a very long time, you know."

"Yes, I do," Lord Riversleigh said more seriously. The land agent was almost the only person he'd met since he'd come into Sussex who could remember his father, and that alone recommended him to Jack.

Charity looked at him curiously. He was gazing down at the fire with unfocused eyes, and she wondered what he was thinking, what memories her words might have triggered. But she didn't ask. She was warm and relaxed, and in his company the silence didn't worry her.

She tucked her feet up beneath her, settled herself comfortably back against the wing of the chair, and took a sip of the brandy. Though neither of them realised it, they made an incongruous pair as they sat before the hearth.

Jack was still wearing the formal, very elegant clothes he had worn to the Leydons' rout. The black velvet of his coat glowed in the firelight and, despite all his exertions, the crisp white lace at his wrists remained as unsullied as it had been when he had dressed for the party—yet nobody could have mistaken him for a fop. Even in repose, he possessed an unmistakable aura of determination and power.

Charity, on the other hand, was entirely and bliss-fully relaxed. Earlier that evening she had been as elegant as Jack, dressed in hoops and silk, with a fashionable train on the back of her dress—but no one could curl up in front of the fire in such a gown.

Now, in her simple nightdress and robe, with her dark curls falling back around her shoulders and her feet tucked up beneath her in the large wing chair, she was far more comfortable. It never occurred to her that there was anything shocking about her presence in the library in such a state of undress—perhaps because she felt so much at ease in Jack's company.

He didn't say anything for some time—he was still apparently thinking—but the continuing silence didn't worry her. She sipped her brandy now and then and gazed into the fire, watching the dancing orange flames with unfocused eyes, until at last it became too much of an effort even to lift the glass, and she rested it on the arm of the chair. She was neither quite asleep nor quite awake, but she was overwhelmed by a delightful languor which made even the thought of rousing herself unthinkable.

The glass began to tilt as her hold on it relaxed, and Jack reached out and took it gently from her.

"You should go back to bed," he said. "You can't go to sleep here. At least…you could, of course, but you'd be more comfortable in bed."

"I'm not going to sleep," Charity said drowsily, because she felt too pleasantly tired to move. "What are you thinking about?"

Jack grinned, well aware that she was simply trying to delay the need to get up. "You're not awake enough to listen to me, even if I tell you," he said. "Come on, stand up."

He took her hand and tried to pull her gently to her feet.

Charity didn't move; she simply let him pull at her arm. Her feet were still tucked up beside her and, until she chose to set them down on the floor again, it wasn't really possible for Jack to get her to stand up.

She looked up at him, a faint challenge in her eyes. She was too close to sleep to be self-conscious, and she was vaguely curious to know what he'd do next—but mostly she simply wanted to stay where she was.

"You'll be cold when the fire goes out," Jack said.

Charity glanced at the grate. "It won't go out just yet," she replied.

Jack looked down at her, a half-smile in his eyes. She'd woken up slightly, but not enough to retreat behind the barrier of reserve she usually erected around herself, and there was a humorous gleam in her eyes as she returned his gaze.

He was still holding her hand, though he was no longer trying to pull her to her feet. The moment stretched out and, as Charity gazed up at Jack, she felt her heart begin to beat faster. His clasp on her hand tightened, and the expression in his eyes changed. He wasn't laughing anymore, and the intensity of his steady gaze nearly hypnotised her. No one had ever looked at her that way before.

Very gently he began to draw her towards him, and this time she didn't resist. Almost without knowing what she was doing, she let her feet drop to the floor and stood up.

Her gaze was still locked with his and for an instant longer she remained unaware of anything but the look in his eyes. Then he put his free hand on her waist and she gasped as his touch sent tremors rippling through her body. He let his hand track very gently around the belt of her robe until it reached the small of her back, and as she felt herself begin to tremble anew he bent his head and kissed her parted lips.

For a moment surprise and confusion held her motionless, but then, as his lips continued to caress hers, the rigidity melted from her body and without realising what she was doing she slid her arms about his neck and pressed herself even closer against him. At some point she had closed her eyes, and now she was lost in a world in which touch was the most important sense. She could feel his arms around her, and she could feel and taste his lips on hers, and nothing else mattered.

Her responsiveness heightened Jack's desire even further, and he too began to lose all sense of his surroundings. Her shawl had long since fallen unheeded to the floor and now, somehow, her robe had become unbelted. His hand slipped within, and through the thin fabric of her nightdress he touched her breast.

Charity opened her eyes, but she didn't pull away, and there was a curious mixture of trust, wonderment and desire in her expression as Jack briefly cupped her breast in his hand before once more holding her tightly against him.

The first shock of surprise at what was happening to her had passed, yet if anything she now felt more intensely aware of everything Jack did than she had before—and more able to savour the pleasure of it. She let her head fall back as he kissed the base of her throat, her own hand caressing the nape of his neck while he began to undo the fastenings of her nightgown.

Then two of the candles, which had been burning for some hours, suddenly guttered and went out almost simultaneously, and Jack looked up, finally recalled to time and place.

His right hand was still beneath Charity's robe, pressing her to him, and he moved his other hand gently to cup her head. At that moment it was more than he could bear to let her go or put her away from him, but he also knew that he couldn't continue as he had been.

Even his experience at the party hadn't prepared him for the way Charity now dominated his thoughts and feelings, and he was shaken to realise what an effect she could have on him—was still having on him. It was only with the greatest difficulty that he resisted the temptation to kiss her again. But, however great the pleasure of this moment, Charity deserved more than this: a wedding and a bridal night to remember—with no regrets to plague her in the morning.

The moment's respite gave Charity time to think, though at first she was aware only of the rapid beating of her heart, and an overwhelming regret that Jack was no longer kissing her.

"I'm sorry," said Jack rather hoarsely, and with an effort he let her go and stepped back. "I didn't intend... I think it would be best if you went back upstairs."

He hadn't intended the words to come out so harshly, but he also hadn't realised how hard it would be to move away from her—or how hard he would find it to crush down his desire for her—and he was too disturbed to frame an elegant speech.

"Sorry!" Charity's eyes flew to his face, suddenly convinced that in some way he had found her wanting and was sending her...

Of course! Well-bred young ladies didn't...

Horror filled her as she remembered what had happened between them, and she blushed crimson and turned her back on him, unable to lift her eyes to what she imagined must be his disapproving gaze.

"No, I'm sorry," she replied, her voice sounding muffled and uncertain. "I don't... I'm not usually... I didn't mean to offend you with my lack of propriety."

"Offend *me!*" Jack exclaimed, relief and amazement mingling in his voice. When she'd turned her back on him he'd been afraid that her action had been prompted with disgust at *his* behaviour.

"You haven't offended me! It was I who took advantage of you."

Despite his earlier resolution, he couldn't help taking a step towards her as he spoke and slipping his hands around her waist.

Instinctively she leant back against him, and his hold on her tightened, one hand lifting to caress her breast, and she felt fresh thrills of pleasure course through her.

"You have nothing to be sorry about," he murmured, his lips brushing her hair.

She closed her eyes and smiled, her hand instinctively covering his at her waist as he bent his head lower and kissed her just below her ear. Her momentary embarrassment was forgotten as fresh ripples of delight radiated from the spot his lips were touching, and she almost felt she no longer had the strength to stand without his support. Without conscious thought she began to turn in his arms to face him…

And then she remembered Owen.

This time she gasped with horror—not pleasure—and Jack felt the change in her immediately.

"What is it?"

"Nothing." With an effort Charity pulled herself out of his arms and moved away from him.

"I— Oh, dear, the candles have gone out," she said, speaking at random.

"Charity, what is it?" Jack looked at her, a slight frown of anxiety in his eyes. Her unexpected change of mood had thrown him off balance.

"Nothing," she said again. "I must have been more tired than I thought." She laughed uncertainly and tried to fasten her robe with hands that trembled uncontrollably.

She was betrothed to Owen! Only that evening she had agreed to marry him and urged him to speak to her mother as soon as possible, yet here she was, a scant few hours later, letting—encouraging—another man to make love to her!

How could she have been such a fool? How could she not have known that this was where her friendship with Jack was leading—was where she wanted it to lead? All the signs had been there, at the party, and earlier—she just hadn't understood them.

But what did Jack really want from her? She began to feel cold as she remembered that he hadn't said anything to indicate his intentions towards her. He had apologised for his behaviour, but he hadn't excused it on the grounds of love, and she began to realise how little she knew about him. He had said once that he had no immediate plans to marry: was that because there was no one he cared for—or was it that he did have an agreement with a lady, though for some reason the wedding had been delayed?

He was standing in front of her now and, as she

stared up at him with huge, frightened eyes, he put aside her cold hands and carefully fastened her robe. Then he picked up the discarded shawl and put it back round her shoulders.

"What's wrong?" he asked gently. "You look as if you've seen a ghost. Have I frightened you? I didn't mean to."

"No," she whispered. It was true, he hadn't frightened her, though perhaps she had frightened herself with the intensity of her response to him.

"It's just…so much has happened that it's… I think I'm just confused."

"Yes, yes, I know," he said quietly, almost ruefully. "Can I help?"

For a moment Charity stared at him, but for once her famous outspokenness failed her and she couldn't bring herself to ask the one thing she most wanted to know—what did he feel for her? And did she really want to hear the answer anyway? All her customary self-confidence had deserted her and she felt that if he told her he didn't love her she wouldn't be able to bear it—because she loved him.

But he had no plans for marriage—he had said so. It would be better not to hear the worst tonight, not when she was so tired and so confused. Tomorrow she would be strong, tomorrow she would be able to face anything—but not tonight.

"No, no, I don't think so, thank you," she said at

last, and knew that now she ought to leave. But she couldn't quite bring herself to do so.

In the morning Owen would ask her mother for her hand in marriage, Mrs Mayfield would consent and Jack would congratulate them.

There would be no more private conversations then, no more rides and no more comfortable evenings by the fire. The thought was so terrible that tears welled up in her eyes. She was so tired and so overwrought by everything that had happened to her in that very crowded evening that it didn't occur to her that she was being foolish.

Jack didn't know exactly what lay behind her sudden distress, but he guessed how she felt far more accurately than she realised. He had still not entirely recovered himself from the fire of their embrace, yet not only was he more experienced, but he had also been partially prepared for it by the strength of his response to her earlier at the party. It wasn't surprising that Charity should find herself overwhelmed by such powerful and unaccustomed feelings. She needed some time to recover and Jack knew he must give it to her.

But it would do no good to send her to bed just yet, he told himself, she wouldn't sleep; but he was honest enough to admit to himself that he didn't want to part from her with so much unsettled between them. He wanted to banish the haunted expression from her face—and he wanted to rekindle the warmth he had seen glowing in her eyes only minutes before. No, he couldn't send her to bed yet.

"Come, sit down," he said, and gently guided her back to the chair she had occupied before. "Would you like some more brandy?"

"Thank you." She took the glass from him and held it cupped in cold hands as she watched him kick the dying fire back into life. Circumstances had gone beyond her control and she felt an odd sense of unreality as she waited for him to speak.

Jack looked down at her ruefully, finally realising that there was nothing he could say to her tonight that would help. Too much had happened to her too quickly, and now she was too tired to understand—perhaps too tired even to feel anything.

"You must go to bed," he said, reluctantly accepting the situation. "I'll take you upstairs."

"No, no, I can manage. Thank you."

A brief resurgence of pride and independence brought Charity to her feet. If he wanted to get rid of her she could at least leave with dignity. She took a couple of steps towards the door, and suddenly the question which had been hovering on the edge of her thoughts for some time rose unbidden and unexpectedly to the surface of her mind.

"Why were you still sitting here after you'd tidied up?" she demanded, both sounding and looking far more like herself. "You said it was a puzzle. Is there something you haven't told me—do you *know* what the burglars were looking for?"

For a moment Jack looked at her, then he smiled faintly. He hadn't intended to mention his suspicions tonight, but if she was actually asking…

"I don't know exactly," he replied. "But I have a pretty good idea of what they think they were looking for."

Chapter Ten

"But what was it?" Charity asked.

"Treasure," said Jack simply.

"Treasure!" she exclaimed. "In our *library!* You must be mistaken. There's no treasure here!"

"Possibly not," replied Jack equably, "but the thieves certainly think there is."

"Good heavens!" said Charity blankly.

"Don't worry about it now," Jack said. "I shouldn't have said anything about it to you when you're so tired. Go to bed; I'll tell you in the morning."

"Certainly not," said Charity indignantly, and now she sounded just like her old self. "It's my library. I want to hear exactly what the man told you. Treasure at Hazelhurst! He must be mad! Or—are you sure you understood him properly? Owen said he was incomprehensible."

"He certainly wasn't the most articulate man I've ever spoken to," Jack agreed. "And he'd obviously had the fear of God—or the Devil—put into him by his master. But some things he said were plain enough. He didn't know what the treasure was, and he didn't know why they were searching here—but they were definitely looking for something in the library. Something they had to find before the end of February."

"Good God! They must be crazy!" Charity declared again. "There's nothing here but books and ledgers. Perhaps they've got the wrong house. I mean…" She looked around at the dimly lit library, shadows from the firelight flickering on the walls and the bookshelves. "There's nothing here," she said again.

"You may be right," said Jack. "But I think it bears investigation. There are one or two things about what he said, and about what else has happened here recently, that…" He paused abruptly and held up a warning hand as Charity looked at him questioningly.

In the silence she heard the creak of wooden floorboards outside and felt a sudden flare of alarm as she wondered wildly whether the prisoner had overcome Charles and was escaping—or was it the master thief returning for his apprentice?

Then she remembered Jack was there and her fear subsided. She turned to him for guidance.

Jack was looking at the door, one hand in his pocket, the other still holding his brandy glass.

There was a moment of silence—then the door

burst open and Owen plunged into the library, a poker upheld in his hand.

He lowered it slowly as he saw them, and Charity watched the look of astonishment on his face change to one of outrage as he took in her presence.

"Charity!" He goggled at her for a moment, then he looked at Jack, his expression redolent with suspicion.

"Ah, Leydon," said Jack smoothly. "I hope I didn't wake you. I'm afraid I must have made more noise than I intended when I was putting the furniture back in its place. Miss Mayfield has already come down to investigate."

"Putting the furniture back?" Owen said disbelievingly.

"I'm afraid I have an obsession with tidiness," Jack explained, straight-faced. "The thought of a disorderly room can keep me awake all night."

"Really?" Owen looked at Jack as if he were mad, and Charity had to restrain a sudden urge to laugh, though at the same time she was on tenterhooks in case either man said anything to arouse the other's suspicions—they both had good reason to suppose they occupied a privileged position in her affections.

"Oh, yes," said Jack, blandly enlarging upon his theme. "I've been known to drive servants mad with my insistence that everything *has* its place and that everything is kept *in* its place. But I assure you there's no cause for alarm. It's quite safe to return to bed; I'll do my best not to disturb you again. Indeed, as soon as I've put these books back on their shelves, I shall feel able to retire myself."

"I see," said Owen, for once almost lost for words, though he retained sufficient presence of mind to feel scornful of what he considered to be a very unmanly—almost housewifely—weakness.

Jack's lips twitched slightly, but he didn't say anything, and Owen was so disconcerted that he started to turn away without continuing the conversation.

Then he remembered that Charity was still in the library—and wearing only her nightdress!

Owen's conventional soul was horrified and he swung back to face Jack, new suspicion dawning in his eyes.

"There's no need for Charity to help you tidy up," he said, so belligerently that Charity felt a flicker of alarm.

"None at all," Jack agreed calmly, taking the wind out of Owen's sails.

"Come, Charity, I'll escort you back upstairs." Owen held out a masterful hand, trying to regain the initiative.

"For heaven's sake! Owen!" Charity exclaimed, exasperation at his high-handedness overriding her anxiety that he might provoke a scene. "I'm quite capable of finding my way upstairs in my own house. Do go back to bed!"

"I'm not leaving you downstairs alone," said Owen magnificently, ignoring Jack.

"But I'm not alone," Charity pointed out. "Besides, there's something I want to ask Lord Riversleigh. Do go to bed, Owen. I won't stay up much longer, I assure you."

"I'll wait," said Owen stubbornly.

Charity sighed in exasperation and glanced at Jack. His wooden expression was belied by the twinkle in his eye, but he clearly wasn't going to give her any help. If she didn't want to include Owen in a discussion about real or imaginary treasure she was going to have to submit gracefully.

She frowned, and walked over to the door Owen was holding open for her. Just before she went through it she looked back at Jack, and he grinned at her. Indignation flared in her eyes and she turned her head away, walking upstairs with great dignity.

Jack closed the door that Owen had neglected to shut and leant back against it. Then he looked around the library, though he was actually thinking about Charity. It still hadn't occurred to him that she might actually have succeeded in getting herself betrothed to Owen when he so obviously infuriated her at every turn, and Jack was hoping that he would have an opportunity to talk to her again in the morning. But first he had other things to do and, after a moment or two, he pushed himself away from the door and headed towards the section of shelving where the first intruder had been standing when Charity had surprised him.

The sun was high in the sky when Charity woke the next morning. Despite her weariness the previous evening, sleep hadn't come quickly and even when she had fallen asleep she'd been restless and uneasy. It had only been just before dawn that she had at last fallen into a profound and deep sleep, and for once she'd overslept badly.

The pale winter sun was streaming in through the curtains, which despite the horrified protests of her mother and the maids, she never allowed to be closed. If she turned her head she could see the tops of the trees outlined against the sky. If she moved her head she could make the pictures through the window shift from one leaded glass pane to another. As a child it had been a game she had played with herself. Does the holly branch look better through this glass pane or that one? She turned her head experimentally. This one, she decided. A perfect picture in a perfect frame.

What had happened last night? Now the sun was shining it was hard to believe that the interlude in the firelit library could be anything more than a dream. But Charity knew it wasn't. Even now she could feel her body begin to glow anew with the remembered ecstasy of his touch. What *had* happened? What did he want from her—and what did she want from him?

She thought of her coolly laid plans to marry first Edward, and then Owen. There had never been any question of love. She liked Edward and she was fond of Owen, but marriage to either would be a practical arrangement to meet practical needs—and she'd always thought that that was what she wanted. Now she knew that it wasn't—and she didn't know what to do.

She felt reluctant to get up and go downstairs to face either Jack or Owen. She was still too uncertain of her feelings—or Jack's—and today was the day Owen was going to ask Mrs Mayfield for permission to marry her!

For one craven minute she thought about claiming she was unwell and staying in bed. But that would have been cowardly and Charity never turned her back on a challenge—even when she was hungry. It suddenly occurred to her that she was, in fact, extremely hungry. She got up and dressed quickly. Things always look better after breakfast, she thought, and for the first time wondered why she'd been left undisturbed for so long. Normally she was up before the maids to go to the dairy and plan the day ahead.

She hurried downstairs and found her mother at breakfast.

"Hello, dear, do you feel more rested now?" Mrs Mayfield asked placidly. "Lord Riversleigh thought you looked tired last night and suggested you be allowed to sleep in. I must say, I thought myself you were looking very weary. It must be the worry of all the arrangements—not to mention the excitement of having burglars."

"Burglars!" Charity's first flush of embarrassment at the mention of Jack's name was forgotten as she suddenly remembered what Jack had said about treasure. In the light of day the notion seemed even more fantastic than it had the previous night, yet she realised now that Jack had been quite serious when he had spoken about it.

"Where is Lord Riversleigh?" she asked urgently, hardly noticing her mother's unusual complacency.

"He's a very nice man, isn't he?" said Mrs Mayfield. "So thoughtful, and very reliable in a crisis. I'm sure all the rumours about him are just spite."

"Yes, Mama."

Charity blushed uncomfortably. She didn't want to think about all Jack's good qualities now—it made her nervous. She preferred to concentrate on the probably apocryphal treasure.

"Where is he?" she asked again, interrupting her mother.

"I was saying to Lady Dalrymple only yester-day…" Mrs Mayfield broke off and looked at Charity in mild surprise, though inwardly she was delighted by her daughter's impatience to seek out Jack.

"He went to ask one of the stable-lads to take a message to Riversleigh," she said.

Charity turned and hurried out of the room, but at the doorway she checked and swung round to face her mother.

"And where's Owen?" she asked suspiciously, suddenly afraid that he might already have declared himself to her mother.

"He's already on his way to fetch Sir Humphrey." Mrs Mayfield dipped another piece of toast into her tea.

"Good." Her mind relieved of one of its cares, Charity hurried off to find Jack.

She came face to face with him, re-entering the house through a side-door, and stopped suddenly. For the first time she felt shy in his presence, and she didn't know what to say.

He was standing with his back to the light and for a moment she couldn't see his expression. Then he turned slightly and smiled, and she felt quite breathless.

"You said something about treasure last night," she said somewhat incoherently, knowing she was blushing and hoping she didn't look as foolish and unsure of herself as she felt.

"So I did." Jack closed the outer door and came towards her. For an instant he was standing beside her, looming over her, then he moved past her and opened the door of the back parlour—politely holding it for her.

"If you have a moment, Miss Mayfield, I think there are a few things we ought to discuss before Sir Humphrey gets here."

Miss Mayfield? He'd called her Miss Mayfield. Last night he'd called her Charity. What did it mean?

"Yes, of course," she said sedately, and went into the parlour.

"What did...?" she began as he was closing the door—and stopped mid-sentence as for the first time she realised that there was an aura of suppressed excitement about him.

"You don't mean you found something?" she demanded.

Jack laughed. "How did you know?" he asked. "I meant to surprise you."

"You have!" said Charity emphatically. "Good heavens! What is it? Show me!"

"Here." Jack took a beautifully made box from his pocket and handed it to her, watching her expression as she opened it.

There was a jewel inside, but a jewel unlike any she had ever seen before. It was an oval pendant of gold, set with diamonds and three blood-red rubies, and it looked as beautiful and perfect as the day it had been made.

Almost without thinking, Charity went over to the window, and in the better light the precious stones seemed to take on new life.

Jack reached past her and picked up the jewel. He opened it carefully and handed it back to her, taking the jewel case from her as he did so.

She took the pendant in her hands, almost afraid to touch it, and saw that it was in fact a locket, containing the most exquisite miniature portrait she had ever seen. It was a picture of a lady, painted against a brilliant blue background and dressed in the style of the Elizabethans. Her glowing hair was drawn back from her face, there was a ruff around her neck, and roses on her breast.

Charity gasped, because it was almost as if the lady were alive. She seemed to be looking straight into Charity's eyes and she was smiling with a joyous happiness which was almost painful to behold.

"I believe it's by Nicholas Hilliard," said Jack quietly; he'd been watching Charity's expression. "He was a miniaturist during Elizabeth's reign. He painted many pictures of the Queen, some of them placed in jewelled settings every bit as magnificent as this one, but he painted other people as well."

"I've never seen anything like it," Charity murmured. "Hilliard? I've heard of him, of course, but I never guessed that *this* was what he could do. An engraving of a dead Queen in a book doesn't prepare you for this glorious colour. It's so *beautiful*."

She couldn't take her eyes away from the picture; she was entranced by its beauty and by the exquisite detail of a portrait barely more than two inches long. How could there be so much life in something so small?

"He was a goldsmith," said Jack quietly. "The definition of craftsmanship was wider in those days. He probably didn't make that jewelled setting himself, but he *could* have done. A goldsmith, a jeweller, and a painter."

Something in Jack's voice caught Charity's attention and she looked up at him.

"You're a goldsmith too, aren't you?" she said. "Not just a banker. Could you do this?"

"I'm not a genius," he replied.

"But you'd like to?"

"Would I?" he said musingly. He took the pendant from her and held it up. "Perhaps I would, but I have little time for such things now. And fashions change—this isn't what I'd seek to make. He was a genius, but in many ways he was still painting in the medieval tradition. You can't see it in these close portraits, but he had no idea of perspective!"

"I haven't either," said Charity. "Edward explained it to me, and I understand the theory, but every time I try to put into practice it goes all wrong."

She sounded so aggrieved that Jack laughed, and that made her laugh.

"You should make time," she said more soberly, laying her hand on his arm. "We all have so little time to do what we really want. That's what I used to think about Edward; I used to worry about him. I'm so glad that things have turned out for him as they have. I'd hate to think that..."

"I'm not unhappy." Jack looked down at her, and covered her hand with his. "I still spend time in the workshop, I still make things—one day I may even create a masterpiece." He smiled self-deprecatingly as he spoke. "But I have a responsibility to the partnership not to neglect our banking interests, and I enjoy that also. You should understand, after all, what I do is not so very different from what you've been trying to do here at Hazelhurst."

Charity looked at him searchingly. She was concerned about him, and because she wasn't thinking about herself her self-consciousness had completely vanished.

"Yes, I see," she said at last. "But you'll get busier, everyone always gets busier. You must be careful that one day all your time doesn't get eaten up by your business."

"Some people might say that was a good thing." Jack smiled. "You've never seen an example of my work!"

"I don't need to," she replied, and for the first time she became aware of his hand on hers. She blushed and drew her hand away.

"What are we going to do about that?" she asked, nodding towards the jewel, and trying to speak normally, though suddenly her heart was racing.

"And now I come to think of it, where did you find it? And how did it get there?"

"In the library." Jack took the case out of his pocket and handed it to Charity. He too had been affected by their touch, but he had himself well in hand this morning.

"I *know* that," Charity replied exasperatedly as she opened the box and held it for him to replace the pendant.

"Well, considering that you thought the whole idea was nonsense…" he said tantalisingly.

"I was wrong, I admit it," Charity said hastily. "Where did you find it?"

"There was a concealed cavity in the wall behind the bookcases," Jack explained. "Once I'd taken all the books off the shelves I discovered a mechanism for swinging the entire bookcase away from the wall. It's on hinges, you see, but the design and the weight of the books usually disguise the fact. And, even when I'd done that, the hiding-place wasn't obvious. But it's easier to find something if you have a rough idea of what you're looking for, so it didn't take long."

"But what was it doing there in the first place? And how did those thieves know about it?" Charity demanded.

"I'd like to know the answers to those questions too," Jack admitted. "I'm assuming that you have no idea of its existence?"

"None at all!" she replied emphatically.

"And your father…?"

"He never said… I'm sure… No," she finished decisively. "He didn't know. He was never any good at keeping secrets, and he was always in need of money for one scheme or the other. I don't think over the years, he would have been able to resist…" She stopped as she suddenly realised what she was saying was hardly flattering to Mr Mayfield.

"That's what I thought," said Jack calmly. "Even if your father had never before had any occasion to sell the locket, he might have considered doing so when the future of Hazelhurst was at stake—but he obviously never mentioned the matter to your lawyer. Besides, there is other evidence to suggest he knew nothing of its existence."

For a moment Jack tapped thoughtfully on the pendant's case, which he was still holding in his hands. He made no attempt to explain himself, and Charity frowned, not quite sure what he was getting at, but before she had an opportunity to ask any questions he spoke again.

"It would be very interesting to know where the pendant came from—but I think there's a far more pressing problem that we ought to tackle first, don't you?"

He looked at Charity, his eyebrow slightly lifted, and she gazed back, not immediately sure what he meant, but pleased that he seemed to value her opinions; then she understood.

"The thief!" she exclaimed. "He's tried twice already—he'll be back. Of course he'll be back. And this time we must catch him. What are we going to do?"

"I've been thinking about that," said Jack, "and I'm not sure you're going to like what I suggest, but we probably haven't got much time now before Sir Humphrey arrives—"

"What is it?" Charity interrupted.

"Do you want to tell anyone what we've found?"

Charity thought about it quickly. "No," she said at last. "I will, of course, but at the moment there are too many other things to worry about, and I don't want Mama to be any more alarmed than she already is. Besides, apart from anything else, I'm expecting to see Lord Ashbourne's agent this morning."

"Really?" Jack said thoughtfully. "Perhaps it would be better if… Well, we can decide that later. What I *was* going to suggest was that you and your mother go and visit the Leydons for a few days. They won't be surprised if you don't feel comfortable here any more—not after two break-ins—and particularly since you'll be leaving here soon anyway."

"Leave?" Charity exclaimed. "Run away? This is our house! We're not going anywhere—not until we have to—and certainly not because we're *afraid!* How *can* you think I'd agree to such a thing?"

"I didn't," said Jack. "I knew you'd argue about it. But we haven't got time, and the situation is too serious, for you to be offended by my high-handedness. If you're determined to quarrel with me it would be better if you postponed it until *after* you're settled with the Leydons and we've caught the thief."

"Postponed…" Charity glared at him. "You've already arranged it, haven't you?"

"I mentioned the idea to Owen, and your mother," he admitted. Then, "Don't, Charity!" He'd seen the look of fury in her eyes and seized her shoulders before she had a chance to say any of the outraged words hovering on her tongue.

"I've seen you lose your temper before," he said. "But, believe me, now is *not* the time. I don't know whether the thief has been frightened away or not, but we need him—and not only to bring him to justice. So I'm not just sending you away to keep you out of danger, but to encourage the thief to think that with you gone the house will be less well guarded. With any luck he'll try again—and this time we'll have him." He paused, but Charity didn't say anything; she simply looked at him.

"That's why I agree with you about not telling Sir Humphrey," he said more quietly. "We must make the thief think that we still don't know what he's looking for—that we think it was an ordinary burglary. If he knows we've found it he won't go back to the library—"

"He'll try to take it from whoever's got it!" Charity interrupted. "What are we going to do with it?"

"I was going to suggest you leave it in my care," Jack replied. "I'll give you a receipt for it. It doesn't really matter where it is as long as no one knows it's been found."

"No, of course it doesn't." Charity sighed with relief. "For a moment I thought…what else have you arranged?"

"I've sent for my man Alan. He's intelligent and quite capable of independent action. You can tell your people that he's here to help with the move. If they think it's odd you can always imply that it's my fault, that I'm being embarrassingly over-attentive. It does happen." There was a question in his eyes as he spoke, but Charity didn't see it.

"I can deal with the servants," she said. "I take it you won't be staying here all the time."

"No, I must go back to Riversleigh. But I'll return later, after dark, before the moon has risen. I think it should be possible for Alan to let me into the house without either your servants or the thief knowing I'm here."

"But you can't keep on doing that," Charity protested. "Are you sure—?"

"I think Sir Humphrey has arrived," Jack interrupted her. "I doubt if I will have to do it many times. In fact, if we don't catch the thief tonight or tomorrow I shall be very surprised—he'll have to make his move within two weeks. We must greet Sir Humphrey."

"Why so soon? And what's this?" Charity asked as he handed her something and at the same time took her arm and pulled her towards the door.

"The receipt. Keep it carefully. I'll explain *why* the first chance I get, but Sir Humphrey is already harbouring enough suspicions about me, without giving him any more grounds for disapproval by keeping him waiting," Jack said. "Particularly when we're going to such lengths to make everything seem normal."

"Yes, all right." Charity went with him unresistingly. "But you can come and visit me at the Leydons' and explain then."

"Very well. But I've already got Lord Travers waiting for me at Riversleigh. I must deal with him first."

"Lord Travers! What's *he* doing there?" she stopped dead.

"Charity! Later!" Jack took a deep breath. "I'll explain later," he said. "Now, come *on!*"

"Yes, my lord," she said obediently.

Chapter Eleven

The Leydon coach jolted across the uneven road surface, and Charity braced her feet firmly to prevent her from being thrown against her mother. Mrs Mayfield was sitting beside her, and Tabitha, the maid, sat opposite. They'd asked Mrs Wendle, the housekeeper, if she also wanted to come. But she'd refused, ostensibly on the grounds that she had too much to do, but really because she couldn't abide the Leydons' housekeeper and had no intention of spending even one night under the same roof as her.

The ladies in the coach formed the first part of a cavalcade; behind them rode Owen and Sir Humphrey on horseback, with the captured burglar under guard. The unfortunate thief was to be taken to Horsham gaol, but the first part of the journey was the same for all of them.

Once again Sir Humphrey had demonstrated why he was such a good magistrate. He might dislike change and react badly to innovation but, faced with a straight-forward situation, he was usually able to respond in a straightforward manner. He believed that the Mayfields had been the victims of commonplace burglary and he had dealt with the matter appropriately.

But Charity, who had asked as a favour to be present when Sir Humphrey initially interviewed the captured intruder, thought that he had failed to pick up some of the things the prisoner said. Of course, that could be because she already knew what the man was hinting at but, on the whole, she was glad that Jack had been the first person to question him.

She thought about Jack now, and then about Owen. The next few days were going to be very awkward. Owen was showing increasing signs of possessive-ness, which was only natural—considering he thought she was betrothed to him. It was going to be very difficult telling him that she didn't want to marry him when she was a guest under his roof, but she knew that she had to.

And she was going to lose her wager with Jack. Was she pleased or sad about that? She began to feel dis-turbed by the trend of her thoughts and tried to con-centrate instead on the pendant. Perhaps they could use that to save Hazelhurst. Perhaps they could—

There was a shot, and the carriage swayed as the horses plunged.

A voice outside the carriage roared a command for

everyone to stand still—and then there was silence, disturbed only by the sound of the restless horses.

"If you stand still, you're safe. If anyone moves, I'll kill them."

From inside the carriage Charity couldn't see who was speaking. But the voice came from one side, and slightly towards the rear of the coach. Sir Humphrey's coachman could do nothing—the horses were too restless for him to concentrate on anything but controlling them. And though she thought Owen and Sir Humphrey had their mounts under better control, Charity guessed that they were too well covered to make any move against the man with the voice.

Her first thought was that this must be an attack by a highwayman, but then she heard the attacker ordering the release of the prisoner—and she knew it was the master thief.

Tabitha was looking grim, but beneath the fixed line of her mouth Charity detected fear, and Mrs Mayfield looked terrified. Charity was too worried to be afraid. This wasn't a normal highwayman—he had no interest in the valuables of the party he held up; he simply wanted his henchman back. They were safe in the coach. It was Owen and Sir Humphrey who were in danger—Owen and Sir Humphrey who might try to prevent the seizure of their prisoner and end up being killed.

Charity put a comforting hand on Mrs Mayfield's wrist, then she edged forward cautiously in an attempt to look through the window. But Mrs Mayfield caught her arm and pulled her back, terrified that Charity might show herself and be hurt.

"You won't get away with this," she heard Sir Humphrey say, his voice shaking with rage.

"I already have, you fool," replied the mocking voice of the thief, and she clenched her fists in angry helplessness, only half aware that it was the voice of a gentleman.

"Quickly, Luke! Mount the spare horse I've brought." That was the thief to the prisoner.

He was in a hurry; of course he was in a hurry. One man against so many. He held the advantage only so long as the situation didn't change. A chance traveller, a moment's distraction and he would be lost. A chance—that was all Owen and Sir Humphrey needed. Charity looked desperately around, trying to think of a way of giving it to them. Should she scream, distract the thief just long enough for the Leydons to arm themselves?

Then she remembered how her father had died and she grew cold. The best laid plans went wrong—and would the Leydons really be able to deal with the thief, or would she kill them with her good intentions?

She sat still and afraid, and willed the man to go without hurting anyone.

Then it happened. A sudden movement, a shot—and a roar of rage and despair from Sir Humphrey.

There was a pistol in one of the pockets of the coach—like most men, Sir Humphrey preferred to travel armed. Charity wrenched herself free of Mrs Mayfield's grip and seized it. Then she opened the door and almost fell out of the carriage on to the side of the road.

One quick glance around and she saw that Owen was down, blood already spreading across his shoulder, and the two thieves were galloping across the fields—getting further away with every passing second.

Charity was filled with a cold, unaccustomed fury. She lifted the pistol, aimed it at the nearest man, steadied it with both hands—and fired.

The second thief fell forward, but he stayed on his horse, and the first thief slowed in his headlong chase to pick up the trailing reins and lead his companion to safety.

Charity's hands were shaking as she dropped the pistol, but, though she was afraid of what she would find, she didn't hesitate as she ran to Owen's side.

He wasn't dead. The bullet had entered his shoulder and she thought nothing vital had been hit. But blood was pouring from the wound and she knew that if something wasn't done quickly he would bleed to death.

Sir Humphrey was in a state of shock. He'd almost

fallen from his horse and he was kneeling at Owen's side, but he'd done nothing to stop the bleeding. If it had been anyone else who'd been hurt he'd probably have dealt with the situation—but it was his son, and for a moment he was paralysed with despair.

Charity dropped down beside Owen on the cold ground and opened his coat. The amount of blood he'd lost horrified her, and she had nothing to staunch the flow but her hands.

Owen wasn't a slight man, but she hauled him up against her and pressed her hand against his wound, desperately trying to slow the loss of blood.

"Open the cases and get me some linen!" she ordered. "Sir Humphrey! Now!" She didn't recognise the sound of her own voice, but it roused Sir Humphrey.

He stood up and staggered towards the boot of the carriage, while the men who had been guarding the prisoner stood around and looked on in horror.

"Will this help, miss?" One of them offered her his scarf and she seized it gratefully.

"Yes, yes. Now, help me get his coat off. We must tie up the wound as tightly as possible," she commanded.

To her relief the guard was willing and obeyed her instructions implicitly, though she didn't know what he would have done if she hadn't been there. It wasn't so much that the men were stupid, it was just that they were as bewildered and horrified as Sir Humphrey by what had happened. Given time, they would have taken the appropriate action—but Owen didn't have time.

Sir Humphrey had brought the linen and Charity contrived a makeshift bandage. She still had to keep her hand pressed tightly into the wound, but she thought that it would now be safe to transport Owen back to Leydon House. She was about to give orders to move him when she heard the sound of hoof-beats.

She looked up and she saw Jack.

He'd heard the shots as he'd been riding to Riversleigh and had come as fast as he could, estimating their location from the sound they had made. He had paused only once, just before he'd nearly reached the carriage, because he too remembered how Charity's father had died and he didn't want to precipitate a similar tragedy. But even from a distance it was clear that the highwaymen were no longer present, and he had urged the bay into one last burst of speed.

He left the saddle while the horse was still running, and three paces brought him to Charity's side.

Charity stared up at him with huge dark eyes, and in them he read not only relief, but also an absolute conviction that he would be able to deal with the situation. Her confidence in him was absurdly gratifying—but he did no more than smile reassuringly at her and lay his hand briefly on her shoulder, before turning his attention to Owen.

"Good," he said. "You've bound him up well. I don't think he's losing much blood now. We'll get him into the carriage."

As he spoke he lifted Owen gently in his arms and stood up. Owen was still unconscious and his head lolled distressingly against Jack's shoulder. Charity reached up to support it and to keep her hands pressed against the bandages, hurrying along beside Jack.

"Get in. I'll hand him in so that you can support him," said Jack.

"Yes, of course. Oh, Mama!" Mrs Mayfield had fainted and Tabitha was trying to revive her. "I'm sorry, Tabitha," said Charity firmly as the maid shuddered at the sight of Owen, "but you're just going to have to support Mama in the corner of the coach, and if she wakes up, comfort her. I'm ready," she said to Jack.

It wasn't easy lifting an unconscious man into the carriage, but Jack managed it with the minimum of fuss, lying Owen across the entire width of the seat with his head and shoulders supported in Charity's arms. There was no help for it but to bend his legs, but the drive to Leydon House was a short one.

Jack emerged from the carriage and ordered the coachman to drive on. Then he turned to Sir Humphrey, who was beginning to recover his wits.

"I think he'll be all right, sir," he said gently. "It's his shoulder only that's hurt. With proper care he'll soon be hunting again."

"Yes, yes, yes," said Sir Humphrey eagerly. "For a moment there I was quite…but it's not serious. All that blood, but it's not…I must stay with him." He made a move as if he was about to climb into the carriage, but Jack restrained him. He didn't know whether it would be better for Sir Humphrey if he travelled in the coach, but he was sure it would be easier for Charity if he didn't.

"I think it would be better if you went straight home," he said. "A bed and dressings must be prepared for Owen, and you must warn Lady Leydon. It will be very distressing for her. I think she'll need your support more than Owen does right now."

"My wife?" Sir Humphrey looked dazed.

"Yes. You wouldn't want anyone else to tell her, would you?" Jack said. He beckoned to one of the guards as Sir Humphrey turned away.

"Go with Sir Humphrey," he said. "Make sure that there will be a bed, bandages and warm water waiting when the coach arrives. Do you understand?"

"Yes, sir." Like the others, the man felt better now that someone had taken charge. He hurried after Sir Humphrey, and Jack heard him say encouragingly to his master, "Come along, sir. We mustn't delay. We must get there before the coach does so there's time to get everything ready."

The carriage was still lumbering along, jolting over each rut, getting slowly further and further away.

The remaining guards were still standing in an untidy circle around Jack, waiting to be told what to do.

Before he said anything he whistled, and the bay gelding came back to him. He took up the reins thankfully, glad that he had devoted so much time to training the animal, and looked around at his companions.

"You," he said, indicating the guard who had originally offered Charity his scarf, "do you know where the surgeon is to be found?"

"Yes, sir," the man answered immediately.

"Good; take my horse and fetch him. Don't delay, but don't lame the horse either—it'll take longer if you do."

"Yes, sir." The guard mounted the horse and set off down the road. Jack watched him critically for a moment. It wasn't just that he was worried about his horse. He was genuinely concerned that an accident might delay the arrival of the doctor. But, if not a master horseman, at least the man appeared to be an adequate rider, and Jack turned his attention to other matters.

"How many men held you up?" he asked the two remaining guards.

"One, sir."

"Who fired the shots?"

"The highwayman." The guards looked bewildered.

"There were three shots," said Jack. "The first was a warning shot?" He looked at the men interrogatively, and they nodded. "Who fired the second—Mr Leydon?"

"No, sir. The more talkative guard shook his head. "He tried to get to his pistol, but he never had a chance. That was the shot that hit him.""

"I see. So who fired the third shot?"

The two guards looked at each other. Until that moment they'd hardly been aware that there had been three shots. They'd been so shocked by the sight of Owen's lifeless body that they'd been only dimly aware of what Charity had done.

"It must have been Miss Mayfield," said the first guard disbelievingly at last. "There was a shot from beside the carriage, and when I looked up I saw that one of the highwaymen had been hit. It couldn't have been anyone else; it must have been Miss Mayfield. But I don't…"

"That's all," said Jack. "One last thing. Did the man give any sign that he wanted to rob the coach? Or was he only interested in rescuing the prisoner?"

"He never said anything about the coach," said the guard definitely.

"Thank you. Go back to Leydon House now," said Jack.

The two men nodded respectfully and set off across the fields, following the same route that Sir Humphrey had taken earlier. It was only the coach that had to stick to the rutted, winding road.

Jack looked thoughtfully after them for a moment, then he turned and set off after the coach. He was on foot now, but the coachman was forced to drive so slowly over the bad road that it wasn't difficult for Jack to catch up.

Charity stood in the Leydons' drawing-room, resting her head against the cool glass of the window-pane. She was alone. Mrs Mayfield was resting in the comforting presence of Tabitha and the Leydons' housekeeper, and Lady Leydon was with Owen.

Mrs Mayfield had been inclined to be hysterical, but Lady Leydon had been remarkably self-possessed. She was one of those retiring women who could always rise to the occasion when there was genuine crisis—and she had the doctor's assurance that her son was not fatally injured. Charity suspected, rather guiltily, that once Lady Leydon had recovered from her initial shock she had even been able to find some compensations in the situation. For the first time in years one of her children was dependent on her again, and Lady Leydon was feeling a renewed sense of purpose.

The door opened, and Charity turned to see Jack. She felt a sudden urge of relief at the sight of him, still so calm and assured after all the terrible things that had happened.

"How is Sir Humphrey?" she asked, not entirely able to conceal her anxiety.

"Much better." Jack crossed to her side. "The

doctor has convinced him that Owen will survive, and now he's putting all his energies into raising a hue and cry against the attacker. By the time Sir Humphrey has finished I doubt if there'll be a magistrate or a constable this side of London who doesn't know what happened."

Charity smiled uncertainly. "I can imagine," she said. "And I dare say you encouraged him."

"I did," Jack admitted. "He's doing something constructive—and it might flush out our man."

"Perhaps," said Charity. She was trying to be sensible and rational, but it was difficult. There had been no time for her to give way to her feelings earlier, but, now that her whole attention was not devoted to the task of keeping Owen alive, she felt weak and tearful.

"You saved his life," said Jack quietly. "Sir Humphrey knows that—the doctor told him. He's very grateful. You were very brave."

"I was terrified," Charity whispered, and the tears she had been holding back so doggedly ever since she had at last been relieved of the responsibility for Owen finally overcame her.

Her head was lowered and she didn't see Jack come towards her; she only felt him take her in his arms. For a moment she tensed, then she relaxed and leant against him, feeling the gentle touch of his hand against her hair. She would have fallen without his support and Jack knew it, and his arms tightened about her.

He had loved her before, and now his love and respect for her had grown beyond all measure. It was only the inappropriateness of the moment which prevented him from speaking—or was it really the memory of the haunted, almost horrified expression he had seen in her eyes when she had pulled away from him the previous evening? Something had certainly upset her, and now, in the cold light of morning, he was increasingly afraid that it might have been his own unrestrained ardour which had appalled her. One thing was certain—he never wanted to see that look in her eyes again.

Charity had never felt so comfortable, or so safe, but after a moment she forced herself to step away and look up at Jack. His hands were still resting on her waist, he hadn't let her go, though he was no longer holding her so closely, and she could only bring herself to meet his eyes very briefly.

"I'm sorry, I didn't mean to be so foolish," she murmured. She was confused and unsure of his intent, and in the back of her mind the illogical fear lingered that there might be some other woman. No *immediate* plans for marriage, he had said…

"Foolish is not the word I'd have used," Jack replied, his voice deeper than ever. "If you don't feel afraid—how can you be brave?"

Charity looked up at that, this time meeting his gaze steadily.

"I shot a man," she said.

"I know."

"I was so angry that I wanted to kill him, but now…" She broke away from Jack and went to stand by the window, staring out at the tree-studded lawn.

"My father taught me to shoot," she said. "I wanted to learn, but when it came to it I hated killing things. Sometimes it's necessary, but…" She sighed.

"Did you see him fall from his horse?" Jack asked.

"No." Charity remembered how the man had fallen forward, but he'd still been riding.

"Then perhaps you didn't kill him. Owen was shot and he'll recover—but he would be dead if you hadn't acted so quickly. What you did was difficult, but in the circumstances it was necessary." Jack put his hands on her shoulders. "It's always easy to say what should or shouldn't be done—much harder to be the person who has to do it." Jack turned her round to face him.

"No one else showed much presence of mind," he said. "You should be proud of yourself—I am."

"*Proud of me?*" There was a note of almost disbelief in Charity's voice. She had been expecting…what? Horror? Shock at her unladylike behaviour? It was one thing to nurse the wounded, but quite another to fire upon their assailants. Mrs Mayfield still didn't know what she had done, and Charity was dreading the moment when she found out.

"Of course," he said.

Charity looked at him searchingly, still not quite sure that he meant it, but then she saw from his eyes that he did, and she felt a sudden, overwhelming happiness that he should have such a good opinion of her.

The moment lengthened and neither of them spoke. The urge to pull Charity back into his arms was very strong, but Jack resisted it. He was convinced he had upset her the previous evening, and she meant too much to him to risk distressing her again, particularly after all the other events of the morning. She was trying hard to hide it, but he knew she was still feeling shocked by what had happened.

"Come and sit down," he said, guiding her to a chair.

"I *am* being foolish," Charity said with a weak attempt at humour. "Whenever I think Mama's upset I always make her sit down too."

"Possibly," said Jack doubtfully. "But in this instance I think it would be more honest if I admitted that I'm trying to make myself useful. You don't *have* to sit down, of course—but I'll feel better if you do. That way I can deceive myself into thinking I've done something constructive too."

Charity blinked at him. He smiled back at her, the expression in his grey eyes kind and self-deprecating, and at last she felt the final vestiges of the horror caused by the events of the morning fade into oblivion.

"Thank you," she said. "You came to the rescue

again. I don't think I have ever been so happy to see anyone in my life. I was feeling quite desperate!" She held out her hand impulsively as she spoke.

"You'd left me very little to do," he replied, taking her hand. "But I'm glad if my presence expedited matters. Now," he added more briskly, "we must decide what to do next."

"The pendant!" Charity exclaimed. "Is it still in your pocket?"

"Yes, I've got it." Jack sat down opposite her. "And I think our original scheme is still a good one. Your highwayman was interested in only rescuing his henchman; that could be because he's a devoted master—or it could be because he was afraid he'd talk. Either way it seems to indicate that he doesn't know we've found what he's looking for. If he did know he might have wanted to search the coach."

"Oh, my God!" said Charity. "You mustn't carry it around with you any more—it's not safe!"

"Yes, it is. He doesn't know I've got it," Jack reminded her, feeling ridiculously pleased by her obvious concern for his welfare.

"But even so…" Charity wasn't convinced.

"I'll put it somewhere secure as soon as I can," he reassured her.

"But that won't make any difference if he finds out you've got it, or that you've had it," she protested.

"Even if you tell him you haven't got it now, he won't believe you; he'll—"

"Charity!" Jack interrupted firmly. "The pendant and I are both quite safe and will continue to be so. He doesn't know I've got it, and he won't find out. And, even if he does, I'm forewarned of his intentions, which gives me the advantage."

"Yes," said Charity. "Yes, I suppose it does."

"Good. Now, as soon as I've taken my leave of Sir Humphrey, I must return to Riversleigh, and then I'll go back to Hazelhurst. I don't know if the thief will come tonight or not, but, judging by the speed with which he acted this morning, I wouldn't be surprised. We won't underestimate him again."

"We?" said Charity with a flash of spirit. "I thought you'd already decided that I was to be relegated to the role of nervous female in this whole affair?"

But inwardly she felt her heart begin to sing. Would he really be doing all this on her behalf if he felt no more for her than simple friendship? Of course he would! He was too much a gentleman not to offer his help to anyone who needed it. All the same...

"Now you're trying to provoke me," said Jack. "You know perfectly well that that was *not* what I thought—even before you went out of your way to prove me wrong!"

"I *didn't*..." Charity began indignantly, and then relaxed as she saw that he was teasing her. "I thought of creating a disturbance," she admitted. "Anything to give Owen or Sir Humphrey an opportunity to turn the tables—but then I remembered all the things that could go wrong and I decided to sit quietly and pray that the man would leave without hurting anybody. I wish he had."

"Yes, I know," said Jack. "I never thought you'd do anything foolish."

"I've done a great many foolish things," said Charity. "But not at a time like that—at least, I hope not."

As she finished speaking the door opened, and they turned their heads to see Sir Humphrey entering the room.

"I've been thinking," he announced without preamble, "and it seems to me that there's something damned fishy going on."

Chapter Twelve

"In what way, sir?" asked Jack mildly, standing up at the magistrate's approach.

"That attack on the coach," said Sir Humphrey, so intent on his train of thought that he'd barely registered Charity's presence. "Didn't occur to me before, but damned risky business! And for what? To save a stuttering idiot! And why? That's what I'd like to know. You don't want to believe any of that nonsense about honour among thieves," he added, glaring at Jack belligerently.

"I don't," said Jack.

"No, well…quite," said Sir Humphrey. He'd been about to argue the point, and now he was feeling somewhat disconcerted.

"But what do you think we should make of it?" asked Jack.

Charity glanced at him doubtfully. She was afraid Jack was making fun of the squire and she didn't approve of it. But there was nothing in Jack's expression or in his tone of voice to suggest he was secretly mocking Sir Humphrey, and in fact he was simply curious to hear the magistrate's opinion.

"I don't know," Sir Humphrey replied honestly. "It doesn't make sense to me. Nothing that idiot said made sense. But the hold-up isn't the only odd thing. There are the two break-ins as well. Thieves don't usually go back to the same place twice—not in my experience, at any rate. And I think we can assume that the man who rescued our prisoner *was* one of the thieves from last night."

Jack nodded. Sir Humphrey's summing up of the situation might be slightly disjointed, but it was far from inaccurate. On the whole, Jack was inclined to think that the magistrate deserved to know the truth—as far as he and Charity knew it themselves—but he was reluctant to say anything without Charity's agreement.

He glanced at her, a question in his eyes, and when she nodded imperceptibly he said to Sir Humphrey, "We think there may be a great deal more to the affair than just a simple burglary."

"You mean, you *know* something?" Sir Humphrey demanded. "What do you know?"

"Nothing very concrete," Charity intervened suddenly.

She was prepared to tell the magistrate about

Jack's original suspicions, but she still didn't want him to know that they'd actually found the pendant. She couldn't overcome the belief that Jack would be in danger if anyone knew the jewel was in his possession, and she wasn't prepared to let anyone else in on that secret.

"Well, come on! Come on! Either you know something or you don't," Sir Humphrey said, looking from one to the other impatiently.

"Perhaps, since Miss Mayfield is so closely involved, it would be better if she explained," Jack replied, his relaxed expression belied by the intent look in his eyes as they rested on Charity's face.

He wasn't quite sure why she was equivocating, but he had every faith in her good sense, and he had no objection to following her lead—at least until he knew what was in her mind.

"Well?" Sir Humphrey stared at her.

"We didn't say anything at first because it seemed such a foolish idea," Charity said composedly. "But when Lord Riversleigh questioned the thief last night the man said certain things that seemed to suggest he was looking for treasure—and in our library!"

"Well! I'll be damned!" said Sir Humphrey after a moment. "Treasure, you say? In the library! Good God!"

"Lord Riversleigh mentioned the matter to me," Charity continued when Sir Humphrey seemed to have recovered from his initial astonishment. "And of course I said the whole thing was nonsense. But..." she paused ruefully "...we were talking about it just now before you came in and, if it's true—that they really believe there's treasure in our library, I mean—it might help to explain what's happened. The return of the thieves to the same place, and the desperate rescue of the captured man. The first man might have been afraid in case the prisoner gave any information away, so he wanted to rescue him before he could talk."

"But good God! Treasure in your *library!*" Sir Humphrey wasn't really listening to her any more; he was still trying to grapple with the outlandish suggestion about treasure.

"The important point is not whether there is any treasure, but whether the thieves believe there is," Jack said smoothly.

It was now clear to him that Charity wanted to conceal the discovery of the pendant and, although he hadn't guessed her true reason for doing so, he was inclined to think it was a good idea.

The callous attack on Owen had made Jack more determined than ever to catch the master thief, and the thief would be far more likely to make a third attempt on the library if he didn't know the pendant had been found. It wasn't that Jack didn't trust Sir Humphrey, it was just that the fewer people who knew, the less likely the information was to leak out.

"Yes, you're quite right, of course," said Sir Humphrey. "But what an *incredible* notion. I wonder where they can have got it from?"

"I'm rather curious about that myself," Jack admitted.

"Most unaccountable—treasure, indeed," said Sir Humphrey. "We're not used to all this excitement, are we, Charity?"

"No, sir," Charity smiled at him. "Actually, I think I could do with a great deal less."

"So could I." The magistrate's smile faded. "When I saw Owen…" His words trailed away and his expression clouded as he remembered the painful events of the morning.

He had submerged his grief and worry in a flurry of magisterial activity, and then his attention had been diverted by his sudden suspicion that there was something odd about the whole affair—but beneath his impatience and his bluster there was genuine fear and concern for his son.

"Owen's very strong," said Charity gently, taking the magistrate's hand. "And nothing vital was hit. You know the doctor said it won't be long before he gets his strength back. Please don't worry."

Sir Humphrey blinked, and then focused his gaze on her face.

"You're a good girl," he said, patting her hand. "I haven't thanked you yet, m'dear, and I know you saved him. I wasn't much help to you. But it shook me, do you see? I wasn't expecting it, and when I saw him lying there..." He stopped and dashed a hand across his eyes.

He was still standing—somehow it hadn't occurred to him yet to sit down, or to invite Jack to do so— and now Charity stood on tiptoe and kissed his cheek.

"Owen's safe now," she said. "And Lady Leydon will make sure he gets better quickly. Everything will soon be back to normal."

"I hope so." Sir Humphrey sighed. "Well," he continued more briskly, "what are we going to do about catching the scoundrels? My dear..." it suddenly occurred to him that he'd shown remarkably little consideration for Charity's sensibilities "...don't you think you ought to go and lie down? After all you've been through, I wouldn't like to cause you any more distress."

"I think it would probably be a good idea if Miss Mayfield stayed," Jack said quickly before Charity could reply. "After all, it is her family home that seems to be at the heart of the puzzle. If you feel up to it," he added blandly to Charity.

"Certainly." She returned his quizzical look with dignity.

"Of course she's up to it," said Sir Humphrey inconsistently, but with great good humour. "I've never yet known Charity overset by anything."

"Thank you," she replied, slightly overwhelmed by this tribute.

"Good," said Jack firmly, and in what he hoped was a decisive manner. He could see that unless they were careful they were going to end up completely side-tracked from the main issue. "But to return to the matter in hand…"

"Catching the thieves," said Sir Humphrey. "I have a piece of information which may be helpful. Apparently one of the thieves—the prisoner, I think—was shot while they were riding away. That should make it easier to find them. A wounded man is harder to hide than a fit one. I don't know who shot him," he added, frowning. "When I questioned them the men were quite clear that one of the villains had been wounded, but none of them seemed to know who had fired the shot. Most odd. It certainly wasn't me. I would have remembered."

Jack didn't say anything. He hadn't given the men any instructions to keep quiet on the subject and he suspected that either they'd simply found the idea of Charity firing the pistol too remarkable to be believable—or else they'd decided not to say anything to protect her from embarrassment. They all knew her and it was quite likely that they didn't want to make trouble for her.

"It was me," said Charity awkwardly, after a brief pause.

"You?" Sir Humphrey looked at her incredulously.

"I was angry." She looked at him anxiously. She still hadn't quite come to terms with what she had done, and she was afraid he would think badly of her.

"Well, well." He gazed at her with narrowed eyes, almost as if he was seeing her for the first time.

Somehow he hadn't really been surprised that she had dealt with Owen's injury so competently—but it did surprise him that she had the determination to respond so decisively to their attackers.

Sir Humphrey was always inclined to create comfortable mental images of the people he knew and, when they did something which didn't fit the character he had created for them, he would often ignore the implications of their action. The habit was too deeply ingrained for him ever to lose it, but, for a moment at least, he did become aware of an aspect of Charity's character which he had never before fully appreciated. For a moment his reaction was uncertain. Did he approve of her determination—or disapprove of her reckless and unladylike behaviour? But he was usually generous in his judgement of others, and not the man to let knowledge of his own failings sour his opinion of others.

"Well done, my dear," he said heartily. "You had more courage and presence of mind than any of us."

"You mean, you approve?" Charity was surprised.

"Well, it's not quite the conduct I'd expect from a young girl—but courage and quick wits are very important qualities to have," Sir Humphrey declared. "It's a pity you're not a man."

Charity blinked, and then opened her mouth indignantly.

"I'm not sure that I'd agree with you on that point," said Jack hastily, frowning at Charity slightly. "But I think we are in danger of becoming side-tracked here. May I be so bold as to suggest that we all sit down, and consider the matter in hand sensibly?"

There was no doubt that his last few words had been directed specifically at Charity, and she closed her mouth and simmered quietly.

"My dear fellow, of course. I'm so sorry. Do sit down," Sir Humphrey exclaimed, dismayed that he should have proved so inhospitable a host. "Would you like some burgundy, claret, brandy—tea...?" He remembered Charity's presence.

She started to laugh. "Sir Humphrey, you hate tea," she said.

"No, no, my dear," he assured her. "I confess, I'm not as fond of it as you ladies seem to be, but..."

The door crashed open and Lord Travers strode into the room, angrily stripping off his riding gloves.

"I have spent hours cooling my heels waiting for that jumped-up jackanapes and I'm damned if I'll wait any longer. *I'm* not answerable to any misbegoten son of a…" He stopped dead, the colour draining from his face as he saw Jack.

Jack stood up slowly.

"You were saying?" he said. There was no expression on his face, but his eyes were cold, and his voice was quiet and dangerous.

"Nothing." Lord Travers stared transfixed at Jack.

"What were you saying?" Jack repeated implacably.

"I…I believe my remarks were not addressed to you, my lord." Lord Travers finally regained the power of speech, and even attempted a casual laugh—but his effort failed dismally.

"Nevertheless, I suggest you retract them," said Jack. "You would be most unwise to rely any further on my forbearance."

He paused. There was something terrible in the silent intensity of his manner and, in the silence that followed his words, the only sound to be heard was Lord Travers's uneven breathing.

"I…I must have been misinformed," said Lord Travers breathlessly.

"Misinformed?" Jack's eyes narrowed. "Then you have been discussing the matter with others?"

"I…I mean, I was mistaken," Lord Travers stammered, seeing another trap opening before him. Later he would writhe with self-reproach at his craven response but now, as he felt the full force of Jack's anger and contempt, he did not even think of trying to save face. Lord Travers was deeply afraid, and he would have abased himself before Jack if doing so would have preserved him from Jack's revenge.

"You *were* mistaken," said Jack. "Don't ever doubt it."

"N-no."

"Good. And no doubt in future you will remember that I do not care to have my affairs discussed in public."

"Y-yes, my lord." Lord Travers looked so wretched that Charity was almost inclined to feel sorry for him. But then she remembered how prejudicial his slanders could have proved to Jack's acceptance by his new neighbours, and she no longer felt any sympathy for Lord Travers. The gossiping lord was not only a fool who gave no thought to the ultimate consequences of his actions, but he was also a coward at heart, with all the instincts of a bully. He neither could nor would repeat his slanders to their victim, and his fear of Jack reduced him to grovelling imbecility.

For a moment longer Jack continued to look steadily at Lord Travers, then he seemed satisfied, and some of the tension left him.

"I sent you a message that I would be delayed," he said. "Unfortunately the delay proved to be greater than I had expected. It is no longer convenient for me to see you now. We will postpone our meeting until a future—but not too far distant—date. There are several things we must discuss."

"Yes, my lord." Lord Travers bowed jerkily and turned to Sir Humphrey.

"Sir Humphrey, I have so much enjoyed my stay, but, I regret, I must...that is, I have urgent affairs...so sorry...very pleasant time...apologies to Lady Leydon...excellent hunting...and must leave at once." Lord Travers backed out of the room, still talking.

"Well!" said Sir Humphrey, taking a deep breath. "What the *devil* did you do to him?"

"Nothing in particular." The sparks of cold diamond fire had left Jack's eyes, and now his expression was as mild and faintly humorous as always. "I believe you were about to offer us some tea," he said.

"In a minute," said Sir Humphrey with uncharacteristic inhospitality. "Now, there has been something odd going on between you and Travers ever since you arrived, and I want to get to the bottom of it. Travers is—was—a guest in my house. I have a right to know."

"There's nothing to discuss," said Jack pleasantly. "Lord Travers made certain...unfounded allegations, which you have since heard him retract. That's all there is to it."

"Yes, but—" Sir Humphrey began doubtfully.

"Oh, for heaven's sake!" Charity interrupted, quite out of patience with both of them. "Lord Travers borrowed money from Jack's—I mean, Lord Riversleigh's bank, but because he's a mean-spirited man he resented having to put himself at such a disadvantage. I dare say telling all those lies made him feel powerful and important—he's too stupid to realise the consequences until too late. Now he's gone scurrying home, to try to persuade himself that it never happened—at least…"

She looked at Jack, suddenly concerned. "You don't think he'll try to take his revenge in a more… more devious way, do you?"

"Waylay me in a dark alley?" Jack asked. "No, I don't think he'll do that. Words are his chosen weapon, and I don't think he'll deviate from his custom."

"But, all the same, I think you should be careful," Charity insisted.

"That *blackguard!*" Sir Humphrey burst out, paying no attention to Charity.

It was true he'd already begun to have doubts concerning the truth of the rumours about Jack, and the events of the morning had completely driven his earlier suspicions out of his mind. Nevertheless, it was still a very unpleasant shock to discover exactly what kind of man had been enjoying his hospitality.

"My lord," said Sir Humphrey with stiff formality, "I owe you an apology. I believed what Travers said and now I see that I have been guilty of gross injustice. I trust that you will forgive me."

Jack smiled and held out his hand. "You didn't know me," he said. "There was no injustice."

"That's generous—"

"I think you mentioned tea earlier," Jack interrupted. "I think perhaps Miss Mayfield…"

"Of course, of course." Sir Humphrey relieved his feelings by tugging at the bell-pull so vigorously that Charity was half afraid he was going to yank it down.

She glanced at Jack and saw the amusement in his eyes and had to look away before she started to laugh.

"Well, you'll live, but you'll be no good to me for weeks." The master thief dried his hands on a rough towel and looked down at his henchman irritably.

"I-I-I'm s-s-sorry, s-sir," the man stammered wretchedly.

"You should be," Ralph Gideon replied curtly. "Were you questioned?"

"Y-y-y—"

"Did you say anything?" Gideon interrupted sharply.

"N-n-n-no, sir!" The man lay on his uncomfortable bed and looked up at his master fearfully. He really didn't think he had said anything, but he was afraid of Gideon.

"I hope you didn't. Dear God! I shall be glad to be out of this place." Gideon had been about to ask some more questions, but he was suddenly recalled to a sense of his surroundings by the aggravating bite of a flea, and instead he looked round the cheap inn room in some disgust. Then he turned his attention back to his servant.

"Remember, if anyone questions you, we were attacked by footpads on Horsham Common. It happens all the time, I'm told. Do you know who shot you?"

"N-n-n…" At the time Luke had been too preoccupied to turn and look, and now he didn't understand the gleam in his master's eyes.

"It was the girl," said Gideon softly. "She was the one who foiled me the first time. When this business is over, I think I shall turn my attention to taming her."

For a moment he gazed into space, contemplating some vision of his own, then he recollected himself and tossed the towel on to the floor.

"Go to sleep," he said abruptly. "I have work to do." He opened the chamber door and went downstairs, and Luke heard him calling for the innkeeper's daughter to bring him ale.

Charity opened the door quietly and crept over to where Lady Leydon was sitting beside the bed on which Owen lay. He appeared to be sleeping comfortably, and his mother was sewing with an expression which was almost peaceful.

She glanced up at Charity but, though she smiled,

it was clear that her thoughts were elsewhere. She was remembering the long-distant days when she had been the most important person in Owen's life. Not like now, when all too often his affection was tempered with impatience and even irritability. He was becoming increasingly like his father and, though Lady Leydon knew how important she was to Sir Humphrey's comfort, she also knew he was very unlikely to tell her so—or to think she needed telling. The magistrate might be prepared to allow *Charity* a certain latitude in her opinions and actions, but he would have thought it a very strange thing if his wife had been equally independent.

"How is Owen?" Charity asked in an undertone.

"Sleeping. He woke earlier, and I was able to give him some broth," Lady Leydon replied.

He'd also asked after Charity, but Lady Leydon didn't mention that. She would lose Owen again soon enough when he was no longer dependent on her, she had no intention of doing anything to bring that situation about more quickly than necessary.

"I'm so glad," said Charity impulsively. "I was worried earlier—but I was just being foolish. With you to look after him, he'll soon be well again."

"Yes," said Lady Leydon baldly.

It was unusual for her to be so abrupt, even curt, and for a moment Charity was afraid Lady Leydon blamed her for Owen's injury. She didn't know what to say. She couldn't apologise for something that hadn't been her fault, nor could she say that Owen had been shot because of his own hasty temper.

"I shall be sorry to leave Sussex," she said instead. "You have been such good neighbours to us all these years. I know this isn't the last time we shall be seeing each other, but I did want to thank you for all your kindness to Mama and me."

"But you won't be far away," Lady Leydon said slightly more cordially.

"Far enough," Charity replied, surprised that Mrs Carmichael had obviously failed to pass on this piece of information to Lady Leydon. "We're moving to London, did you not know?"

"I thought you were going to Horsham!" Lady Leydon exclaimed.

"That was our first plan," Charity admitted, "but Mama never really cared for it. We're going to London instead. We're in the middle of making the arrangements now."

Even as she spoke she wondered why she was telling Lady Leydon all this. With the discovery of the pendant it might not be necessary for them to move at all.

But perhaps she was telling Owen's mother that she was leaving Sussex because she couldn't tell Owen that she wasn't going to marry him. She had never regretted anything so much as she regretted her folly at the party the previous evening. She should never have encouraged Owen to believe they were as good as betrothed, and now, with Owen sick, there was nothing she could do to put her mistake right. She must wait until Owen recovered—and hope that he wouldn't be too disappointed.

Perhaps the gentlemanly thing to do would be to go through with the marriage—but Charity was too honest to contemplate such a course. In the past she had always believed that love was not necessarily essential for a successful marriage, but now she knew that, for her at least, it was. She wanted Jack, and if she couldn't have him she didn't want anyone.

"London!" Lady Leydon exclaimed, interrupting Charity's thoughts. "I had no idea. We'll all miss you so much—I know Owen will," she added significantly.

"Thank you. It will be sad for us too," Charity replied sedately, trying not to look self-conscious. "But you know how Owen and I are always arguing. You'll be able to have some peace for a change!"

"No such thing," Lady Leydon assured her, but there was a warmth in her expression which had been lacking previously. She had suspected that there was more between Owen and Charity than either had admitted and, though she didn't dislike Charity, she was relieved that her suspicions had apparently been unfounded.

"You must come back and visit us whenever you feel homesick for your old haunts," she offered generously.

"Thank you. And when we are settled in London you must come and visit us," Charity replied, though inwardly she hoped the suggestion would never come to anything. She was grateful that the undercurrent of tension that had seemed to exist between Lady Leydon and herself had disappeared—but she had no desire to pursue their friendship. It would be too awkward.

There seemed to be very little more to be said and so, with one last look at Owen's recumbent form, she took her leave of Lady Leydon and returned to her bedchamber.

It was nearly dark, and Mrs Mayfield was still resting after the upsets of the day, but Charity sat quietly in her room, knowing that Sir Humphrey and Lord Riversleigh were already on their way to Hazelhurst, ready to lay the trap for the master thief.

When they had finally managed to discuss the problem of trapping the thief Sir Humphrey had insisted that he take part in the scheme. Jack had tried to dissuade him, pointing out that if too many people were involved the thief was more likely to become suspicious and perhaps not even come.

But Sir Humphrey would not agree to remain behind. He had invoked his authority both as a Justice of the Peace and as the father of one of the thief's victims—and Jack had made no further attempt to exclude him. He would have felt happier without the magistrate's presence, but in all fairness he could not deny Sir Humphrey's right to be involved.

With that decided, they had laid their plans quickly, the only further matter of slight dissension being the number of men they took with them—Sir Humphrey wanted four; Jack didn't want any. In the end they compromised on two, but Jack was beginning to despair of how they would get so many men into the house unobserved.

He was certain that the thief would be watching the house, if not all day then at least for an hour or two before he made another attempt to enter it. It was for that reason that Jack wanted his party to arrive in the late afternoon before dark. There was a possibility that the thief wouldn't be watching the house during the day, especially since he already had the problem of finding somewhere to take his wounded confederate.

But if he didn't return that evening he would certainly be back the next—if he didn't come during the day. It was unlikely—even with the house apparently unoccupied by its owners, there were still several people about—but it was possible. That was why Jack had arranged for his own servant to be present while he himself was absent. He could rely on Alan to react quickly and effectively during an emergency—unlike Charles, who invariably needed guidance in any unfamiliar situation.

Charity had listened to the discussions quietly. She had made one or two suggestions as to how they could best enter the house unobserved, but apart from that she had taken no part in the arrangements. She had seemed rather withdrawn, but she couldn't help smiling at the enthusiasm Sir Humphrey displayed for the plan.

"Well, we've some time yet before we must leave," Sir Humphrey had declared at last. "How about a game of piquet while we wait, Riversleigh?"

"Certainly," Jack had smiled.

"Good, good. I'll just go and set things in motion, then we can play a quick hand or two." Sir Humphrey's eyes had lit up in anticipation as he had hurried off to order his servants to be in readiness later in the afternoon.

It was then, when she had been left briefly alone with Jack, that Charity had spoken. And it was that moment which she remembered now as she sat on the edge of her bed in the gathering darkness at the end of the short winter day.

"You will be careful, won't you? Sir Humphrey is sometimes too impulsive," she had said.

"I will act as a restraining influence," Jack had replied lightly.

"It's important," she had insisted. "He's a ruthless man, this thief. He'll hurt you if he has to—perhaps even if he doesn't. And it's my house you're defending. If anything happens to any of you—I will feel responsible."

"That's nonsense," Jack had said firmly, a slight frown creasing his forehead as he looked at her. "You aren't responsible for what he does—or for us. Don't ever think it."

"I'm not sure I agree, but, anyway, do be careful," Charity had repeated as she had heard Sir Humphrey returning.

She remembered her words now, and she couldn't rid herself of the feeling that she *was* responsible, and that she should be at Hazelhurst. If her father had been alive he would have been waiting with Jack and Sir Humphrey. It was her home and they were her friends—she should be there.

She came to a decision and stood up briskly. It wasn't difficult to leave the house without being observed, and once outside she made her way quickly to the stables.

Chapter Thirteen

The house was dark and still. The candles had been extinguished and the fires banked. The doors were bolted and the windows locked, and the only movement in the library came from the gentle billowing of curtains caught in the gentle draught from the closed casement. Upstairs the servants slept; downstairs the only sound came from the ivy leaves brushing against the windows—but six silent men were waiting for the thief.

Only Alan, Lord Riversleigh's manservant, had known that Jack would be returning, and he had let Jack and his party in at a side-door while the rest of the household was at supper. It would have been relatively easy at that point to conceal their presence in the house, but both Sir Humphrey and Jack had agreed that such excessive secrecy was probably not advisable.

Jack in particular was anxious to avoid the kind of chaos which might arise if there was a disturbance and the rest of the household was unaware of his and Sir Humphrey's presence. At the very least there would be some confusion, but it would be far worse if the thief managed to escape because the men who should have been defending the house were tripping each other up in the dark.

So they had spoken to Charles and Mrs Wendle. The alarmed housekeeper had agreed to remain in her room until she was told it was safe to come out, but Charles had been determined to join the others, and now he was waiting in the parlour with Alan and the two men Sir Humphrey had brought.

Only Jack and the magistrate waited in the library. Jack had been firm on that point and, on reflection, Sir Humphrey had agreed with him. After all, he had brought his men to guard his anticipated prisoner—not get in his way while he was catching the villain.

But they had been waiting a long time in the dark, and Sir Humphrey, never the most patient of men, was beginning to get restive.

"Riversleigh," he hissed, "why don't we open a window a little bit? It might encourage the scoundrel."

"I don't think so," Jack replied in a low voice which gave no hint of the exasperation he felt. "It would make the trap too obvious. Our man is not a fool."

The magistrate sighed, because he knew Jack was

right, and shifted uncomfortably. He found such in-activity more trying than a hard day in the saddle. In the darkened library all he could see were shadows. If he hadn't known that Riversleigh was waiting on the other side of the room he would have been con-vinced he was alone. How was it possible for a man to be so still, and so silent? Apart from that one comment, Jack had made no sound since they had begun their vigil.

Sir Humphrey became aware of how noisily he seemed to be breathing. He tried to breathe more quietly, taking shallow, careful breaths, but it didn't seem to help. He was making less noise, but he was also becoming extremely self-conscious about the whole mechanical process of breathing and in-creasingly desperate to gulp in a huge lungful of air. With an enormous effort of self-discipline he did no such thing, and instead his tortured imagi-nation became obsessed with the notion that his lungs were like bellows. He put his hand on his chest to feel the rise and fall of his ribs and found himself becoming more and more fascinated by his flight of fancy. What a remarkable creature a man was, how admirably designed, how exqui-sitely made—how loud.

Riversleigh didn't seem to be having similar dif-ficulties, Sir Humphrey thought resentfully. Perhaps he'd solved the problem by not breathing at all—he was certainly making no more noise than a dead man. The magistrate was just about to enquire about his companion's welfare when all thoughts of lungs and bellows were driven completely out of his head.

He plunged to his feet, his hand reaching instinctively for the hilt of his sword as a woman's scream splintered the silence.

She was outside, desperate with terror and, even as Sir Humphrey listened, the sound of her screams began to recede. She was being carried away.

"Good God! The villain's attacking a woman!" Sir Humphrey burst out. "Come on, Riversleigh!" he shouted and dived towards the door, nearly colliding with the horrified men who'd erupted from the parlour.

The woman's despairing screams could still be heard. She was being carried further away, but the intensity of her fear was as palpable as if she'd been standing beside them.

Sir Humphrey tugged at the bolts on the front door, the others crowding behind him. Alan looked at his master for guidance and Jack nodded. Then the door was open and they burst out on to the drive, running across the gravel towards the despairing cries of the woman.

At that moment she gave one last, panic-stricken scream—and all was silent. Sir Humphrey checked for a moment, horrified by the dreadful implications of that silence—then he forced himself to run even faster. But already the younger men were overtaking him, forging their way through the shrubbery.

Then they were all gone, the distant sounds of their running feet only emphasising the silence of the empty and deserted house.

A man stepped out from behind the holly tree and ran lightly towards the house. In one hand he carried a shuttered lantern—in the other a pistol.

The front door was still ajar and he pushed it gently open and stepped cautiously inside. He listened carefully, but no sound came to him from within the unguarded house and he moved quickly into the library.

He could no longer be certain that the booty he sought was still there, but he had no intention of abandoning his search while there was a possibility that it might be. He knew his servant had been questioned, and the fact that a trap had been laid for him at Hazelhurst seemed to indicate that his opponents had guessed something at least of what he was doing. But he was hoping they'd either failed to understand, or else discounted his servant's story as nonsense. If they *had* found the pendant he would have to approach the problem differently.

He dropped the pistol into his pocket, removed the shutters from the lantern and held it up to look at the bookshelves. Nothing seemed to have changed. The books were still on the shelves and there was no indication that anything had been moved—or that anyone had been searching here.

He felt an inward surge of relief and set the lantern down on the desk. He knew he would have to work quickly, but he knew what he was looking for; there should be time.

He reached up to lift down a handful of books, and a voice behind him said, "You're wasting your time, Gideon. It's not there any more."

For a moment the thief froze, disbelief suspending his actions. Then he spun round, his hand reaching for his pocket—and heard the sharp click as Jack cocked his pistol.

"I'll kill you if you make another move," he said pleasantly, and the thief believed him.

"Damn you!" he said viciously. "Meddling, impertinent…"

Jack smiled. "Until you walked in and unshuttered the lantern I had no idea it was you," he said quietly. "It was quite as much a surprise to me as my presence must be to you. But I'm not sorry. One day you were bound to fail—and I'm glad I'm here to see it. Put your hands in the air and turn round."

"And if I don't?" Insolent blue eyes locked with cold grey eyes in an unspoken contest of will. The tension between the two men was almost visible in its intensity.

"If you don't I will put a bullet through your leg," said Jack."

Gideon stared at him for a second longer, but the steady grey eyes were implacable, and he knew that if he didn't obey Jack would do exactly as he'd said.

The thief turned round slowly, cursing himself. He'd known that Riversleigh was in the neighbourhood, he'd even heard the rumours and laughed scornfully at the credulous Sussex yokels. But it had never occurred to him that *he* would have to deal with Jack before he was through. He should have questioned his servant more closely.

He felt Riversleigh come up behind him and take the pistol from his pocket, but he made no attempt to retaliate. Some men might drop their guard when they believed their mastery of the situation was complete—but not Jack; no, certainly not, Jack, not after what had happened before.

Gideon was aware of a grudging flicker of respect—the same respect he'd first had for Jack nearly sixteen years ago when they'd both been schoolboys, and Jack the younger of the two. He frowned; the memory of what had happened all those years ago had sparked an idea for escape. He was no longer interested in searching for the pendant, only in saving his own life. If he hadn't gone by the time the others returned he would almost certainly hang for what he had done.

"May I turn round?" he said.

"Yes." The pistol in Jack's hand didn't waver, but he was curious to know more of his opponent. It had been half a lifetime since they had last encountered each other, but all the old animosity still existed between them.

"Are you going to keep me covered with that pistol like a common criminal until your friends return?" Gideon asked insolently. "I am a gentleman."

"No, you are a thief," said Jack. "A thief, a liar and possibly even a murderer. I wish I could say that you've improved since last we met—but I can't."

"When last we met I proved conclusively that a money-lender's son is no match for a true gentleman," Gideon replied arrogantly.

Jack smiled. "Is that what you proved?" he said quietly. "My recollection of the affair is somewhat different."

"Of course it is," Gideon agreed. "No loser can bear to remember honestly how he came to be defeated!" He paused, watching Jack closely. "I could do it again," he continued softly. "You and I both know that. That's why you're hiding behind that pistol until your friends can come and tie me up. Because if we met with our swords as gentlemen—you wouldn't stand a chance."

The scorn in his voice would have roused a marble statue to fury, but the only indication that

Jack had heard was a slight narrowing of his eyes as he looked at Gideon.

Then he laughed. "No," he said. "Not this time."

For a moment Gideon thought he'd failed, that he'd have no opportunity to cross swords with Jack, but then he saw the look in Jack's eyes and knew that he'd have his fight after all.

But not because of anything he'd said. His words hadn't roused Jack to blind fury, only to cold and calculating anger. Perhaps he'd even wanted the fight and Gideon's words had only furnished him with the excuse he'd needed.

Gideon had no lack of faith in his own ability, but the unexpected thought chilled him, and for the first time he began to wonder whether his plan would be successful.

"Push back the desk," said Jack. "And the chairs."

"Are you afraid you'll trip over them?" Gideon taunted, but he did as Jack said. He had no desire to fall over furniture in the half-light either.

"Draw your sword," said Jack.

They met in the centre of the room, barely saluting each other before their blades tangled. Both men were intent on their opponent; neither of them knew they were no longer alone.

Charity had been standing in the hall, listening to what they said and trying to make sense of it. But now she stood in the doorway, watching them fight by the flickering light of the lantern.

She could see Gideon's face and his expression chilled her. He would kill Jack if he could, even though he only needed to disable him to escape.

She was terrified. She had never known that such fear could exist. Her thoughts were so paralysed that she did not even berate herself for not having intervened sooner. She could only watch—and pray.

She couldn't see what was happening properly. Jack's back was towards her, and she was afraid to move into his line of vision in case her presence distracted him. But she had to know what was happening.

She'd been clutching convulsively at the doorframe, but now she released it and began to edge along the wall into the corner of the library. She was still behind Jack, but now she could see more.

The blades moved so fast that she could never have described the encounter, but she had a sense that neither of the two men had fully committed himself to the attack. They were waiting, watching, trying to discover the other's weaknesses.

The swords gleamed dully in the inadequate light, and Charity began to feel dizzy and confused, uncertain of what was happening—or of who was winning.

Gideon lunged, his movements so fluid that his sword seemed like an extension of his arm. Jack parried and Charity heard the sickening slither of steel. She saw that his sleeve had been torn, and she began to feel as if she were suffocating.

This could not go on. The pace had quickened, both men were fighting hard now, and Jack was beginning to press the attack. Gideon's blade missed him by less than half an inch and Charity closed her eyes.

Then she opened them resolutely. She must not be afraid and she must not flinch, because if Jack fell— God forbid—then it would be up to her.

Before she had left Leydon House she had spent several minutes debating the wisdom of bringing a pistol. She could not forget that she had already shot one man—she didn't think she ever would—and she never wanted to repeat the experience. But, though she had been sorely tempted to come unarmed, in the end it had seemed to her that to do so would not be to show common sense—but simply to surrender to her fear. So she had taken one of Sir Humphrey's duelling pistols from his study.

She had never really thought she'd need it, but now she took it out with shaking hands and pointed it at Gideon. She mustn't tremble—she *must not* tremble! She blocked out all other thoughts and kept the pistol levelled at the thief. Her concentration was complete and her hands were steady. Whatever happened, there would be no escape for Gideon now.

Gideon didn't even know Charity was there. His

breath was coming in short sharp gasps and the sweat was trickling into his eyes, but he didn't dare to wipe it away. There was nothing casual about this encounter and he was growing desperate.

He was running out of time. Soon the other men would be back, and if he didn't finish Jack soon he would be caught like a rat—so he fought like a rat. But he couldn't find an opening. Whatever he tried, Jack anticipated it. It seemed as if he were surrounded by an impenetrable barrier of steel.

At last! Gideon thought he saw an opportunity. He lunged forward, fully committed to his attack—and realised too late that it was a trick. He staggered back, his sword falling from his nerveless hand as Jack's blade penetrated his right shoulder.

He was lying on the shabby carpet, dizzy and sick, and Jack towered over him. Gideon blinked and tried to clear his head. He saw the tip of Jack's sword, slowly dripping blood, then he looked up and met Jack's quizzical eyes.

"You should have killed me," he gasped.

"No doubt you deserve it," Jack replied mildly; he was breathing heavily, but he wasn't winded. "But you can't answer questions if you're dead."

"You calculating bast…" Gideon tried to struggle up, fury in his eyes, but he was too dizzy, and in too much pain, and he finally lost consciousness.

Jack looked down at him thoughtfully, shaking his

head a little. Then he wiped his sword and sheathed it, before kneeling down beside Gideon. It was only then, as Charity made a slight sound, that he turned and discovered her presence.

She was still holding the pistol before her, though she'd lowered it so that it was pointed at the ground. She was deathly pale, and when she looked at Jack her eyes hardly focused; it was almost as if she didn't recognise him. It had taken so much effort for her to block Jack out of her thoughts and concentrate only on Gideon that now she was finding it equally difficult to return to normal.

Jack stood up and crossed swiftly to her side. Her hold on the pistol was so fierce that it was only with difficulty that he took it from her and laid it on the desk.

"Charity, it's all right now," he said.

She looked at him uncomprehendingly, her eyes dark with remembered fear and reaction, and he put his hands on her shoulders.

"Charity! It's over!" He shook her slightly.

She stared at him a moment longer, then her eyes cleared and she began to tremble.

"Oh, my God!" She put both hands up to cover her face and leant against him.

He put his arms round her and she began to cry.

Jack drew her closer, speaking in a low, soothing voice—but knowing she wasn't listening to him. She needed time to recover, and he gave it to her. Perhaps he needed some time himself. It had been a hard fight, made harder by the fact that he had never wanted to kill Gideon. In that respect, Gideon had always held the advantage; because Jack had had his own reasons for fighting, and the death of Gideon was not the victory he sought.

At last Charity became aware of where she was. She could feel the touch of Jack's hand on her hair, and the warmth of his body against hers as he continued to support most of her weight. She felt his lips brush her hair, and felt a renewed flutter in her breast, but this time it wasn't caused by fear.

"Charity," he said softly.

She looked up, shyly, but quite openly.

"You shouldn't have come," he said. "It was a crazy thing to do."

"I had to," she said simply. "It's my house; besides—"

"Riversleigh! Where the devil are you, man?" roared Sir Humphrey from outside.

There was the sound of running footsteps on the gravel and the next minute Alan burst into the house, followed by Charles.

"Sir, where…?" Alan checked on the threshold of the library, stunned by the evidence of violence before him.

"Ah, Alan," said Jack calmly, guiding Charity to a chair. "You must learn to be less impetuous. Now you're here, you can bind up my…victim. It would be most inconvenient if he bled to death!"

"Yes, sir." The manservant hastened to obey, rather crestfallen at Jack's remark, but when he saw Gideon he swung round in surprise. "Sir! It's…"

"I know," said Jack quietly. "I want him alive, Alan."

For a moment their eyes met and held, then Alan looked down. "Yes, sir."

Jack smiled faintly. "Where's Sir Humphrey?" he asked.

"He's coming, my lord," Charles replied, dragging his eyes from Gideon's recumbent form. "We caught a *woman*."

"Yes, I thought you might," said Jack. "I think you'd better fetch some linen and some warm water."

"You mean, you knew it was a trick?" Alan demanded, looking up from Gideon and quite forgetting himself in his indignation. "Why didn't you stop us…sir?" he added as an afterthought.

"Of course he couldn't stop you," Charity said. She wasn't fully recovered, but she was more than capable of holding up her end of any conversation. In fact, for some reason she felt better than she had done for a long time. "It was only because you all ran out that *he*," she nodded at Gideon, "came in. And that was the whole point."

Jack glanced at her, amusement in his eyes. Once again she had proved herself to be far from lacking in wit, and there were a number of questions he wanted to ask her—but now was not the time.

Sir Humphrey arrived, followed by the other two men, dragging a girl between them. She was struggling half-heartedly, but they had no difficulty in restraining her.

"Where are you taking me?" she demanded. "You ain't got no right to do this to me. I ain't done nothing wrong."

"Well, you may be correct," Jack agreed, apparently unconvinced. "I'll leave it up to Sir Humphrey to decide that point. In the meantime you might tell us why you were creating such a disturbance."

"*He* told me to do it." She jerked her head at Gideon. "He told me it was for a joke, and I'd earn some money if I did it well. Doesn't look as if I'm going to get paid now, does it?"

"No, I think not," said Jack. "In fact, it has been an extremely unprofitable evening for you, hasn't it? In the circumstances, I think the best way for you to help yourself will be for you to help us—don't you, Sir Humphrey?"

"Yes," the magistrate grunted. Strictly speaking, he should have been the one conducting this interrogation, but he didn't object to Jack's taking charge. He'd already seen Gideon and he knew now that he had been tricked. He was angry with himself, but he was too fair-minded to resent Jack for having been less gullible.

"You mean, you'll let me go if I answer your questions?" the girl demanded.

"Possibly." Jack made no promises, but on the whole the girl thought it would probably be wisest to do as he wanted.

"How did you meet our friend?" he asked.

"He was staying at my father's inn."

"Alone?"

"No, he had a servant with him. The man's hurt." The girl looked at Jack with appraising eyes. "Is that what you wanted to know?"

"How badly?" Jack ignored her question.

"Bad enough to be laid up in bed, but he won't die," she replied scornfully.

"Did he explain how he'd been hurt?" Jack asked.

"Footpads, *he* said." Once more she was referring to Gideon. "He said they were held up on Horsham Common." The girl watched Jack suspiciously.

"And you believed him?"

"Why shouldn't I?" she demanded belligerently. "It happens all the time."

Jack smiled. "Is the wounded man still at the inn?" he asked.

"Was when I left. Where would he be going?"

"Where indeed?" Jack murmured. "How long have they been at the inn?"

"A week, maybe a little longer. Can I go now?"

"No. Tonight you stay here. In the morning you can

show us the way to your father's inn." Jack looked at Sir Humphrey as he spoke, and the magistrate nodded.

"Have you any other questions you wish to ask, my lord?" he asked.

Jack shook his head. Sir Humphrey smiled grimly and turned to the two men who were still standing on either side of the girl.

"Take her to the kitchen and guard her," he ordered. "What are we going to do with him?" he added, looking at Gideon, who was now being tended by both Alan and Charles.

"He'd better stay here," said Charity firmly. "There's no point in moving him. Beside, he's got to answer some questions, and the quicker he's able to do so, the better."

"Quite, quite." Sir Humphrey nodded his agreement. Then he looked at her as if he was registering her presence for the first time. "What the devil—?"

"Is there a bed ready for Gideon?" Jack interrupted, addressing himself to Charles.

"No, sir," the man answered; he seemed rather puzzled. "We didn't know he was coming."

There was a moment of silence as the assembled company absorbed this piece of information.

"Come on, Charles, I'll tell you what I want you to do," said Charity at last.

She was grateful that Jack had intervened before

Sir Humphrey could begin interrogating *her,* but she couldn't help thinking he was amusing himself at their expense. There was certainly a distinctly humourous glint in his eyes as he briefly met her gaze.

Chapter Fourteen

Jack and Sir Humphrey were playing cards in the library when Charity finally rejoined them. She had arranged rooms for everyone who needed them, and supervised the bandaging of Gideon's wound. In fact, for someone who wasn't even supposed to be there, she thought she'd been very useful.

Jack looked up and smiled as she came into the room. Sir Humphrey looked up too, but he frowned.

"Now, miss," he began, "perhaps you'll explain exactly what you're doing here."

"It's my house," she said, just as she had done earlier to Jack.

"It's your mother's house, or it is until the end of February," said Sir Humphrey precisely. "And, in any case, you had no business interfering in such a matter. Good God, girl! You might have been hurt. It might have been you we heard screaming! How would I have faced Mrs Mayfield then?"

"But it wasn't me," said Charity calmly. "Sir Humphrey, if someone had told you Leydon House was about to be burgled, would you have stayed behind and let someone else protect it for you?"

"The case is entirely different," Sir Humphrey protested. He'd intended to give Charity a good scold, but somehow the conversation wasn't going as he'd planned. "If you were my daughter..." he began.

She laughed. "I dare say you're glad I'm not," she said.

"No, m'dear," he said unexpectedly. "I would have been very happy to have had you as a daughter." He put down his cards and stood up.

"I'll talk to you in the morning, Riversleigh," he said to Jack. "We must go and see the man at the inn, and we must also decide what we're going to do about the fellow we've got upstairs. There are one or two things I don't understand...and I wonder..." he frowned, looking around the library "...perhaps we did ought to see if there's anything here. No doubt it's nonsense, but after all this it would be a pity if we missed something."

Jack glanced at Charity, but she was looking uncharacteristically subdued—stunned, even. And she certainly didn't show any signs of wanting to enter the conversation.

"You're quite right, sir, we should discuss it," he said, and stood up, offering Sir Humphrey his hand.

"We achieved a lot tonight," he said. "I enjoyed working with you."

Sir Humphrey flushed. "I'm not sure I was much help, or only by accident," he replied. "But it's been a pleasure. You're a man after my own heart, my lord. It was a lucky day for all of us when you inherited Riversleigh." He shook Jack's hand vigorously.

"Thank you, Sir Humphrey." Jack smiled. "I had my doubts at first. I was bred to be a banker, not a baron. But I think it will work out."

"I'm sure of it," the magistrate replied emphatically. "I'm sure of it. Goodnight, m'dear." He glanced at Charity.

"Oh, goodnight, Sir Humphrey." She roused herself to reply. "Thank you for your help."

"No thanks necessary," said Sir Humphrey earnestly. "I'll be indebted to you for the rest of my life. I'll always be at your service."

He took her hand in both of his for a moment, then he nodded to Jack and left the library. A few seconds later they heard him stub his toe against the bottom stair and swear under his breath. Then he climbed the stairs and the library was silent again.

Charity stood up uncertainly, not sure whether she should stay—or go to bed. She couldn't forget that on the previous evening Jack had seemed so anxious for her to leave. She glanced at him shyly and saw that, although he was smiling at her, there was an uncharacteristic gravity in his expression. Suddenly she was afraid of what he would say.

"I must go…" She started to move towards the door.

"Not yet." He was still some distance away from her, but his voice stopped her almost as effectively as his touch might have done.

She turned slowly, looking up at him with surprised and almost fearful eyes.

"How long were you waiting outside?" he asked.

She blinked; that had been the last thing she'd expected him to say and for a moment she could hardly frame a coherent reply.

"Oh, a couple of hours, I think," she said at last.

"You must have been cold." He had come to stand right in front of her and now she had to tip her head back to meet his eyes.

"Not really," she murmured. "I had my cloak, there's no frost…"

"You shouldn't have come." He lifted a hand to brush a stray tendril of hair from her face, and she saw that his grey eyes were darker than usual. "Sir Humphrey was right. It could have been you we heard screaming, and if it had been…"

For the first time, Jack's voice faltered, and at last Charity realised that it was retrospective fear for her that had briefly quenched his customary humour.

The past twenty-four hours had been filled with so much anxiety and worry that her sudden insight left her feeling quite weak with happiness. She had hoped that she was important to Jack—and now she could see in his eyes that she was. It was true she still didn't understand everything he had said, or done—and, most of all, she still didn't understand why he had seemed so anxious to be rid of her on the previous evening—but at last she could no longer doubt that he cared deeply for her.

With no other thought than the need to reassure him that she had come to no harm, she reached out to touch the velvet of his coat, and smiled up at him.

"There was no need to be afraid for me," she murmured. "It was not I who deliberately put myself into danger. Why *did* you do it?"

Jack didn't answer; he might not even have heard the question. His whole awareness was dominated by the way she had reached out to him, so naturally and unself-consciously. Could she—would she—have done that if he had frightened her on the previous night?

He remembered the relief he had seen in her eyes when he'd arrived after Owen had been shot, and her absolute confidence that he would know how to deal with the situation. And he remembered how she had allowed him to take her in his arms to comfort her after she had seen him fight Gideon. There had been no indication then that she did not welcome his presence—or his touch. So why had she seemed so horrified when she had wrenched herself out of his arms last night?

She was standing only inches away from him and he desperately wanted to crush her against him—yet he was afraid that if he did so he would see the expression in her eyes change to fear or disgust.

"Last night…" he began, and saw the colour flood into her cheeks at his words.

She dropped her arms awkwardly to her sides and moved away from him, afraid of what he might say. "I love you, but I'm already committed to someone else"—would that be it? Could she bear to hear it?

"I didn't mean to frighten you," he said, half lifting a hand towards her and then letting it fall. "You must know that the last thing I'd ever want to do is hurt you… I don't think I shall easily forget the look of horror in your eyes," he finished, his manner far less assured than usual.

"Frighten me!" Charity turned back to him in amazement. "You didn't frighten me. I told you so at the time—I think." To be honest, she wasn't entirely sure what they had said to each other; her memories were rather confused.

"But you seemed so appalled!" he protested, relief and excitement flaring through him as he began to realise he might have been mistaken in her feelings.

"Did I?" She sighed, and glanced down for a moment, then looked up and met his eyes. "Perhaps I did, but not because of anything you'd done. It was just a trifle…unexpected. You didn't frighten me," she said again, very earnestly.

Very soon she would have to tell him about Owen, but not yet, not while so much else was still unsettled between them.

"Unexpected?" Jack repeated softly, reassured as much by her manner and the glow in her eyes as by her words. "It was certainly that. After all, despite your very flattering proposal, when I first came into Sussex I had no intention of getting married."

His hands were on her waist and he began to draw her towards him.

"And now?" Charity whispered, his words thrilling her almost as much as his touch. Did he mean…?

"Now I think it's a pity I didn't know you better when you first put the question." He paused, smiling down at her, his eyes filled with a gentle, teasing light. "I might have given you a different answer," he said.

"Might?" she questioned gently.

"Well…" for a moment longer he continued to tease her, then his expression changed, and she saw a new light blazing in his eyes "…if I had known you better," he said, "I would have pre-empted your proposal with one of my own."

She smiled, joy filling her at his words.

"I'm so glad," she murmured and, as he bent his head to kiss her, she closed her eyes and gave herself up shamelessly to his embrace.

He had lost his earlier unaccustomed hesitancy, and she could feel the strength in his arms as he held her against him, claiming her for his own—now and forever.

Then he relaxed slightly, without releasing her, and let his hand glide leisurely down her spine from the nape of her neck to the small of her back. Even through the fabric of her riding habit his touch could ignite a fire deep within her soul, and she clung more tightly to him, feeling his lips on her cheek, her eyelids and her hair. She was lost in a world in which only they existed, and when he put his hand up to the lace at her throat she made no protest. He held her slightly away from him and slowly unbuttoned first her jacket, and then her waistcoat. Then he paused, a question in his eyes, and Charity smiled and drew his head down to hers again.

"I wasn't afraid, I'm not afraid," she murmured, her lips moving delightfully against his.

For a moment longer Jack made no effort to restrain his desire, but then he lifted his head and drew back slightly, though his hands still rested on either side of her waist, within the folds of her waistcoat.

Charity sighed; she was still feeling dazed with passion, yet it took only an instant for her to read the intention in his eyes, and regret and relief mingled within her as she finally understood what had prompted some of his actions on the previous night.

"Now you're going to send me to bed," she predicted. "It's not...I mean, I don't..." she blushed and glanced down, then looked up again, an expression of shy, almost rueful humour in her eyes.

"People have been telling me for years that I'm unladylike," she said, "but I never knew before how true it was! Last night you were being a gentleman, but I thought..."

Her voice trailed away, but Jack had understood and a wave of relief washed over him as he realised that one more misunderstanding had been cleared up.

He smiled. "That particular aspect of the situation hadn't occurred to me," he admitted. "But, if you must know, you make it very difficult for me to be...a gentleman. You see?"

As he spoke his hands drifted higher until they were resting just below her breasts and, instinctively, Charity leant towards him—then she leant back again.

"I shouldn't... Oh, dear, am I too forward?" she asked, with such a comical look of anxiety on her face that he nearly laughed.

But he had heard the anxiety in her voice, and he chose instead to reassure her.

"No." He drew her towards him until their bodies were just touching, in subtle, tantalising proximity. "Sincerity in your dealings with others is always a virtue—you could never lose my respect because you don't play conventional games."

"Sincerity?" she murmured as he kissed her again. He was still holding her no closer than he had been a moment before, but the feel of his lips on hers, and the delicate tracery of his hands beneath her waist-coat, along her sides and across her back, filled her with trembling, shimmering pleasure.

It was hard to pull away, but she knew that she had to. She had to tell Jack about Owen. It never occurred to her that she might terminate her engagement without Jack's ever knowing about it. She had to tell the truth, and she had to tell him now. She should probably have told him sooner.

She stepped reluctantly away from him and, when he tried to take her back into his arms, she braced her hands against his chest, holding him off.

"Wait, there's something I have to tell you," she said. "It's not...I mean, I'm going to do something about it as soon as I can, but..."

"What is it?" Jack's smile faded as he saw the expression in Charity's eyes.

"Owen thinks I'm betrothed to him," she said baldly.

For a moment there was silence as Jack stared at her in disbelief.

"Good God!" he said at last. "I never thought you'd bring it off!"

"You mean, you don't mind?" Charity gasped in confusion and broke away from him.

"Well, yes, actually," he said quietly, and from

his voice she knew she had shaken him more than he wanted to admit. "I hadn't thought… When did it happen?"

"At the party," she said sadly, regretting more than ever what had happened. He had said earlier that hurting her was the last thing he ever wanted to do—and now it seemed that it was she who had hurt him. "I didn't even understand what Owen was asking at first!" she continued. "I wasn't really listening—it was just after you'd gone to get me some lemonade. I wasn't really…" She broke off, looking at Jack. "Something had happened, hadn't it?" she said.

"To me, certainly," he replied, his calm manner not entirely hiding his underlying tension. "I nearly kissed you in front of all the other guests! You were—you are so…" He smiled almost apologetically at her. "I had to leave you," he said. "I'd have caused another scandal if I hadn't! But that was when Owen asked you?"

"I was trying to make him go away," she said. "I didn't want to talk to him just then—but I realised what he was asking, and it was what I'd said I was going to do, so…"

"So you went ahead and did it," Jack finished for her.

The first stab of pain he'd felt when she'd told him what she'd done was easing. He couldn't blame her for feeling bewildered by everything that had happened, and in the circumstances it wasn't surprising that she'd stuck to her original plan when everything else must have seemed so uncertain and confusing.

"I knew I'd made a mistake almost immediately," she said quickly. "Please believe me. I was going to tell him this morning, but he was gone before I woke up, and after that…" She sighed as she remembered what had happened to Owen. "Oh, I do hope he'll be all right."

"He will be," said Jack quietly.

He no longer sounded upset, but it suddenly occurred to Charity that perhaps, once again, she had been less than tactful.

"I didn't mean…" She looked at him anxiously. "It's just that I've known Owen so long. I don't…"

"No, I know." He smiled at her. "Mind you, if it had been Edward you'd accidentally found yourself betrothed to I might have been less understanding."

"Edward!" she exclaimed. "Why…?" Then her lips curved deliciously and she smiled up into his eyes. "Jealous, my lord? You can't be jealous of Edward."

She was standing very close to him and she lifted her hands and laid them against his chest. She had done the same thing before, to hold him off, but now she let her hands slide sensuously across the black velvet of his coat until they were linked behind his head.

"He *was* your first choice of husband," Jack pointed out, resisting the urge to put his arms around her.

"True," Charity admitted. "But in the past few days what I'm looking for in a husband seems to have changed. I used to be so sensible too," she added. "It's a sad fact that you've turned me into a heedless and frivolous woman."

As she spoke she leant against him, pressing her slim body against his until his resolution began to disintegrate. He let her draw his head down until their lips met, and lost himself in the passion of their kiss, his hands moulding her against him.

Then he sighed and held her away from him.

"This will not do," he said.

"You're not going to send me to bed!" she protested.

"I don't want to, but I've got to get some sleep too," he pointed out mildly. "Besides, I'm afraid this business isn't over yet, and we'll need our wits about us when we question Gideon in the morning. So I really think—"

"Gideon!" Charity exclaimed, the other events of the evening suddenly recalled to her mind. "Of course, that's what I was going to ask you! How could I have forgotten? How do you come to know the thief? And why did you fight him?" she demanded, ignoring Jack's smile at the first part of what she said. "You didn't have to. All you had to do was wait for the others, but instead you let him goad you into nearly getting yourself killed!"

"No, that's not quite what happened." With an effort Jack put Charity away from him, and guided her to a chair. Then he sat on the edge of the table, one foot braced on the floor, the other swinging freely. He felt almost bereft now that she was no longer in his arms, but rational conversation wasn't really possible when they were too close to each other.

"It's what it looked like." Charity looked at him squarely, puzzlement and something like disapproval in her eyes.

At the memory of what had happened, the fear she had felt at the time rose within her, chilling her and making her almost angry with him. It seemed so wanton to have deliberately put himself into danger.

"You think I let my temper get the better of me?" he asked, sensing her change of mood. "That I fought him to prove myself because he had belittled me?"

"N-no. I don't know," she stammered, startled by the momentary, uncharacteristic harshness in his voice.

"I'm sorry." The tension left him and he smiled crookedly. "And, in a way, perhaps you're right. But it was the end of something—not the beginning."

"I don't understand."

"We attended the same school once, a long time ago," Jack explained. He was gazing into the fire, re-membering, and Charity suspected that, for the moment, he had almost forgotten her presence.

"He's two years older than I am, and at that age two years makes a lot of difference."

"What happened?"

"We fought a duel."

"At school! How old were you?"

"I was fourteen, he was sixteen. He won."

"But why? For God's sake!" Charity exclaimed. "They can't have permitted duelling at school!"

"No, of course not. It was...unusual, even at Westminster." Sudden amusement flared in Jack's eyes, and just as quickly died.

"It's a simple story," he said. "It happened because one of the masters temporarily had a large supply of money in his quarters with which he intended to buy a home for himself and his mother. His elder brother had inherited the family home, you see, and his wife didn't want her mother-in-law living with her."

A log collapsed, hissing in the hearth, and Jack went over to tend the fire.

"Nobody knew he had the money," he said as he stood up. "Except Gideon. I don't know how Gideon found out, but he has a way of hearing things. He stole it."

"Then what happened?" Charity demanded; she was watching Jack intently.

"One of the servants was blamed. There was evidence against him. That was Gideon's doing. He always liked to cover his bets. But I didn't believe it." Jack's smile was slightly twisted. "And, being young and impetuous, I thought it was up to me to do something about it. Besides, I had no proof, so no one would have believed my accusations."

"But what about the money?" Charity asked. "If Gideon had it, the servant couldn't have had it. So how could they prove he'd taken it?"

"It was assumed he had a confederate," Jack explained. "They were going to hang him. And the master didn't have his money, and his mother didn't have a home. So I confronted Gideon. I knew where the money was by then, but I had a misplaced notion that he deserved a chance to put right what he'd done. After all, he was supposed to be a gentleman— he'd taunted me with the fact often enough."

He moved restlessly over to the table and swept up the cards that were still lying where they'd been left in the middle of the game Sir Humphrey had interrupted earlier.

Charity watched him riffle through the cards, shuffling them with quick movements. She didn't think he was aware of what he was doing; he was just giving himself time to think before he carried on with his story.

She was beginning to see the obstacles he must have encountered all through his life. He was the grandson of both a baron and a man who had begun life as penniless apprentice, but he did not completely belong to the world of either. Perhaps there was nowhere he felt entirely at home.

Gideon had mocked Jack for being a money-lender's son, and he must have been referring to

Richard, who had chosen to become a banker rather than continue to live at odds with the late Lord Riversleigh. Jack was proud of his father, she knew that, but he must have been hearing such damning comments for most of his life.

She began to understand why he had been so sympathetic to her own fear of gossip, and to see why he had been so moved by her defence of him at the Leydons' rout. He too must have spent a great deal of his life defending himself against the unkind or unfounded judgements of others, and there must have been times when he had held to his principles at considerable cost to himself.

It did not occur to Charity that she had done the same; she was too preoccupied by her sudden increased understanding of Jack.

"You confronted Gideon," she prompted gently when he showed no sign of continuing.

"Yes." He put the cards down on the table and turned back to face her. In the flickering candle-light she could see his expression was tense.

"He chose to assume I'd challenge him. Naturally he accepted. And, since I'd issued the challenge, he had the choice of weapon. He chose swords."

"So you fought," said Charity. It was a statement, not a question. Even if he hadn't said as much earlier she would have had no doubt of it.

"I thought he was going to kill me," said Jack. "I

don't know if he intended to or not, but in the end he just put his sword through my side and stood laughing at me. That was all."

"No, it wasn't," said Charity. "What happened about the master and his money and the servant?"

"Oh, yes." Jack roused himself from his rather painful recollections. "Well, Gideon and I were discovered before he had time to leave. There was no scandal—too many of the people concerned wanted to hush up what had happened. But before I completely lost consciousness I was able to say where the money was, and who had taken it. I was ill for several days—the wound became infected—but when I finally regained my senses I found that Gideon had been sent down and the servant exonerated. I left school at the same time to take up my apprenticeship. I don't think anyone was sorry to see me go."

"They should have been," said Charity. "Particularly the servant and the master."

"I think they were both grateful," said Jack. "Alan certainly was—he insisted on coming with me."

"Alan!" Charity exclaimed. "Good heavens!"

Jack smiled. "There's a happy ending for you," he said.

"I should say so!" she agreed. "And for you?"

"And for me." Jack frowned thoughtfully. "For a long time I thought I hated Gideon, then I realised it was myself I was angry with. I haven't seen him for years—I didn't know he was in Sussex. But when I saw him tonight I wanted the chance to re-fight the duel. I'm a fool, you see." He looked at her steadily. "I had to prove to myself that I was no longer afraid of him, that he is no longer better than I am."

"He never was," said Charity. "He was just older than you—older and unscrupulous."

"Don't you think I should have known that, and let it rest?" Jack asked. "It would have been the sensible thing to do, and I would have saved you a lot of anxiety!"

It would be a long time before he forgot the look in her eyes when he'd turned and discovered she'd seen the duel.

"It might not have been the right thing," she replied. "And now it really is over. Sometimes it's not enough just to know; we have to prove it to ourselves. You wouldn't believe the number of trees I've fallen out of, and the number of ponds I've fallen into, to prove I can do what I say I can. Owen used to dare me," she explained.

"Yes, I think you two would make a fatal combination," Jack agreed. "Climbing trees is one thing; marriage is another!"

"I know I made a mistake, but I feel badly enough about it as it is!" she exclaimed. "You don't have to rub it in."

He raised his eyebrow, a distinct gleam in his grey eyes.

"And I still don't really know who Gideon is," she said hastily before he could speak. "He must have a name and a family. What are they going to say when they find out he's going to be on trial for his life? What is it?"

Jack was looking at her with a strange expression on his face.

"No, you don't know, do you?" he said slowly. "And, what with one thing and another, I haven't thought to mention it. His name won't mean much to you—it's Ralph Gideon. But you might be interested to learn that he's Lord Ashbourne's nephew."

Chapter Fifteen

"He's awake," said Charity. "We can talk to him now."

It was morning, and Sir Humphrey and Jack were just finishing their breakfast when she came to tell them that Gideon was conscious.

He had been left all night in the care of Alan and one of Sir Humphrey's men, though in fact he hadn't been in a condition to escape. But Jack knew Gideon was both cunning and vicious, and he had no intention of underestimating him.

"We?" Sir Humphrey frowned. "I really don't think it's appropriate for you to be present, m'dear."

"No, but I'm going to be," she replied inflexibly. "This matter concerns me more closely than anyone, and I want to know what he's doing here, and what part Lord Ashbourne has played in the whole affair."

Sir Humphrey stared at her worriedly. There was something implacable in her determination. He was becoming more aware than ever of her uncommon strength of will, and it almost frightened him. He didn't know what she would do next.

"I don't think it will do any harm if she's present," said Jack quietly. "And she certainly has a right to be. Shall we go up?"

He opened the door for the others and held it as they passed out of the room. Sir Humphrey looked up at him anxiously and he nodded reassuringly.

Gideon's eyes were closed when they entered the room in which he lay, but there was a crease of pain in his forehead, and he certainly wasn't asleep.

He turned his head at their approach and his expression was hostile. He wasn't going to answer questions willingly; perhaps he wasn't going to answer them at all.

"Hiding behind a woman's skirts," he sneered, and Sir Humphrey started forward angrily.

Jack caught him by the arm and held him back.

"How did you know there was something in the library?" he asked almost pleasantly.

"I had a dream," Gideon replied insolently.

Jack smiled. "So did I," he said. "It told me you're going to hang."

Gideon's eyes narrowed. He had certainly committed enough capital offences for that to be the case, but he still thought he could evade the rope.

"No, I won't," he said. "Do you think my uncle is

going to let me hang? He has the ear of the King. Even if I'm convicted, I'll be pardoned."

Sir Humphrey opened his mouth to speak. It was his son that Gideon had nearly murdered, and he was angry. Then he felt Jack's grip on his arm tighten and he suddenly decided to leave the questioning to Riversleigh.

"Perhaps you *might* be pardoned, even acquitted," Jack said calmly. "But only if you survive long enough to stand your trial. And there are so many misfortunes that can befall a man—particularly when he's already injured. The wound may become infected, or you may fall and open it again. It's so easy to bleed to death."

Gideon stared at him, understanding dawning in his angry eyes.

"You wouldn't *dare!*"

Jack smiled coldly and Gideon began to feel doubtful. He knew that neither Jack nor Alan had any cause to love him—perhaps Jack really would carry out his threat.

"If I answer your questions, will you tell my uncle where I am?" he demanded.

"I think that could be arranged," Jack agreed.

"What do you want to know?"

"What made you think there was something hidden in the library?"

"I found some papers in my uncle's desk. He should

have locked them up, but on one occasion he was inter-rupted before he could. He doesn't know I saw them."

"I don't suppose you'd be here if he did," said Jack. "What did the papers say?"

"They were notes Uncle made. I think he'd taken them from a diary. That didn't interest me. I was only concerned with finding the pendant. It was there, wasn't it?" He looked at Jack.

"Why did you want it?" Jack asked, ignoring Sir Humphrey's amazed gasp.

"Because it's worth a fortune, you fool," Gideon said savagely.

"But, when you realised there was a trap set for you last night, you must have suspected it had already been found. You took a risk; you must have wanted it badly," Jack said.

"That's none of your business," Gideon replied sullenly.

"It wasn't. It is now," said Jack implacably. "Anything you do is my business now."

The two men stared at each other, they might have been alone, for all the notice either of them took of Charity and Sir Humphrey. The balance of power had changed, but their mutual dislike remained unaltered.

"Perhaps it was because you wanted a bartering point with Lord Ashbourne," Jack suggested. "I'd heard he'd finally had the good sense to disown you. But everyone knows he collects such things."

Charity looked at him sharply. She didn't entirely understand what was happening, but it was becoming clear to her that Lord Ashbourne lay at the back of everything that had happened.

"What *does* Lord Ashbourne want?" she demanded harshly. "Why were those notes in his desk in the first place?"

Gideon turned his head on the pillow and looked at her.

"He wants the pendant," he said softly. "Any way he can get it. He nearly cheated your fool of a father out of a fortune he didn't even know he possessed! But if it hadn't been for *him*," Gideon looked at Jack with hatred, "*I* would have got there first."

Charity's eyes burned with fierce indignation and anger. She was standing on the opposite side of the bed to the others and, as she took a step towards Gideon, Sir Humphrey tried to intervene.

"M'dear, I think this is a matter…"

She looked up at him and as he met her gaze he faltered into silence.

"What did he do to Papa?" she said, her voice low and dangerous.

"You don't think my uncle normally demeans himself by playing cards with country bumpkins, do you?" Gideon said scornfully. "As I said before, your father was a fool."

"Gideon!" The sound of Jack's voice was so compelling that both Gideon and Charity were startled.

Gideon turned his head towards Jack and began to regret the petty revenge he had taken on Charity. At that moment he was convinced that Jack was going to carry out his earlier threat, and he was afraid.

"Be careful," said Jack with dangerous softness. "Be very careful."

Beads of sweat stood out on Gideon's brow and upper lip, and his mouth was so dry that he couldn't speak.

"So, let us be clear," said Jack, after a moment. "Lord Ashbourne tried to trick Mr Mayfield out of possession of the pendant—and you tried to get hold of it first so that you could use it to force your uncle to acknowledge you again. Have I that correctly?"

Gideon nodded, unable to say a word.

"You'll hang, Gideon. In the circumstances, I don't think your uncle is going to lift a finger for you."

"But the scandal," Gideon croaked. That was how he'd always escaped the consequences of his actions in the past, right from the moment when he'd almost killed Jack. Lord Ashbourne didn't care for scandal.

"We'll see," said Jack. "Alan!" He summoned his servant. "Watch him!"

"Yes, sir." Alan looked at Gideon with dislike.

"Charity," said Jack quietly. She looked at him as if she didn't know who he was, but when he held out his hand imperatively she walked over to him and allowed him to guide her out of the room.

Sir Humphrey, still too staggered to think of anything to say, followed them downstairs.

"We must send someone to the inn to see the wounded servant", Jack said as he closed the library door.

"What? Good God! I'd quite forgotten the fellow! What a head you have," Sir Humphrey exclaimed.

"I don't think what we've just heard has come as such a surprise to me as it has to you," Jack said apologetically. "I've had my suspicions for some time. Though I admit I hadn't guessed that Gideon was involved."

He was looking at Charity as he spoke. She seemed to be in a daze, and he knew that she had not been prepared. He took her hand and led her to a chair. She sat down obediently, but she hardly seemed to know that she wasn't alone. Her whole awareness was taken up by the sudden and unexpected knowledge that her father had been cheated out of Hazelhurst— and out of an inheritance he hadn't known he had.

Until that moment she had felt more exasperation than sympathy for the situation in which her father had found himself. She had been angry with Mr Mayfield for what she had seen as his folly. But now she knew he had been the victim of another man's duplicity, and the full force of her rage and dislike was directed towards Lord Ashbourne. *He* had caused all the misery and pain her family had suffered in the last year.

"Suspicions!" Sir Humphrey was still preoccupied by what they had learnt from Gideon, and by the amazing notion that Jack seemed to have anticipated it. "And a pendant? You said you'd found a pendant?"

"The night before last. It was hidden in a cavity behind the bookshelves. It's by Hilliard," Jack said, his eyes still on Charity.

But Sir Humphrey had never heard of the miniaturist and he didn't care who the pendant was by.

"You mean that, when we were discussing it yesterday, you knew all the time that there was really treasure here?" he demanded.

"It was my fault," said Charity distantly. She was looking pale and almost unnaturally calm. "When Jack first showed it to me I didn't want to tell anyone until I'd decided what to do with it."

"And then events rather overtook us," Jack continued. "I'm sorry, Sir Humphrey."

"Well, I'm not sure that I blame you," the magistrate confessed. "All this is beyond my experience. I wouldn't have taken that stuttering fool's ramblings seriously. Is that when you first started to be suspicious?"

"That's when my initial nebulous doubts were confirmed," Jack replied. "And it was also the point at which it became obvious that Lord Ashbourne must be involved in some way."

Charity looked up at that. "You mean, you *knew* he was behind everything?" she said. "Why didn't you tell me?"

"I did try, at least once," Jack said. "But we were interrupted and the subject never arose again."

"I don't understand," she said. "When did you try to tell me?"

"It was after I'd first shown you the pendant," Jack explained. "We were discussing my plan to trap the thief and I said we wouldn't have to wait long, that he'd have to make his move within the next two weeks. I was just about to tell you why when Sir Humphrey arrived."

"I still don't see…" She frowned; she didn't seem to be thinking as clearly as usual.

Jack took her hand.

"In two weeks, in less than two weeks' time now, Hazelhurst will belong to Lord Ashbourne," he said gently. "The stuttering thief said they had to find the pendant—only he called it the treasure—quickly, within that time period. But that amount of haste could only be necessary if the new owner knew what they were looking for. They had to find it before he arrived."

"I see." She took a deep breath. "I've been a fool."

For a moment she frowned distantly into the fire; then she stood up in sudden decision.

"I'm going to London," she announced. "I thought when we caught the thief this business would be ended, but it isn't. Gideon was only a distraction; Lord Ashbourne is the real villain. I'm going to confront him."

"But you can't…" Sir Humphrey began, confused and appalled by the speed at which events were over-taking him.

"Wait!"

Charity was already on her way to the door when Jack seized her arm and swung her round to face him.

"What are you going to say to the Earl when you meet him?" he demanded.

"I'm going to tell him what we know. I'm going to ask him why he did it—and I'm going to make sure he never does anything like this again. Ever."

Charity's eyes burned with a greater rage and a more implacable sense of purpose than she had ever before felt. She was impatient of restraint and she tried to pull her arm away from Jack's grasp in her haste to start for London.

"How?" Jack put his hands on her shoulders and almost shook her. "How are you going to make sure he never does it again? The law can't help you—I don't think the Earl has done anything illegal. So what are you going to do—shoot him?"

He had had a horrifying vision of Charity turning up at Lord Ashbourne's house, armed with a pistol and bent on vengeance. He had never seen her so angry. "Then you'll be the one to hang," he finished harshly.

"What do you mean, he didn't do anything illegal?" Charity demanded. "He cheated Papa. He *stole* Hazelhurst."

"It's not as simple as that. Gideon was lying to you."

"I don't understand." She stared up at him. The immediacy of her rage had passed, but not her determination. "Are you saying that Lord Ashbourne isn't responsible? You just said he was."

"He is." He met her eyes squarely. They had both forgotten Sir Humphrey's presence. "What he did was immoral—but not illegal. And I don't think you really understand what he *did* do. You think he lured your father into a card game and then cheated him out of a fortune, and ultimately out of his home, don't you?" His eyes bored relentlessly down into hers. "But there's one thing I'm certain of," he continued, "the Earl never cheated in a card game."

"Gideon said he did. Why shouldn't I believe him?" Charity was beginning to feel confused, almost suspicious. She didn't understand why Jack seemed to be defending Lord Ashbourne. She'd expected him to support her, to feel the same outrage that she felt—why was he protecting the Earl?

"Why shouldn't I believe Gideon?" she said again.

"Because he was trying to hurt you," Jack said.

He was desperately trying to make Charity understand what he thought had happened, but he was still haunted by the vision of what she might do if he failed, and in his anxiety for her he was neither as gentle nor as conciliatory as he might have been.

"He had to tell us nearly the truth—he was too afraid of me not to do so. But you spoiled all his plans and he wanted revenge—so he twisted the story just enough so that it would still be believable, but so that it would also cause you the maximum amount of pain. It would amuse him to set you and Ashbourne at each other's throats."

For a moment there was silence in the library. Then Charity lifted Jack's hands from her shoulders and stepped away from him, deliberately distancing herself from him, and Jack felt a stab of pain at the coldness in her voice.

"Then what do you think did happen?" she asked.

"I think Lord Ashbourne knew about the pendant, and I think he might well have flattered your father into playing cards with him to get it," Jack replied. "But he didn't cheat. The Earl is a devious, and in many ways an unscrupulous man—but he has his own peculiar code of honour, and he would never cheat. It wouldn't accord with his own image of himself."

"I don't see that what you have said makes any difference at all," Charity said inflexibly. "I don't care whether he cheated or not. It seems to me that everything that has happened to us has been the Earl's fault. I don't care whether what he did was legal or not. He's not going to get away with it."

"I didn't say he should get away with it," Jack replied. "I said you should know what you're blaming him for—and what he isn't guilty of."

Charity looked at him sharply and Jack gave a twisted half-smile in response. He knew she wouldn't welcome what he was about to say, he knew he might even alienate her completely—but he was still afraid of what she might do.

He was also certain that in the long run it would be far better if she didn't persist in blinding herself to some of the more distressing aspects of the situation, though later he wondered if he should have given her more time before he said anything.

"What do you mean?" Charity demanded, and now there was an underlying hostility in her tone.

For the first time it had dawned on her that Jack and Lord Ashbourne came from the same world—and that they'd known each other for years. What a fool she was! All the time she had been thinking of the Earl as the outsider in her world—but that wasn't how it was. It was *she* who was the outsider in Jack's and Lord Ashbourne's world! No wonder Jack was defending the Earl.

If Jack had known what she was thinking he might have approached the situation differently—but he didn't; and he was still trying to prepare

Charity for what she would have to face if she confronted Lord Ashbourne.

"I believe you can blame the Earl for encouraging your father to play cards with him," he said slowly. "But not for forcing him to do so. You can also blame him for having done so with a secret ulterior motive. And you can blame him for having continued the game until Mr Mayfield was twenty thousand pounds in debt—there was always something slightly odd about the fact that your father lost almost exactly the same sum as his estate was worth."

That was one of the things which had always seemed strange to Jack, even before he had suspected there was anything more sinister behind the debt.

"But you can't blame Lord Ashbourne for not having given your father enough time to repay his debt—he gave him a whole year," he continued, even though he knew that Charity might not accept what he was saying. "Perhaps the Earl thought that by doing so he was giving your father a fair chance to recover himself. Nor can you blame him for Gideon's presence, the Earl certainly wouldn't have permitted that if he'd known anything about it—and, most important of all, you can't blame him for your father's death," he finished more gently, because he thought it was that belief which lay at the root of Charity's distress.

She stood, shocked and still. Jack's words washing

over her like icy water. She knew he was right about Gideon; the Earl would have been as much a victim of his nephew as she and her mother would have been if Gideon had been successful.

But she couldn't be as dispassionate as Jack apparently was about what the Earl had done. And Mr Mayfield had died so quickly after that bitter card game that in her mind the two events were inextricably linked. She couldn't rid herself of the notion that her father must have been feeling desperately unhappy, despairing even, when he died. Lord Ashbourne might not have caused Mr Mayfield's death, but he was certainly responsible for the distress he must have been feeling at the time.

Jack was watching her closely and he saw the hardening of her purpose in her eyes. She still intended to confront the Earl, and to do so half armed, because she still hadn't accepted one basic, unpleasant fact.

There was one last thing for him to say. He knew that if he did so not only would he hurt her, but she might also never forgive him for it. But he also knew that there were others involved who would be less considerate, and he wanted her to be prepared.

"Your father must always have had a choice," he said gently. "No one, not even the Earl, can force a man to play cards with him against his will."

To Jack, that was the key to the whole affair. What he believed Lord Ashbourne to have done was immoral, devious and dishonest. But everything he knew about the Earl convinced him that Lord Ashbourne had neither cheated, nor forced Mr Mayfield to play cards with him. So Charity's father must have had a choice—and he had made the wrong one. He was not blameless for what had happened to his family. No man needed to gamble with his home.

But Charity didn't want to hear that: it hurt too much—and it was too close to the truth.

"Why do you keep defending the Earl?" she demanded. She was flushed and breathing rather quickly. "Is he your friend? Yes, of course, he must be. How else could you claim to know so much about him?"

"Charity…" Jack began. He was appalled at the hostility in her eyes.

"I dare say you knew all along what was happening," Charity swept on, ignoring his attempt to speak to her indignation and fury. It was difficult to know whether she really believed what she was saying, but in her own pain and distress she lashed out as hard as she could at Jack.

"No wonder you found everything so amusing, such *country bumpkins* as we are. I dare say his lordship will be very grateful to you for rescuing his pendant—and all the time I thought you were keeping it safe for me. Well, you haven't won yet, my lord. I want it back. You haven't had time to go home; you must still have it."

She held out her hand imperatively.

Jack was very pale, but he didn't say anything. He simply put his hand in his pocket and drew out the box which contained the pendant.

Charity took it and opened it. Jack smiled, rather bitterly, at that.

"It's still there," he said, not angrily, because he wasn't angry. It was too easy for him to understand why she thought as she did—but it still hurt him.

"I had no intention of stealing it—or of delivering it into any hands but yours," he said.

Charity looked up, and for a moment her eyes met his—then she looked away again. Her anger had passed now, but she felt drained and confused. The ground seemed to be shifting beneath her feet, and she turned with relief to Sir Humphrey, who was always the same, and who hated change.

"Will you look after this for me?" she asked. "I don't want to take it to London—something might happen to it."

"Of course, my dear," he said instantly. "But I think you're doing Riversleigh an injustice."

The magistrate hadn't entirely followed everything that had happened, and he wasn't sure if he approved of everything Jack had said—but he also thought Charity had been less than fair.

"Am I?" she looked at Sir Humphrey bleakly. "I don't feel certain of anything any more. Perhaps things will seem clearer when I've seen Lord Ashbourne."

"You can't go to London on your own," said Sir Humphrey gruffly, knowing he'd never be able to persuade her not to go at all. "If you're determined to go I'll come with you."

"Oh, Sir Humphrey!" Charity exclaimed. She could feel tears pricking at the back of her eyes at this evidence of friendship. The magistrate disliked travelling and hated going outside his own county. "Thank you so much, but please don't come," she said. "You know how much you dislike London— and you won't want to leave Owen now. I shall be quite all right."

"My dear, I can't—" Sir Humphrey began.

"I'll escort you to town," said Jack quietly. "You and your mother can come as guests of my mother."

"No," said Charity flatly. "Mama isn't to know anything about this business. You must promise, both of you, not to tell her."

She looked from one man to the other.

Sir Humphrey sighed.

"Very well, my dear," he said.

She looked at Jack.

"And you," she said.

"You have my word," he replied steadily.

"I don't see how it's going to be managed, though," Sir Humphrey protested. "You can't go rushing off to London on your own, or even in Riversleigh's company, without starting a lot of gossip. What's your mother going to say? I really think you ought to let someone go in your stead."

"No," said Charity. "I want to hear the truth for myself, then perhaps things will begin to make sense again."

She was dangerously close to tears; only a supreme effort of will made it possible for her to speak so calmly.

"I don't think there'll be any great difficulty, Leydon," said Jack quickly.

He was still very pale, but his concern now was for Charity. He could feel her distress as if it was his own and he wanted to bring the discussion to an end as soon as possible in the hope that, if something was decided, Charity would begin to feel better.

"We can say that my mother has invited Charity and Mrs Mayfield to visit her, but, since Mrs Mayfield doesn't feel up to travelling at the moment, Charity is to go on ahead—to arrange things. Most people know the Mayfields are planning to move to London; I don't think the news will be too surprising."

"But what about Mrs Mayfield?" Sir Humphrey asked. "Won't she think it odd?"

"Not necessarily." Jack's lips twisted in a wry smile. He was well aware of Mrs Mayfield's matrimonial designs for her daughter, and fairly sure that she wouldn't have any objection to Charity visiting

Mrs Riversleigh. "I believe it was her idea that Charity should ask my advice on where they ought to live in London," he said to Sir Humphrey. "The only problem may be to convince her that she doesn't feel up to the journey at the moment—and I'm sure Charity can manage that."

"Oh, yes," said Charity distantly; she seemed to have dissociated herself from the conversation now. "She hates travelling more than Sir Humphrey. I'll just have to tell her that there's been a lot of rain between here and London. When can we leave?"

"Now, if you like," said Jack calmly. "But it would cause less comment if we set off tomorrow morning. There are several things that need to be arranged."

Charity looked at him and he wondered if she suspected him of deliberately trying to hinder her efforts to see Lord Ashbourne, but if she did, she didn't say anything.

"I must go and speak to Mrs Wendle," she said. "Then I'm going back to Leydon House."

She went out, closing the door behind her, and Jack drew in a deep, slightly ragged breath.

"I take it that that blackguard *isn't* your friend?" said Sir Humphrey quietly.

"No." Jack sat down on the edge of the table. "No, he's no friend of mine."

"Why didn't you tell her?" Sir Humphrey demanded. "Why did you make it sound as if you were protecting him? It was bad enough for her to hear what she did about her father, without it sounding as if her…friends are on the side of her enemy."

The magistrate hadn't been blind to the growing intimacy between Charity and the new Lord Riversleigh; that was partly why he found Jack's attitude so difficult to understand.

"You think I shouldn't have rammed it down her throat that her father shared responsibility for what happened?" Jack said. "You're right, of course. But you don't know the Earl. You have to see things clearly when you deal with him—otherwise he manipulates everything to his own advantage. If Charity marches in and accuses the Earl of forcing Mayfield to play cards with him—or of cheating—the first thing Ashbourne will hit her with is the fact that Mayfield *didn't* have to play. That he was a fool to be flattered by a great man's praise!"

Jack caught himself up. There was no point in justifying what he'd said. He'd been motivated by fear for Charity more than anything else, but he knew he'd handled the situation badly. Ironically, he suspected that if he had cared less he would have done better.

"It's a complicated situation," he said more quietly. "The Mayfields still owe the Earl twenty thousand pounds, and I think the law will favour Ashbourne."

"But good God, man!" Sir Humphrey burst out. "Even if he didn't cheat, he will have obtained

Hazelhurst under false pretences—and now we know—"

"As far as we're aware, there were no witnesses to what happened at that card game," Jack interrupted. "And by the time they came to sign the agreement everything seemed to be in order—Mayfield's lawyer certainly thinks so. So do I. I saw the agreement the night this place was burgled and I tidied up for Charity. Ashbourne was very clever; there's no mention of a gambling debt in the agreement—the courts are notoriously reluctant to enforce gambling debts. The agreement merely mentions a loan for a non-specified purpose secured against Hazelhurst. We might be able to overturn it—but it would be a long and costly legal battle."

"Then they're still going to lose Hazelhurst!" the magistrate exclaimed, quite horrified by the idea.

"Unless we do something to avert the inevitable," said Jack grimly. "That's what I was trying to explain to Charity, though I'm afraid I didn't do it very well. Righteous anger is a very poor weapon when you're dealing with a man like the Earl."

"Good God," said Sir Humphrey blankly. "Do you have a better one?"

Jack looked thoughtfully into the fire, and drummed his fingers against the edge of the table.

"I think I may be able to lay my hands on one," he said at last. "This isn't the first time I've had dealings with the Earl. Besides," he glanced up, with the first glint of real humour in his eyes that morning since they'd spoken to Gideon, "I don't imagine any of us care for the idea of having the Earl for our neighbour."

"I should say not!" the magistrate exclaimed. "I hadn't thought of that. He may not be a cheat—to be honest, Mayfield was such a poor card-player that he probably didn't need to be—but he certainly doesn't sound like the kind of man *I'd* care to welcome into the area!"

"I didn't think he would be," Jack murmured, and looked up as Charity came back into the room.

She was still very pale, but quite composed.

"Shall we go?" she asked, looking at Sir Humphrey.

He hesitated for a moment. He wanted to help her in any way he could, but it was in his mind that it would be better if he left her alone with Jack in the hope that they settle their differences.

"I'd be glad to escort you, my dear," he said at last. "But I'm afraid my duty obliges me to go to the inn to see the other scoundrel involved in the house-breaking. I'm sure Riversleigh will be pleased to accompany you."

He took her hand.

"I'm sure everything will turn out all right in the end," he said gruffly. "If there's any way I can help, don't hesitate to ask. And don't fear that I won't keep your mother, and the pendant, safe."

"Thank you." She smiled at him, her eyes glistening.

He squeezed her hand warmly and hurried out of the room, leaving Charity alone with Jack.

"Are you ready to go?" he asked quietly.

"In a minute." She turned away from him and went to stand looking out of the window.

"I'm sorry," she said, without looking at him. "I had no right to accuse you of complicity with Lord Ashbourne."

"Charity!" He came towards her.

"No! Don't touch me." She turned to face him. "I believe that you're not working with the Earl—if you had been there would have been no need for you to show me the pendant at all."

She saw the sudden leap in his eyes and smiled without much humour.

"But there are still too many things I don't understand," she said. "You're a stranger from a world that's foreign to me, a world where all kinds of despicable tricks seem to be acceptable as long as you don't actually break some peculiar code of honour— and I'm not sure I want any part of it. Take me to London, my lord. I accept your help so far because I have to—but after that…"

She didn't finish what she was saying. Instead she walked over to the door, turning to look back at Jack with her hand resting on the door-handle.

"I'm ready to go now," she said.

Chapter Sixteen

The carriage jolted uncomfortably towards London, and Charity closed her eyes and tried to sleep. She was tired—she had had so little undisturbed sleep over the past few days—but she couldn't close her mind to the terrible thoughts that tormented her.

She couldn't stop thinking about her father and what he must have felt when he'd realised he had lost everything—and that led her to think about Lord Ashbourne. She had never hated anyone in her life before, but she had no doubt that she hated the Earl. She knew she could never rest until she had confronted him, and all through the long carriage ride she rehearsed again and again what she would say to him. Only now and then did her thoughts wander away to other, less compelling matters.

Sometimes, as she braced her feet against the jolting of the carriage, she found herself thinking about Jack. It was a painful exercise, in some ways more painful than her thoughts about her father. She had trusted Jack, and relied on him—now she realised she hardly knew him.

She couldn't understand why he hadn't condemned Lord Ashbourne more strongly for what he had done. He had taken the news so calmly, almost dispassionately. Did he not find Lord Ashbourne's actions shocking? Did he even *admire* the Earl for his cunning?

She shied away from the thought, resolutely putting Jack out of her mind. He was riding beside the carriage, escorting her to London, but she had hardly acknowledged his presence since their departure that morning. At the back of her mind she was dimly aware that he was trying to help her, but she was too confused and too bewildered to make any attempt to understand his point of view. She didn't know what he wanted her to do, but she was afraid that if she listened to him she might be diverted from her purpose—and that would have been a betrayal of her father.

They'd been travelling some time and she wanted to open her eyes and see where they were. She wanted to look at the passing countryside in the hope that the changing scenery would take her mind off her problems; but Tabitha was sitting opposite her and Charity knew that if she opened her eyes the maid would begin talking to her. She couldn't bear the idea of conversation, so she kept her eyes resolutely shut and remembered instead her meeting with Owen the previous afternoon.

"Charity!" Owen exclaimed delightedly.

He looked up at her as she stood beside the bed. A band of pale afternoon sunlight illuminated her face, and he thought she had never looked more beautiful. He didn't notice the shadows in her eyes or her pallor—he was too pleased to see her.

"How are you?" she asked, and smiled at him with something of an effort.

"I'll be on my feet in no time," he declared. "Sit down, sit down."

She obeyed, folding her hands demurely in her lap, though inwardly she felt anything but calm.

"I was hoping you'd come before," said Owen. "I asked for you. I know you saved my life. I wanted to thank you."

"I did what I could," Charity replied. "I'm thankful that it was enough."

"And you shot one of the ruffians," said Owen with satisfaction. Sir Humphrey had told him that, though he still didn't know everything else that had happened at Hazelhurst since he had been confined to his sick-bed.

"Mind, I'm not sure that I like the notion of you having anything to do with guns, but in the circumstances you did well. Not like me. I don't seem to be able to do anything right at the moment," he added bitterly. "I hear Riversleigh came to the rescue again."

"He heard the shots," said Charity.

"He's always in the right place at the right time," said Owen, "but he won't always have the advantage on his side."

"I don't think he does now," said Charity, surprising herself because she wasn't feeling particularly in sympathy with Jack and she hadn't expected she'd have any urge to defend him.

"What do you mean?" Owen looked at her suspiciously, but she didn't reply.

She didn't know how to explain that, whatever else Owen might lack, he had always possessed the one advantage denied to Jack. Owen wasn't rich and he wasn't particularly clever, but he was the squire's son and, from birth, his place in his small world had always been accepted unquestioningly by himself, and by everyone around him.

By contrast, as Charity thought about Jack, she realised his world must always have been a more complicated place, and she was aware of a fugitive notion that perhaps, to survive in a complicated world, it might be necessary to be a complicated person. But then she dismissed the idea. She had other, more important things to think about than Lord Riversleigh.

"Charity!"

At the sound of Owen's voice she recollected herself and smiled at him.

"I'm glad you're feeling better. But you always did have a very strong constitution. It would be very hard to kill you, I think."

Owen looked pleased.

"We're a tough lot, the Leydons," he declared. "We always breed true. When we're married—"

"Owen!"

He looked at her in surprise. "I know I haven't spoken to your mother yet, but as soon as I'm able to stand on my feet I will. I'm sure she won't object. There's no need for you to be anxious."

"I'm not," said Charity with a hint of her old tartness, but it wasn't fair to be annoyed with Owen. This whole dreadful misunderstanding was entirely her fault.

"Owen, I'm sorry…" she began. But then, because she wanted there to be no doubt of what she was telling him, she said simply, "I can't marry you."

"What?"

"When you proposed to me at the party I was…flattered, but I was also confused," she said steadily, trying to make her rejection of him as painless as she could. "I was surprised, and I didn't know what to say—so I said yes. But I shouldn't have done. It was very wrong of me. I'm sorry."

"You mean, you don't *want* to marry me?"

"No. I don't think we'd suit. I'm sorry," she said again.

For a moment he didn't say anything, he just lay staring up at the ceiling. There was an unreadable expression on his face and Charity didn't know what to do.

She didn't know whether he'd accepted what she'd said, whether she'd hurt him, or whether he was angry with her. She didn't know if she should say anything else, or if she should allow the silence to lengthen until he broke it himself.

In the tree outside the window a crow began to make its harsh cry, and Charity thought it sounded as desolate as she felt. So many birds sang in the summer, but the sound of the crow always reminded Charity of winter.

"It's him, isn't it?" Owen said at last, still not looking at her.

"No, it's me," she replied quietly, knowing that he was referring to Jack Riversleigh.

Owen turned his head at that, frowning. "You?"

"We wouldn't suit, Owen. Think how many arguments we've had in the past few days. We would spend the rest of our lives quarrelling. I don't want that."

"No, we won't," he said. "It's true you're headstrong, and not always very…sensible. But one must make allowances for your circumstances. I'm sure things will be different when we're married."

"You mean, I'll change and become more biddable, less opinionated?" she asked, smiling faintly. "But I don't want to change, Owen. I like the way I am."

He looked puzzled; he was very fond of her, but he didn't really understand her. The very qualities in her which he admired when they led to her saving his life distressed him when they resulted in a clash of wills between them. He wanted part of Charity, but not all of her, and he didn't see that that wasn't possible.

"I'm sorry, I can't stay any longer," she said. "I'm going to London tomorrow. I have to get ready."

"London?" He stared at her with renewed suspicion. He couldn't rid himself of the notion that somehow Lord Riversleigh had something to do with Charity's change of heart.

"Mama and I are going to move to London," she said calmly. "Mrs Riversleigh has invited us both to stay with her while we find somewhere to live. It will be easier to make arrangements if we're on the spot. Unfortunately, Mama doesn't feel up to the journey yet, so I'm going on ahead. I hope I'll be able to have everything arranged by the time she arrives."

"You're going to London on your own!" Owen was outraged. "Whatever can you be thinking of? Headstrong! Heedless! It's most improper behaviour!"

"No, it's just practical," said Charity. "I have always made all the arrangements. There's no reason why I should cease to do so, just because we're moving elsewhere."

"I suppose *he'll* be going with you?" Owen said sullenly.

"Lord Riversleigh has business of his own to attend to in London. He has kindly agreed to escort Tabitha and me," she said flatly. "Goodbye, Owen."

Charity sighed, wishing her parting with Owen had been more amicable. Owen still didn't like Jack—perhaps he never would—and it must have been difficult for him to hear that she was going to London in Lord Riversleigh's company.

The carriage was turning off the road. She felt the altered motion and opened her eyes, looking out of the window. They were stopping at an inn. It was time to change the horses and eat a quick meal before they continued their journey.

The door was opened, the steps let down, and Jack held out his hand to assist her. She hesitated for a moment, then she put her cold hand in his and let him help her out.

"Thank you," she said, her voice polite but very cold.

"Charity..." he began, still holding her hand in his.

"Will we be stopping here long?" she asked, drawing her hand away.

He looked at her steadily for a moment, knowing that she was deliberately distancing herself from him.

"No," he replied at last, reluctantly accepting the situation, even though he had a strong desire to take her in his arms and shake her until her eyes lost their blank, desolate expression and sparked instead with indignation.

"No, we won't be staying here long, Charity, but if you come into the inn you can rest for a while, and they'll give you something to eat." He offered her his arm.

"I'm not tired," she said, but she took his arm. It was the only friendly gesture she had made and she would have been surprised if she had known how much comfort Jack took in it.

It was late afternoon by the time they arrived in London, and Charity was exhausted and Tabitha sick. Normally Charity would have been fascinated by the sights and sounds of the metropolis because, though Mr Mayfield had come to town regularly, this was only her second visit. But now she didn't care.

Somehow she had imagined that they would go straight to Lord Ashbourne and she was vaguely surprised when she realised that in fact Jack was escorting her into his mother's house.

He guided her gently into the elegantly yet comfortably furnished drawing-room. Outside it was cold and dark, and for the first time in days it had come on to rain, but inside the house the candles had been lit and the fire crackled welcomingly.

Charity was too tired to feel anything but faint relief at her arrival, but she made an effort to smile as she saw a dark, plumpish woman stand up to greet her. She had no quarrel with her hostess, however mixed her feelings about her son.

"Miss Mayfield! I was so pleased when Jack told me you and your mother would be visiting us," Mrs Riversleigh exclaimed. "I'm only sorry that your mother didn't feel she could face the journey yet. You must be exhausted. Come and sit down."

Mrs Riversleigh was shocked by Charity's exhausted and haunted appearance, but no sign of her feelings could be detected from her voice. Instead she took Charity's hand and led her to a chair by the fire.

"Thank you." Charity's smile was a mere vestige of its usual self. It hadn't yet occurred to her to wonder how Mrs Riversleigh had known she was coming, though in fact Jack had sent a messenger on ahead, warning his mother of their arrival.

"I'm sorry." She roused herself with an effort. "You must think it very rude of me to arrive unannounced like this."

"No, of course not," Mrs Riversleigh replied firmly. She was a kind woman and, even if she hadn't known Jack wanted her to welcome Charity, she would still have greeted her warmly. "But you must still be very shaken from the coach. Let me take you up to your room so that you can rest. Or are you hungry?" she added as an afterthought. "I can never eat when I first get out of a carriage, so I always assume that no one else can, but I know it's not the case with everyone. Would you like something to eat first?"

"No, no, thank you." Unintentionally, Charity's expression indicated that the thought of food at that moment was as nauseating to her as it obviously was to Mrs Riversleigh after a long journey.

"Come, then." Mrs Riversleigh took Charity upstairs herself and saw that she was settled in a very pretty room before she left her alone.

"Would you like me to send some food up to you later? Or will you come down?" she asked as she opened the door.

"Oh, no, I'll come down," Charity said quickly. "I'm sure I'll be more myself soon, it's just that, at the moment, every time I close my eyes I have the foolish notion that I'm still being tossed about in the coach." She smiled apologetically, a distinctly self-deprecating expression in her eyes, and Mrs Riversleigh felt herself warming to her unexpected guest.

She closed the door quietly and went down to join Jack.

"That poor girl looks quite exhausted," she said as she sat down in her favourite wing chair. "Why have you brought her to London?"

"She has some family business to attend to," Jack replied mildly, though his voice sounded slightly strained. "Where's Fanny?"

"She's gone to dinner with the Markhams. When I received your note I sent my apologies. I thought you would want me to be here when you arrived."

"I did. But I'm sorry to spoil your evening." Jack sat down in a straight-backed chair, sideways to the table, and selected an apple from the fruit bowl.

"You haven't," said Mrs Riversleigh calmly. "The Markhams are very nice people, and Fanny is fond of Lucinda—but an evening in their company bores me to distraction! This promises to be much more interesting."

Jack had been peeling his apple, but he looked up at that, an unforced gleam of amusement in his eyes that pleased his mother. She wasn't unaware of the tension which filled him, and it both puzzled and slightly concerned her.

"You are quite reprehensible," he said. "Sometimes I blush for you."

"No, you don't. You agree with me," she replied.

"Touché." He flung up his hand and laughed.

"What is this all about, Jack?" she asked more seriously. "Miss Mayfield looks as if she's seen a ghost."

"I think, in a way, she has," he said. "No, I can't tell you any more. I think you must ask Charity if you want to know anything else."

"Certainly not," said Mrs Riversleigh firmly. "I don't know her!"

"Not yet," said Jack. He smiled faintly. "It doesn't usually take long to get to know Charity. She may ask your advice on finding a house in London," he added more briskly. "I don't think it's likely; she's got a lot of other things on her mind at the moment. But that *is* the ostensible reason for her visit. So, if she does…"

"If she does I'll give her all the help I can," said Mrs Riversleigh.

"Thank you," Jack said. "Now, I must send a message to Lord Ashbourne." He stood up and went over to an elegant bureau.

"Lord Ashbourne! Is he involved in this business?" Mrs Riversleigh exclaimed.

Jack nodded.

"I don't like the man," said Mrs Riversleigh firmly.

"You're prejudiced," he responded lightly.

"Of course I am," she replied. "His nephew nearly killed you!" She saw a flicker of something in Jack's eyes and a sudden suspicion flared within her.

"Have you seen Ralph Gideon recently?" she demanded.

He folded his note, addressed and sealed it before he replied.

"We ran into each other the night before last," he said as he pulled on the bell rope for a footman to take his letter to Lord Ashbourne.

"And?"

"He is now nursing a wound in his shoulder."

"You're a fool," she said with conviction.

"Yes, I probably am," he agreed reflectively.

Charity sat quietly in a comfortable chair. She hadn't wanted to lie on the bed—she felt too vulnerable in that position. Her eyes were closed and her mind finally empty of almost all thought. It had been impossible for her to remain at the same fever pitch of emotion with which she had begun the day, and by the time she had arrived at the house she had felt quite numb, and drained of all emotion.

But she was resilient, and the time on her own had helped her. After a while she began to feel more like herself. She knew she wouldn't be seeing Lord Ashbourne that evening, and she owed it to her hostess to make some effort to be a charming guest. She didn't want to see or speak to Jack, but it would be rude to hide in her room, or allow her own troubles to worry others—particularly when she had virtually forced her presence on Mrs Riversleigh.

She went over to the mirror and gasped at her appearance. She looked terrible—her hair was falling down, there was a smudge of grime on her cheek, and her dress was creased and dusty. She could never go downstairs like that.

She glanced at the bell rope nervously; despite her

earlier attention, she already knew she was staying in a far grander house than any she had previously visited, and she wasn't quite sure what would happen if she pulled it, but she needed Tabitha's help—if Tabitha was well enough.

She took a deep breath, and resolutely tugged at the rope. Within an astonishingly short space of time a shy maid appeared. She asked for Tabitha, but Tabitha was apparently quite unwell—in fact, she was groaning on a bed, but the maid didn't tell Charity that.

"May I help you, miss?" she asked.

Charity looked at her doubtfully for a second, then she nodded decisively. It took nearly forty-five minutes to repair the ravages of the journey, but when they had finished the maid stood back admiringly.

"You're beautiful, miss," she said shyly.

Charity stared critically at herself in the mirror. Her dark curls shone and the activity had brought a glow to her cheeks, but the beautiful eyes looking back at her seemed tired and sad.

She sighed.

"You're flattering me," she said. "But thank you anyway." She took a deep breath. "I must go downstairs," she said, "but I wasn't really attending when Mrs Riversleigh brought me up here. I'm not sure if I can remember the way back."

"I'll show you, miss," said the maid eagerly.

She really did think Charity was beautiful, and she was quite charmed by her kind manner. Mrs Riversleigh was very kind too, but until that moment the maid had been inclined to think that such considerate ladies were rare.

Charity paused in the doorway. She felt shy, and a little confused, because Jack and Mrs Riversleigh had been joined by another man she didn't recognise.

"I'm sorry," she said hesitantly. "I hope I haven't kept you waiting."

"Not at all," Mrs Riversleigh replied warmly, walking over to her with a stiff rustle of silk. "As soon as I knew you were coming I had dinner set back. It was quite easy, and not at all inconvenient," she added reassuringly as she saw that Charity was looking guilty.

"Come and let me introduce you to Matthew." She took Charity's arm and led her over to the other man.

Charity followed obediently but, as she did so, she couldn't resist the impulse to look across at Jack. He was watching her quietly. There was no humour in his eyes—only a question, and something that was not quite an apology.

"This is Matthew Dawson," said Mrs Riversleigh, unconsciously recalling Charity's attention. "He was my father's partner; now he is Jack's. Matthew, this is Miss Mayfield."

He was a spare man, not above middle height, with stooped shoulders. He was clearly bashful in strange company, but his eyes were shrewd and kind, and Charity found herself warming to him.

He sat next to her at dinner, but, though he replied when she spoke to him, he introduced no new topics of conversation himself. He only felt at ease with his craftsman peers, with his apprentices and with the people close to him that he had known for years. Elegant young ladies—to him, Charity was an extremely elegant and self-assured young lady—made him nervous and uncomfortable. He couldn't imagine that anything he had to say would interest her.

Jack said very little, and Mrs Riversleigh was frankly curious. She knew there was an undercurrent of tension between Charity and Jack and she wanted to know what Charity meant to her son but, though he might have told her if she'd asked, she hadn't chosen to do so. She had never pried into her children's affairs and, on the whole, they had rewarded her tact by being remarkably open with her. She was afraid that this time, it might be different, but she knew that she could only wait, and hope that in the end she would find out what was happening.

When the meal was over she took Charity back to the drawing-room, leaving Jack and Matthew to their wine.

"Would you like some tea?" she asked as they sat down. "There's no knowing how long those two will sit over an empty table. It's not that they're heavy drinkers, you understand. It's just that when they start talking about their craft they forget all sense of time!"

Charity smiled. "Lord Riversleigh told me about Mr Dawson," she said. "I think he must be a very clever man—and a very nice one."

"Yes, he is." Mrs Riversleigh was slightly surprised. She knew that Matthew did not always appear at his best in unfamiliar company. It was not everyone who could see beyond the monosyllabic and awkward replies to the talented and sensitive man he really was. She felt a growing respect for Charity, which increased when Charity said, "You must think it very rude of me to invite myself like this; I don't normally behave so badly. Well…" she paused ruefully "…perhaps I do."

"You seem troubled," said Mrs Riversleigh, because she wanted Charity to feel that she could confide in her, but she didn't want her to think that she was being vulgarly curious.

"Yes," said Charity, "but it's so complicated that I just don't know how to explain. Didn't Ja…Lord Riversleigh tell you anything about it?"

"No. I don't think he felt it was his place to do so," said Mrs Riversleigh. "He would never betray another's confidence."

"No." Charity looked at her hostess rather strangely. "No, he wouldn't."

She remembered the other confidences he hadn't betrayed. He could have made her the target for every gossip in Sussex if he'd chosen to do so—but he hadn't. He had been very kind to her; perhaps she was doing him an injustice—but *why* had he defended Lord Ashbourne?

"I don't think it's a secret," she said at last as she realised Mrs Riversleigh was waiting for her to continue. "I'm afraid I've been treating it like one, but that's only because it feels so much like a nightmare. Does that make sense?"

"We don't always want to talk about the things that upset us most," said Mrs Riversleigh gently. "Sometimes it helps. But sometimes when we're confused, and people ask questions we can't answer—because we don't know the answers—we just end up feeling more confused."

Charity looked at her gratefully. "Yes," she said. "That's how I feel. Do you mind if I don't explain now? I promise I will later."

"There's no hurry," said Mrs Riversleigh, and looked up as Jack and Matthew came into the room. For once Jack had had no desire to linger over the dining table, discussing their craft, and he had made the move to rejoin the ladies long before Matthew had felt ready to do so. Matthew would have been quite happy if he'd never gone back into the drawing-room.

Charity saw his hesitation and guessed how he

must be feeling. It would be a kindness not to embarrass him further by trying to engage him in conversation, but she didn't want to talk to Jack, nor even to Mrs Riversleigh. Jack confused her and, although she liked her hostess, she couldn't feel entirely at ease with her while there was still so much unexplained between them.

Matthew was the only one present who offered no threat, only the challenge of setting him at his ease. To Charity the combination was irresistible, and she took a cup of tea from Mrs Riversleigh and gave it to Matthew, sitting down beside him as she did so. It had occurred to her that the best way to draw him out must be to ask him about his work, and that was what she proceeded to do.

Matthew looked rather alarmed at her approach. But when she was neither patronising nor flirtatious he began to feel more at ease. And when she asked if it had been he who'd made the beautiful silver gilt teapot, and seemed genuinely interested in his reply, he became quite talkative.

Mrs Riversleigh appeared to be concentrating on her embroidery, but in fact she was watching them in some amusement. Even after forty years, Matthew was as enthusiastic about his craft as he had been as a new apprentice. Given the opportunity, he could talk well and at length about what he'd made in the past— and he was always full of his plans for future work.

He described the processes of casting, soldering and annealing to Charity; explained the difference between embossing, chasing and engraving, and even upended the contents of the tea caddy on to the silver tea-tray so that he could show her how he'd finished it.

Charity had begun to talk to him partly because she really was interested, and partly to take her mind off her other problems. But it wasn't long before she became quite engrossed in what he was telling her. She'd always enjoyed the company of people who were good at something and, once he'd lost his initial self-consciousness, Matthew was able to bring his stories and descriptions to life.

"Of course, that was the salvar Hogarth engraved for us," he said at one point.

"Hogarth!" she exclaimed.

"He began life as an engraver," Jack explained, looking up briefly from what he was doing. "I don't think Matthew has ever forgiven him for his fall from grace to become a mere painter!"

"Well, I can see the merit in his pictures too," Matthew admitted. "But it was a sad loss to the trade." And he continued with his description of the early days of the business, when Joseph Pembroke had realised that he would never have a son to succeed him and had taken Matthew into partnership.

Jack didn't interrupt any more. Early in the conversation he had taken some paper from the bureau and begun to sketch Charity and Matthew as they sat talking. Mrs Riversleigh knew what he was doing, but neither of the other two did.

His movements were quick and deft and, when he at last put down his pencil, Mrs Riversleigh got up and went to stand at his shoulder to look at the finished sketch.

Jack was a very fair artist, but Mrs Riversleigh had always believed that he drew best those people that he knew best—and those people that he loved. He was as close to Matthew as he had been to his father and she wasn't surprised to see how well he'd caught the silversmith's likeness. But she had to restrain a gasp when she looked at his picture of Charity, and she knew then that at least one of her unspoken questions had been answered. The girl on the paper was as vibrant and full of life as the girl talking to Matthew. Jack had surpassed himself.

"It's very good," she said softly.

"It is, isn't it?" he looked at the sketch almost as if he was surprised that it should be so.

"What is it?" Charity glanced up, momentarily distracted from her discussion with Matthew.

Jack passed her the sketch, and she looked at it for a long moment without saying anything. Then at last, with her eyes still on the picture Jack had drawn of her, and apparently quite irrelevantly, she said, "When can I see the Earl?"

"Tomorrow morning. I've arranged a meeting."

"Good." For almost a full minute Charity continued to look at the sketch, and Mrs Riversleigh wondered what she saw in it.

"It's very good," she said quietly as she finally handed it back to Jack. "It's not often one sees oneself through someone else's eyes. Thank you."

For a moment her gaze locked with Jack's, almost as if she was seeking the answer to her question. Then she stood up.

"I'm sorry, I hope you'll excuse me," she said to Mrs Riversleigh. "But it's getting quite late and I'm afraid I'm very tired."

"You've had a tiring day," said Mrs Riversleigh. "I hope you'll sleep well."

"Thank you." Charity smiled briefly, and went quickly out of the room.

Chapter Seventeen

"Yes, Bolton?" Lord Ashbourne was sitting at the table, his head bent over the letter he was writing, and he didn't look up at the servant's approach.

"Lord Riversleigh has arrived, my lord."

"Show him into the library. You may tell him I will join him shortly." The Earl's pen continued to travel unhurriedly over the paper as he spoke.

"Yes, my lord. There is a *lady* with Lord Riversleigh, my lord."

"A lady?" Lord Ashbourne finally looked up. "Did she give a name?"

"No, my lord."

"I see." A hint of curiosity gleamed in the Earl's eyes, but he didn't say anything further on the subject. "Provide them with refreshment, Bolton. The lady may care for some tea, perhaps." He dipped his pen in the ink and completed his unfinished sentence.

It was twenty minutes later when Lord Ashbourne

finally joined his guests in the library, and they were twenty very difficult minutes for Charity. She suspected, though she couldn't be sure, that the Earl was making them wait to display his own consequence, and she began to feel angry.

"It's not you he's slighting," said Jack softly. "Don't let it agitate you. I didn't tell him in my note I was bringing anyone with me and, although he certainly knows you're here now, I'm fairly sure he doesn't know who you are. It's *me* he's trying to provoke. I asked for this meeting, which means that I probably want something from him, and that made it almost inevitable he'd keep me waiting."

"Doesn't that anger you?" Charity demanded; she couldn't understand how Jack could be so calm in the face of such an insult.

"It might if I allowed it to," Jack replied quietly. "But it would be a waste of energy—and a victory for the Earl. It's better not to let yourself be sidetracked from your purpose."

He had tried to explain this to Charity before, but without much success and, despite his calm demeanour, he was in fact unusually tense. It was not his forthcoming meeting with Lord Ashbourne which worried him, but how Charity would react in what was bound to be a difficult situation. He had tried to prepare her for the meeting, but she had been unresponsive and distant. She was afraid of being misled, or of having her purpose blunted, and she was determined to deal with Lord Ashbourne on her own terms.

"Riversleigh, my dear fellow. How delightful to see you again. I'm sorry to have kept you waiting." The Earl strolled into the room, calm and unhurried.

"Not at all," Jack replied politely, standing at the Earl's approach. "It was kind of you to grant us an interview at such short notice."

"Us?" Lord Ashbourne queried courteously. "I believe I have not previously had the pleasure of meeting your charming companion."

He turned to Charity as he spoke, and she saw the slightly appraising look in his eyes as he smiled at her.

"No, I don't think you have," said Jack. "This is Miss Charity Mayfield."

Lord Ashbourne clearly hadn't expected that, but he was too sophisticated to show his surprise openly.

"My dear Miss Mayfield," he said, after only a moment's hesitation. "I am delighted to meet you. I was…very sorry to hear of your father's death. He was a remarkable man."

"Thank you." Charity's voice was as cold as the hand she allowed the Earl to kiss, but she was containing her fury very well.

She didn't know Lord Ashbourne and she was sure he was mocking her. It was only Jack, watching his host carefully, who thought there was something odd in the Earl's manner. The Earl was doing his best to conceal it, but Jack was convinced that he had been thrown off balance by Charity's presence.

"I'm all the more delighted to make your acquaintance because my agent has been so impressed by your remarkable grasp of business," said Lord Ashbourne urbanely. "Do, please, sit down again."

He gestured towards a comfortable chair before the fire.

"I hope things are proceeding to your satisfaction," he continued. "Is there any way in which I may be of assistance—or have you come to pay your father's debt?" His voice was almost languid in its lack of emphasis.

"No, my lord," said Charity.

She ignored the chair he offered and sat at the table, her hands clasped tensely before her.

"I've come to ask you why you tricked my father into losing Hazelhurst to you," she said baldly.

"Tricked?" There was a hint of contempt in the Earl's voice now, though the expression in his eyes was quite unreadable. "My dear young lady, there was no trick. Mayfield and I simply amused ourselves with a few hands of piquet. Unfortunately your father lost rather heavily."

"Ashbourne!" said Jack suddenly before Charity could speak, and the Earl swung round to face him. "It may save time at this point if I tell you that we know that your meeting with Mr Mayfield was not entirely...accidental," Jack continued quietly.

He didn't think this was a situation in which there was anything to be gained by fencing, and the quicker they reached some kind of understanding, the better.

"Do you, indeed?" said the Earl, his attention now entirely directed at Jack, almost as if he found Jack easier to deal with than Charity. "May I ask why?"

Jack glanced briefly at Charity, but she seemed surprisingly reluctant to speak, so he continued with the explanation himself.

"Two nights ago I had the misfortune to encounter Ralph Gideon," he said. "He was just about to make his third attempt to ransack the library at Hazelhurst." He saw the look of sharp understanding spring into the Earl's eyes, and smiled grimly.

"Quite. Perhaps I should inform you that during his brief stay in Sussex he has not only helped a prisoner to escape from the custody of the local magistrate, but also shot that same magistrate's son in the process."

"Dead?" Lord Ashbourne asked sharply.

"No. But only because Miss Mayfield was on hand to administer immediate assistance," Jack replied.

The Earl glanced at Charity, a frown in his eyes.

"A most unpleasant experience," he said. "I'm sorry that any relative of mine should have caused you such distress."

"Sorry!" Charity burst out, forgetting her previous intentions as she impetuously rejoined the conversation.

Her unusual silence until that moment had been prompted by the sudden realisation that she might find it more instructive to listen than to speak. It had finally dawned on her in those painful minutes while she had been waiting for the Earl to appear that she was even more anxious to know how Jack would deal with the situation than she was to find out what had happened to her father. And she was afraid that, if *she* took the lead in questioning Lord Ashbourne, she might never find out what Jack really felt about the Earl. Nevertheless, it was impossible for her to remain silent for long.

"It wasn't Gideon who tried to cheat my father out of everything he possessed—and it's not Gideon who is responsible for all the misery my family has suffered this past year!" she exclaimed. She was breathing quickly, her eyes burning with anger and dislike.

"Lord Riversleigh says you did nothing illegal," she continued, her voice quieter now and more compelling than any scream of outrage. "I'm not sure I believe him. But even if he's right—how do you justify what you've done to us?"

Her eyes were locked with the Earl's.

"I'm not sure I know what you think I *have* done," he said at last, his voice stripped of all expression.

"You wanted the pendant, the jewel by Hilliard,"

she said. "I don't know how you knew it was in the house, and it's not important. But you didn't go to my father like a gentleman and tell him it was there—or offer to buy it. Instead you tricked him into playing cards with you, and into losing so much money that the only way he *could* repay the debt would be by selling Hazelhurst—and then you agreed to take our home in lieu of cash. Isn't that what you did?"

She was leaning forward, her arms resting on the table, her eyes blazing with fury. She had forgotten Jack; she had forgotten everything but the man sitting before her who had caused so much pain to so many people.

For a moment there was silence. The Earl was looking at Charity, a curious expression on his face.

"Broadly speaking, you're quite correct," he said at last, and some of the tension left Charity.

"You consider such conduct unforgivable," he said softly. "No doubt you're right, but having admitted my guilt so readily, perhaps I might be permitted to say a couple of things in my own defence."

Charity didn't answer, and after a moment Jack said, "You're the only witness to what happened, Ashbourne. I think it would be best if you told us everything."

"Will you believe what I say?" the Earl asked.

"Perhaps." The two men looked steadily at each

other for a moment, then Lord Ashbourne turned to
Charity. "I didn't cheat," he said. "Please understand
that. Whatever else I might have done, I have never
cheated at cards in my life. I would scorn to do so!"

"You sound very grand," she replied quietly,
meeting his gaze with her honest brown eyes. "No
doubt you are very grand. But beneath the fine
speeches and the fine clothes you're still only a man,
and you can never be any more than that—only less."

The Earl drew in a deep, slightly uneven breath and
turned away to lean his arm on the mantelpiece.

"I tried to buy Hazelhurst first," he said after a
moment. He was staring down into the fire, not
looking at Charity. "Through an agent, of course.
Your father wouldn't sell, even though I offered
nearly half as much again as it's worth. After that I
really had no choice but to pursue other methods."

"You could have told him the truth," said Charity
inflexibly.

"That did not occur to me," Lord Ashbourne
glanced up briefly, "although at first I did wonder
whether he knew about the pendant—but he didn't.
Certain things he said made that plain. But you
mustn't think I lied to him—lying, like cheating, is
something I never do. I simply didn't tell him all the
facts." He paused, but Charity didn't comment.

"Well, I don't suppose you're interested in my
personal foibles," he continued, turning back to face

her. "I arranged for a chance meeting; I believed he was flattered when I invited him back here; he was certainly quite willing to play cards with me—unfortunately for him, his skill was not equal to his ambition."

Charity bent her head and closed her eyes. The Earl's words could have been an epitaph for Mr Mayfield's life. It hurt her to think that he should have exposed himself to the scorn and ridicule of a man like Lord Ashbourne.

"He was a very brave man," said the Earl quietly. "At first he wasn't aware of how much he'd lost, and when he realised he couldn't afford to pay what he owed he tried to win his money back. He didn't, of course, but I stopped the game when the debt equalled the value of the property. There was no need to continue any longer."

"Should I be grateful for that?" asked Charity bitterly.

"No," said the Earl. "But when he left me I did think he would seek out the man who'd tried to buy Hazelhurst and take up his offer. If he had done he would have had ten thousand pounds in hand."

"Would you still have bought it?" Charity asked incredulously. "Even when there was no longer any need?"

"I didn't want to have to wait a year before looking for the pendant," Lord Ashbourne replied.

"Why *did* you give him that year?" Jack asked suddenly.

"I really cannot say," the Earl said, and, whatever his earlier feelings might have been, his mask of indifference was now firmly back in place. "No doubt I had a reason at the time, but I cannot recall it now."

"Then it seems to me you're in danger of being convicted by your own boasts," said Jack.

Lord Ashbourne frowned, then he realised what Jack meant.

"The truth then, if you must have it," he said, a sharper note in his voice. "I won twenty thousand pounds from Mayfield that night. But even when he knew he was ruined he continued to act with dignity and courtesy. I had expected him to be distraught, angry, even suspicious, but he wasn't. I have done many things in my life, but I have never destroyed a man before—and then heard him thank me for giving him a pleasant evening. I told you he was a brave man."

Charity looked away, tears in her eyes. The Earl was the last person she had ever expected to praise her father, and she was thrown off balance. Everything had seemed so simple before; now it was becoming so complicated.

"I still wanted the pendant," said Lord Ashbourne. "But Mayfield deserved a chance to recover—he'd earned it. So I gave him a year. I expected him to sell Hazelhurst to the interested buyer. But when he didn't I thought he'd found another way to pay the debt."

"He was dead," Charity whispered.

"Yes, I know that now. I didn't know it then. I didn't find out until your lawyer contacted me a couple of weeks ago." Lord Ashbourne walked over to stand before Charity.

"I'm sorry," he said.

Charity turned her head away.

"You didn't make any effort to find out *how* he was going to raise the money?" Jack asked.

"No." The Earl looked down at Charity's averted face, then went back to stand by the fireplace. "The cards had been dealt. It was up to Mayfield how he played them."

"An unlucky metaphor, don't you think?" Jack said, an edge to his voice.

"Yes. I apologize. At the time I had no desire to interfere any further. I regret that now. Had I done so I would have discovered that Mayfield was dead—and that you had apparently no knowledge of his agreement with me."

"I found out two and a half weeks ago," Charity said. She was looking pale and stressed, but she was quite calm.

"You are very like your father," said the Earl slowly.

"How can you say you regret not knowing my father was dead?" Charity demanded, ignoring his comment. "Are you trying to suggest it would have made any difference? You have known for more than two weeks that neither Mama or I knew we would have to leave Hazelhurst by the end of this month, but you have done *nothing* to ease our distress. Your words are empty. You still wanted the pendant and you didn't care how much suffering you caused as long as you got it!"

The Earl winced.

"Yes," he said. "I wanted the pendant; I still do. But I wouldn't have kept Hazelhurst as well. A couple of days and I would have had the jewel. Then perhaps an error would have been found in the agreement. Or perhaps I would have discovered that Mayfield had already repaid me and I hadn't been informed because of an inefficient underling." He shrugged. "I wouldn't have kept Hazelhurst," he said again.

"Do you expect me to believe you?" Charity asked.

"My dear, you can believe what you like," he replied tartly. He'd finished abasing himself. "Would you care for some more tea?"

"No, thank you." Charity frowned slightly; she didn't understand the Earl.

Lord Ashbourne turned to Jack.

"I was surprised to see you involved in this business, Riversleigh," he said. "But I recall now, you have land in Sussex, have you not?"

"Hazelhurst and Riversleigh share a common boundary," Jack replied. "Naturally I'm delighted to assist Miss Mayfield in this matter in any way I can."

"Naturally." The Earl smiled faintly. "I trust Ralph was equally gratified to renew his acquaintance with *you?*"

"Not demonstrably," Jack replied.

"You surprise me. Where is he?"

"In the custody of Sir Humphrey Leydon. He believes you'll use your influence on his behalf."

"Does he?" The Earl's expression was inscrutable. "I wonder why?"

"To avoid a scandal," Jack suggested.

He was more relaxed now. They had already discovered most of what they wished to know, and there were only two more matters he wanted to raise. He had no interest in what the Earl decided to do about his nephew.

"To avoid a scandal," the Earl repeated. "In the circumstances, it seems an inadequate reason. It's a pity you didn't kill him, Riversleigh. Think how much trouble you would have saved everyone."

"How did you know they'd fought?" Charity demanded, suddenly re-entering the conversation.

"I didn't," said the Earl calmly. "But in view of their last meeting…"

"Of more interest to me," said Jack, who had no desire to discuss the past, "is how the pendant came to be in the library in the first place. And how you found out about it."

"Yes, I imagine you would like to know that," said

Lord Ashbourne. "Is it beautiful, Riversleigh? Was it worth all that abortive trouble I took?"

"It is beautiful," said Jack quietly. "But I don't think it's worth the distress it's caused. No inanimate object is worth so much pain."

There was an edge to his voice, and Charity looked up at him quickly—but Jack was looking at the Earl.

"A predictable response," said Lord Ashbourne. "I have no desire to waste my time describing how I discovered the existence of a jewel which I failed to obtain possession of. If you're interested you can read its history for yourself in the Duke of Faversham's diary."

He walked across the room and unlocked a bureau with a key he took from his waistcoat pocket. There were a number of papers in the desk, but he ignored these, taking up instead two leather-bound volumes, which he put on the table in front of Charity.

"A present, my dear," he said. "You may read all about the origins of the pendant and how it came to be in your family at your leisure. There is just one other matter."

He returned to the bureau and locked it carefully before turning back to look at both Jack and Charity.

"The ownership of Hazelhurst," he said. "You have the pendant, my dear. And, by catching my nephew, Riversleigh has dragged my family into a very unpleasant scandal. In the circumstances, I think it only fair that I should recoup some of my losses. After all, your father—or his heirs—still owe me twenty thousand pounds."

Charity gasped.

"You said you didn't want Hazelhurst!" she exclaimed.

"I don't," said the Earl blandly. "I want the pendant. Of course, if you'd care to exchange possession of one for the other…but, failing that—" he'd seen the immediate refusal in Charity's eyes— "I'll settle either for ownership of Hazelhurst or for twenty thousand pounds. I'm sure Riversleigh will have no trouble in raising such a sum."

"You are despicable!" Charity burst out, her first reaction simply one of horror as she realised that Lord Ashbourne meant to enforce the debt.

Then she absorbed the implications of his last words and she began to feel angry instead. How *dared* he suggest that she would leave the management of her affairs in someone else's hands—or allow someone else to pay the debt for her?

"I am quite capable…" she began, and felt Jack put his hand on her shoulder "…of managing…" she continued.

Jack tightened his grasp imperatively, and she knew he wanted her to remain silent. In fact, he was *ordering* her to remain silent! The arrogance of it outraged her; nevertheless, she obeyed his unspoken command. Partly because she didn't want to quarrel with him in front of the Earl, and partly because she knew that, apart from righteous indignation, she herself had very little with which to counter the Earl's ultimatum.

Lord Ashbourne was looking at Jack and there was something curious, almost expectant in his expression.

"It would be no trouble at all to raise such a sum," said Jack pleasantly. "On the scale of things, twenty thousand pounds is hardly an enormous investment."

He dropped his hand from Charity's shoulder and moved to one side so that he faced the Earl with no barrier between them. He was quite at his ease—he seemed almost amused.

"I have often encountered men who will invest far more than that if they believe the returns will be high enough," he continued conversationally. "Of course, some ventures are more risky than others. I heard only this morning that Mark Horwood and Adam Kaye have finally found a third investor for their East Indian venture. It must have been a great relief to my friend Horwood. They've been held up for weeks because Adam Kaye is so particular about who he'll do business with. I hope nothing goes wrong for them this time. I'm sure you share my hope."

Jack smiled blandly at Lord Ashbourne, and the Earl looked back, an unreadable glint in his eye.

Then he unlocked the bureau once more and took out one of the documents it contained.

As Charity watched, quite bemused, he wrote quickly on the paper, dusted it with sand, and handed it to Jack.

"Satisfied, my lord?" he asked softly.

"I think so." Jack scanned the paper quickly. "Yes, definitely."

He passed the document to Charity and she saw with bewilderment that the debt had been cancelled. For some reason which she didn't understand, Lord Ashbourne had suddenly renounced all claim to both Hazelhurst and the twenty thousand pounds.

"Well," Jack turned back to the Earl, "that seems to settle things nicely. I don't believe we need take up any more of your time, my lord. Thank you."

"It's always a pleasure to do business with you," Lord Ashbourne replied, inclining his head ironically.

Jack smiled, and picked up the two volumes of the diary that Lord Ashbourne had given to Charity.

"Shall we go?" he asked her quietly.

They completed the journey back to the Riversleighs' house in almost complete silence. A great deal had happened in a very short space of time, and Charity was still trying to make sense of it. She didn't know what she had been expecting the Earl to be like, or what she had expected him to do, but nothing in her imaginings had prepared her for such an outcome to their meeting.

Jack sensed her preoccupation and made no attempt to intrude upon it. Charity had been anticipating disaster for so long that he thought she probably needed time to come to terms with the fact that the whole unhappy business was finally finished with. Soon she would realise that Hazelhurst was hers once more, and then they would be able to get on with their lives. He still had one very important question to ask her.

He took her into the drawing-room on their return, and Charity went immediately to sit by the fire, perched on the edge of her seat, her hands clasped tensely in her lap.

Jack glanced at her, frowning slightly; he didn't entirely understand her mood. He was about to speak to her, then thought better of it and opened the diaries Lord Ashbourne had given them instead. He meant to see if he could find the passage explaining the presence of the pendant so that he could read it to Charity.

He flipped through a few pages in growing bewilderment then, as understanding dawned, he closed the book and started to laugh.

"What is it?" Charity demanded, looking up at him with an almost hostile expression in her eyes.

"Do you remember Gideon told us he'd found *notes* his uncle had made on the diary?" Jack asked, still obviously amused by something. "I should have remembered that. There was a reason—the diary itself is written in a sort of code. Quite unintelligible unless you know the key."

"*What?*" Charity leapt to her feet and went to look. "How can you laugh?" she exclaimed when she saw he was right. "It's not funny."

"It is in a way," said Jack. "The Earl isn't the man to allow himself to be outmanoeuvred on every account."

"You *like* him, don't you?" Charity demanded, her pent-up feelings finding an outlet in the accusation. "After everything he's done, you *like* him! Perhaps you even *admire* him!"

"No." The humour had died out of Jack's eyes. "I don't like him, and I don't admire him either—the Earl is not an admirable man. But I do respect him."

"*Respect* him! More than you respect me, it appears!" Charity's eyes flashed indignantly. The anger she had been feeling ever since he had bidden her to silence in Lord Ashbourne's house over-flowed, and now she hardly stopped to consider what she was saying.

"You certainly seemed quite happy to do business with him, regardless of my wishes on the matter," she said hotly. "How *dare* you interfere in my affairs? How *dare* you pay my debts for me? You had no right!"

"No right?" Jack tossed the diary down on to the table with a thud as he, too, finally lost his temper.

"How dare you talk of rights to *me?*" he said, his voice throbbing with anger. He thought he'd been very patient, but now he was thoroughly roused by what he considered to be her unreasonableness.

"In the past two days you've judged me and condemned me for actions which you don't understand, and without once asking me to explain why I've done what I have," he said, his anger no less terrible because it was tightly controlled. "I've been very patient—I know things have been hard for you— but after all my efforts on your behalf I'm damned if I'll stand here and have my generosity flung back in my face! You've got Hazelhurst *back.* That's what you wanted, isn't it? Whatever your feelings about me, you might have the grace to show a little gratitude."

"Why should I be grateful?" Charity blazed back, all the anger she had felt at her father and Lord Ashbourne finding an outlet in her quarrel with Jack. "I never asked for your help. I never asked for you to step forward in that lordly manner and take over as if you were some kind of king or god. Hazelhurst belonged to my family; it was ours to keep or lose. My father wouldn't have wanted you to give it back to him in that charitably gracious manner—and nor do I!"

Her heart was pounding and she was breathing very quickly, but she met Jack's eyes squarely. Part of her was horrified at what she had done and afraid of Jack's reaction—but on the whole she was too furious to care what he said.

Whatever else he might or might not have done, he had had no right to take over the management of her affairs without even consulting her. It was obvious to Charity that he must have known even before they had arrived at Lord Ashbourne's house how he would deal with the Earl's threat to keep Hazelhurst, yet he hadn't once mentioned the matter to her.

"Hazelhurst is not yours to refuse," said Jack coldly, though his eyes sparked dangerously. "It belongs to your mother. But there is certainly no reason why it should remain in your family if you don't want it—you may transfer its ownership into my name. After all, the fact that I was not obliged to spend any money does not alter the fact that I was instrumental in wiping out the debt which preserved the property from Lord Ashbourne."

"Give it to you?" Charity gasped, paling.

"Certainly." The heat had gone out of Jack's anger, but there was no softening in his expression as he met Charity's eyes. "It would make a very useful addition to the Riversleigh estate," he said. "And I hate to think I'd done anything to offend the obviously inordinate family pride of the Mayfields! No doubt it would be possible for you to have the tenancy of the place. Would you like to come into my study so that we can discuss the arrangements?" He began to move towards the door as he spoke.

"I'm not going to be your *tenant!*" Charity was starting to feel confused and, in her bewilderment, she clung to her anger rather like a losing gambler clung to the cards that were failing him. "Is *this* the way you made your fortune?" she demanded, trying to turn the argument back on to Jack.

"No," he said, looking at her sardonically. "It's not often I end the morning twenty thousand pounds richer than I began it in exchange for absolutely nothing— or for no more than the price of a little gossip. You accused me of being arrogant, Charity; I dare say you're right, but in your own way so are you."

She stood quite still, staring at him almost as if she had been petrified. She tried to rekindle her anger, but it was gone. She was alone in the middle of the room. He was still standing there, still watching her, but he had gone beyond her reach. She had driven him away. She still didn't understand him, but she had denied him the opportunity to explain before, and now she didn't know if he ever would.

He was looking at her coldly; there was no warmth in his eyes, no softening. There was so much she wanted to ask him—but it was too late.

A servant came softly into the room and hesitated, sensing the tension.

"Yes, James?" said Jack without turning his head.

"Mr Sedgewick wishes to speak to you, sir," said the servant respectfully. "He says it's urgent."

"Tell him to wait," said Jack curtly.

"No, don't," said Charity. "I'm sure you should speak to him now."

She smiled uncertainly, but she was glad of the interruption; she was too confused, she needed more time to think.

"Very well," said Jack after a moment. "Where is he, James?"

"In the book-room, sir."

"Thank you." Jack glanced once more at Charity, then he left the drawing-room quickly, closing the door quietly behind him.

Chapter Eighteen

Charity let out her breath in a long, shaky sigh and sat down limply at the table, dropping her head into her hands. She couldn't remember ever having felt more confused or more miserable in her whole life.

She loved Jack. For two days she had been trying to pretend that she didn't care, that everything she had felt when she was in his arms meant nothing—but she knew now that she had been deceiving herself. She loved him, whatever he'd done and whatever he was. To be at odds with him was the worst fate she could imagine—yet she still didn't understand him.

Less than five minutes ago she had condemned him for his arrogance, but she knew that the real cause of her distress wasn't his high-handedness—it was her underlying fear that in some strange way he shared Lord Ashbourne's peculiar code of honour. She had once accused him of defending Lord

Ashbourne and, although she was now certain that the two men were not friends, she still couldn't blind herself to the fact that Jack had openly admitted to respecting the Earl.

Was that all, or did he also emulate the Earl's methods? She didn't know exactly how Jack had persuaded Lord Ashbourne to give up Hazelhurst, but she knew no money had changed hands, and she was fairly sure that the Earl had been blackmailed in some way. Did Jack always use such methods? What kind of man had she fallen in love with?

She lifted her head from her hands and, in a vain attempt to distract herself, she began randomly to turn over the unreadable pages of the Duke of Faversham's diary. For a moment she almost thought of trying to decode it herself, but she didn't really care what was in it. It wasn't the past that interested her—it was the future.

She stood up restlessly and took a turn about the room, wondering what she should do now. It was raining outside, a bleak February day, in tune with her mood. She wanted to go out, but there was nowhere to go. She had nothing to read and nothing to do.

Then she heard voices in the hall outside, exclaiming against the damp, and in a moment or two Mrs Riversleigh came briskly into the room.

"Miss Mayfield, back already!" Mrs Riversleigh exclaimed. "I hope you missed the worst of the rain.

Fanny was caught out in it and got quite drenched. She's had to go up and change."

"We were back before it started," Charity said, smiling with something of an effort. "I hope your trip was successful."

Mrs Riversleigh and Fanny had been shopping.

"I'm glad to say we got most of what we went for," Mrs Riversleigh replied. "I do *not* enjoy shopping, particularly in February, but we both needed new gowns. What about you—has your morning been successful?"

She glanced shrewdly at Charity as she spoke, then turned her attention to warming her hands at the fire.

She hadn't failed to notice the slightly distracted look in Charity's eyes and she was afraid that the interview with Lord Ashbourne must have gone badly.

"Successful?" Charity repeated distantly.

She was thinking of her quarrel with Jack—there was nothing to boast of in that. But then she cast her mind further back to the meeting with Lord Ashbourne, and it suddenly occurred to her that it had indeed been a successful morning.

Hazelhurst was hers again!

Before Mrs Riversleigh's surprised eyes Charity suddenly seemed to lighten up. The dejected young woman of thirty seconds ago vanished, to be replaced by a glowing girl who could hardly prevent herself from dancing around the room in her excitement.

"Yes!" she cried, stretching out her arms in her delight. "I've got Hazelhurst back! I've got Hazelhurst *back!* I don't know why, but until this moment I never really...I'm sorry." She stopped in mid-sentence and looked at Mrs Riversleigh contritely. "You don't even know what I'm talking about."

Mrs Riversleigh smiled. "It doesn't matter," she said. "I'm just pleased to see you so happy. You looked so sad last night that I was worried about you—I know Jack was too."

"Jack?" Charity looked at Mrs Riversleigh quickly, almost doubtfully.

"Of course," said Mrs Riversleigh calmly. "Now, tell me about Hazelhurst. Is that your home? How did it come about that you had to get it back?"

"My father used it to secure a debt," said Charity, and without more ado she told Mrs Riversleigh the whole story.

"Good heavens!" Mrs Riversleigh exclaimed when Charity had finished. "What a terrible business. No wonder you looked so haunted last night. But you seem to have dealt with it all very well. Your mother must be proud of you."

"She doesn't know much about it," Charity admitted. "I couldn't bring myself to tell her. I'll have to, of course, but I just couldn't face... The last year has been very difficult for her," she added quickly, in case it sounded as if she was criticising Mrs Mayfield.

"Yes, I remember how hard it was when my husband died," said Mrs Riversleigh quietly. "I'm sure you must have been a great comfort to her. I know how much I relied on Jack in that first, difficult year. He was only thirteen, and of course my father was still alive then, but Jack still insisted on taking on many of my husband's responsibilities."

"You must be very proud of him," said Charity softly.

It was clear to her that, whatever methods Jack might adopt when he was dealing with outsiders, he would never let down those he cared for. But then, hadn't she always known that? Why else had she been able to accuse him of collusion with the Earl in one breath and in the next accept his escort to London?

Mrs Riversleigh smiled.

"Yes, I am," she said. "But he hates it if he thinks I've been praising him to others, so perhaps I'd better not say any more. Tell me instead, what do you mean to do, now that you've got Hazelhurst back?"

"Do?" Charity blinked at her hostess.

Mrs Riversleigh's brief comments about Jack had given her a great deal to think about, but it would be rude to appear distracted when her hostess had been so kind.

"I suppose I'll put into practice all those plans I thought I'd have to abandon," she said slowly. "We've increased our yield quite considerably over the last few years and I have hopes that, with…" she stopped, smiling. "I'm sure you're not really interested in such things," she said guiltily. "I know I can become quite boring on the subject if I have even half an opportunity."

"I'm not bored," said Mrs Riversleigh, encouraging Charity to continue. It was true that she wasn't particularly interested in the best time to plant wheat in the Weald, but she was fascinated by Charity's obvious knowledge and enthusiasm.

It wasn't often that Charity was given such an opportunity to talk about something which was so close to her heart and, despite her preoccupation, she soon found herself describing some of the innovations she had introduced.

"Of course," she said at one point, "things don't always happen as I intend. Even Sam Burden has a tendency to prefer the old ways, and our other tenant, and many of the farm-workers, are completely resistant to change. But I usually get what I want in the end."

"How?" asked Mrs Riversleigh curiously.

Charity laughed mischievously. "On at least one occasion by proposing an enormous change I didn't want at all," she said. "By the time Sam had managed to persuade me it wasn't a good idea he was so grateful that he agreed to make the change I *really* wanted as a concession to sweeten my defeat on the larger issue." She smiled reminiscently. "I suppose I should feel guilty about my underhand methods," she continued, "but I know for a fact he's done the same to me. It's almost…" Her voice trailed off.

"Almost what?" Mrs Riversleigh prompted her.

Charity was sitting still, staring into space as if she'd been stunned.

"Almost a game," she said distantly.

Jack wasn't like Lord Ashbourne! Why hadn't she seen it before? Of course he respected the Earl's cunning—only a fool underestimated his enemy. Perhaps he even found pleasure in outwitting Lord Ashbourne, as she had enjoyed outmanoeuvring Sam Burden. But he had never approved of the Earl's motives—or his methods.

For the first time she remembered the moment when Lord Ashbourne had asked whether the pendant had been worth all his trouble—and she could hear Jack's reply just as clearly and unambiguously as if he were speaking to her at that very moment.

"No inanimate object is worth so much pain."

She could even remember what the Earl had said next. "A predictable response." He had known Jack better than she had. She had been so wrong.

The revelation was blinding in its force. She leapt to her feet, forgetful of Mrs Riversleigh's presence in her urgency to speak to Jack.

She had to tell him that she did understand. She had to apologise for all her doubts, for her rudeness and her coldness—and she had to thank him for what he'd done for her.

She turned to the door, but she had taken no more than two steps towards it before it opened and a servant came in.

"His lordship's compliments, miss," he said respectfully to Charity. "And would you be kind enough to join him in the library?"

"Oh, yes!"

She picked up her skirts, almost as if she intended to run—and belatedly remembered Mrs Riversleigh.

"I'm sorry, do excuse me," she said incoherently, and left the room so quickly that her hostess had no chance to reply.

"Thank you, James." Mrs Riversleigh dismissed the footman and picked up her embroidery, smiling to herself.

"Jack!"

Charity burst through the library door, every bit as impetuously as she had once burst through the library door at Hazelhurst when she had thought it was Edward who was waiting for her.

And, just as she had on that occasion, she stopped short, uncertain of how to go on. Now she was in Jack's presence she felt shy and unsure of herself. He looked so stern. How could she ever explain she had been wrong?

He had indeed been looking unusually serious when she had opened the door, but now, at the sight of her breathless arrival, his expression softened.

"You never know what's going to be on the other side of the door, do you?" he said, and moved past her to close it.

She revolved slowly so that she could continue to look at him.

"I'm sorry I summoned you in such an arrogant manner," he said without irony, "but I wanted to speak to you alone. I should not—"

"Jack!" she interrupted. I..." She glanced up at him and saw that he was looking down at her intently. He was making her feel nervous, but she was determined to tell him what she had been thinking. "I came to thank you," she said simply. "And to tell you I'm sorry for all the dreadful things I said. I know they weren't true. You were right, I didn't understand, and I wouldn't let you explain. I'm sorry."

She looked up at him quite frankly, making no attempt to excuse herself, though in her eyes he could see her longing that he accept her apology.

"I wouldn't blame you if you're still angry with me," she said quietly when he didn't immediately reply. "I accused you of some terrible things. I even demanded the pendant back as if I thought you were a thief! And you still helped me. I don't deserve it,

I know, but I am grateful for everything, you've done—and for giving Hazelhurst back to me." She paused, but when he still didn't say anything she added rather desperately, "Please say something!"

For one more long minute Jack didn't reply, then he let out his breath in a long sigh and smiled crookedly at her.

"Do you always apologise so devastatingly?" he asked, and Charity could see the relief in his eyes.

"Oh, Jack," she said. "I was so unkind; I wish—"

"You don't have to apologise," he interrupted, taking her in his arms. "And you don't have to be grateful to me. I did what I thought was best, but you were right earlier—I didn't consult you, and I didn't explain."

"But I should have trusted you," Charity whispered. It would be a long time before she forgave herself for her doubts.

"I wonder," he said slowly.

He was still holding her, his hands resting lightly on her waist, but for the moment he made no move to draw her any closer.

"Perhaps I don't deserve your good opinion," he said at last. "Charity, I want you more than I've ever wanted anything in my life, but I can't offer myself to you under false pretences. Sooner or later you would know me for a fraud—and sooner or later I would hurt you. If you come to me it must be because you see me as I am—not as you would like me to be."

She looked up at him seriously. She could feel the tension in his arms, and see it in his expression—and she knew that, whatever it was he wanted to say to her, he wasn't finding it easy.

"What are you telling me, Jack?" she asked quietly.

"You made me angry when you accused me of liking—or even of admiring—the Earl," he answered steadily. "You came too close to the truth, you see. I don't like him—but I do like dealing with him. Owen and Sir Humphrey get their sport from chasing a fox through the fields; I get mine from pitting my wits against men like Ashbourne. I get less muddy, but in some ways I take more risks."

He sighed, gazing down into her luminous brown eyes. She was too honest and too forthright, and he wasn't sure if she would ever be able to understand him.

"I'm a devious man," he said. "Perhaps even more devious than the Earl, though my aims are different. I'm not proud of myself, but I can't change."

Charity tipped her head on one side. From her expression it was hard to tell what she was thinking.

"Did you blackmail Lord Ashbourne into giving me Hazelhurst?" she asked curiously, but without any particular suggestion of condemnation in her voice.

Jack hesitated.

"Yes," he said at last, rather reluctantly. He was afraid she would disapprove. "That is to say, I had information which I knew he would be very unwilling for me to repeat."

"That's not a proper explanation," said Charity firmly. "What information?"

"You heard me tell him that Horwood and Kaye had finally found a third investor?" Jack asked, wondering what she was thinking. He had never expected that she would be able to hide her thoughts so well. "Well, that's Ashbourne, although they don't know it," he continued, feeling very much as if he were on trial. "He's using an agent as usual, and if Adam Kaye finds out before he signs the final agreements he'll withdraw. He hates the Earl. But it should be a very profitable partnership—for all three men."

"What about poor Mr Kaye?" Charity asked, continuing her interrogation. "Shouldn't you warn him?"

"The Earl won't cheat his partners—he'll just taunt them for failing to discover his involvement. Besides, Kaye had just as much chance of finding out as I had—and I'm not responsible for protecting *his* interests," said Jack.

He might also have pointed out that Adam Kaye was both bigoted and unpopular, but he really was trying to avoid giving Charity a false impression of his character.

She gazed up at him thoughtfully, and for a moment he was afraid of what she would say—but then, at last, he saw the growing twinkle in her eyes.

"One day I must tell you how I persuaded Sir Humphrey to sell my father the five-acre field," she said reflectively. "I still don't think Sir Humphrey knows I had anything to do with it."

She began to laugh at his startled expression and looped her arms around his neck.

"We have more in common than you think," she murmured, stretching up to kiss him lightly on the chin.

For a moment longer he continued to stare down at her; then his expression relaxed.

"You little devil!" he exclaimed. "You…" Words failed him, and he silenced her laughter with his kiss.

There had been so much doubt and so much misunderstanding that it was bliss for Charity to feel his arms around her again, and to taste his lips on hers. He was holding her to him fiercely, possessively, as if he never intended to release her again, and she surrendered joyously to his embrace.

"You're quite shameless!" he murmured, brushing his lips against her hair. "There I was, laying my soul bare to you, fearing at any second your disapproval or rejection—and all the time you were laughing at me!"

"I wasn't!" She lifted her head indignantly. "But I thought I'd better find out everything I wanted to know before I told you how I felt. I might not have remembered to ask later."

Her indignation dissolved into a wickedly tantalising smile, and she ran her finger lightly along the line of his jaw.

"No, I don't think that's exactly what you thought," he replied, an answering gleam of humour in his grey eyes. "Are you sure you weren't getting your own back for my arrogance earlier?"

She shook her head, setting her dark curls dancing.

"No," she said quietly. "I finally understood how you must feel about Lord Ashbourne just before I came to see you. That's what I was so anxious to tell you—that I *did* understand how it was possible for you to respect him. But when you started to explain…my good opinion seemed to mean so much to you—and *that* meant so much to *me*."

Jack gazed down at her, wonder and love in his eyes.

"Charity…" he began, but there were no words to describe what he was feeling. "I love you," he said simply.

Her hands were resting on his shoulders, and he took one in his own hand, kissing it almost reverently, then turned it over, kissing her palm, and the deep lace ruffles of her sleeve fell back to above the elbow. His lips followed, caressing the soft skin of her inner arm, tantalising, soothing and exciting her.

She sighed and leant against him, weak with desire and pleasure as she felt him kiss her throat. Then he bent lower, his lips teasing and exciting her as he pushed down the lace of her bodice and kissed the hollow between her breasts.

She caught her breath and clung to him, longing to feel him even closer.

Jack lifted his head and looked down at her; with one arm he was supporting her, with the other hand he started to stroke the nape of her neck. A ripple of pure delight coursed through her and she leant back against his arm, her dark eyes languid with love and desire.

"Did you speak to Owen?" he asked quietly.

"Mmm? Oh, yes," she said, only half listening, and admiring the straight line of his nose.

"What did he say?"

"Who?"

"Owen!" Jack began to laugh softly, his customary good humour completely restored. "Do concentrate, Charity! I'm about to propose to you. Mind you," he added thoughtfully as he saw that she was still not giving his *words* her full attention, "you do seem to make a habit of letting your thoughts wander at crucial moments like this. In the circumstances, perhaps it would be better if…"

Instead of completing what he was saying he suddenly swept her up in his arms and glanced quickly round the room.

"Jack!" she exclaimed. "What on earth…?"

"I'm not having you wriggle out of this betrothal on the grounds that you didn't understand what I was asking until it was too late!" he declared, and carried her over to a chair.

"There, sit here, and pay careful attention to what I'm about to say to you," he said firmly, stepping back and looking down at her. "And while you're about it you can confirm that you really have told Owen you're not going to marry him."

"Of course I have." She folded her arms demurely in her lap and laughed up at him.

"Good. Now, then, Miss Mayfield—" he began briskly, only the faintest twitch of his lips indicating his own amusement.

"You mean you're not going to get down on your knees?" she interrupted in a disappointed voice.

Jack paused and appeared to think about it. "One knee, if you insist," he said at last. "Both knees—definitely not. Most undignified."

"Oh, I beg your pardon. It was a slip of the tongue. Of course I only meant one knee," she replied graciously.

Jack grinned. "In that case..." he began, but before he could continue the door opened and a servant came in.

"A letter for the lady, my lord," said James discreetly. "No reply is expected."

"Thank you," said Jack calmly. "Leave it on the table, please."

He waited until the footman had turned to go, and

then he raised his eyebrow at Charity, who had suddenly been overcome with amusement.

"I'm sorry," she gasped as the door closed behind James, "but I was just imagining…"

"I dare say," said Jack austerely, going to pick up the letter, "but such merriment—" He broke off abruptly, his eyes narrowing as he read the direction on the outside.

"What is it?" Charity asked.

"I'm not sure," he replied slowly. "But I think you'd better open it." He passed it to her and watched her changing expressions as she read it.

My dear Miss Mayfield,

No doubt you will be surprised to receive a letter from me; no doubt, also, you will be sceptical of the contents. I would be disappointed in you if it were otherwise. As I said when we met, you are very like your father in your courage and your composure, but in one respect at least you are immeasurably his superior. If Mayfield had been blessed with your wit, and your clear-sightedness, I would feel less guilt for what I did a year ago. But Mayfield was not my opponent— he was my dupe. A brave, heroic, generous dupe. I will avoid such men in future—they make me uncomfortable.

But you, my dear, are different. I have no doubt

that we shall meet again, and when we do I want no unfinished business lying between us. I fear I'll need all my wits to survive that encounter—and guilt is a bad companion.

So...I enclose the key to decoding the Duke's diaries and, to appease your immediate curiosity and to save you the need to read through the entire two volumes, I also enclose a brief resumé of the pendant's history. Thus I feel I have discharged my obligations to you—and to Riversleigh.

Until our next meeting, I remain,

your faithful servant,
Justin Ashbourne.

By the time Charity had finished the letter she was a prey to so many conflicting emotions that she didn't know what to say. She handed it to Jack without a word and waited for him to speak.

"The man's incorrigible!" he exclaimed as he came to the end.

He glanced at Charity to see what she was thinking.

"He didn't want Hazelhurst, you know," he added more quietly. "By the time you went to see him I think his conscience had given him a lot of trouble. All he wanted was the opportunity *not* to take it—and he was expecting me to give it to him."

"So you did," said Charity, smiling at him. "I

suppose he would have felt as if he was losing face if he'd just given it back to me."

"I think so," said Jack. "What does he say about the pendant?"

Charity scanned the second sheet quickly.

"It's a portrait of the fifth Duchess of Faversham, painted just after her marriage in 1578," she said at last, paraphrasing Lord Ashbourne's more elegant sentences. "It was given by her son, the sixth Duke—the one who wrote the diary—to Thomas Mayfield in 1639 as a reward for his extraordinary loyalty to the Duke's son. Of course!" she interrupted herself. "Thomas was the man who built Hazelhurst. I wonder if he actually built the house to hide the pendant?"

"That was always a strong possibility," Jack agreed, not at all surprised at what she'd told him. "I've suspected from the first that Thomas must have had something to do with it. You never did see where the jewel was hidden, but it certainly seemed to me that the hiding-place was an integral part of the house, and you told me on our very first meeting that Thomas had built it. You also told me that he'd died fighting in the Civil War only a few years later, and that might have been when the knowledge of the jewel was lost to your family. What's the matter?"

Charity was staring at him in amazement.

"You mean you guessed all that the minute you found the pendant?" she exclaimed.

"Not immediately," he said apologetically as he realised that she wasn't entirely pleased. "But you must admit, the man who built the house did have the best opportunity for installing such an elaborate hiding-place. Anyway, I still don't know why he was given the jewel. I'm waiting for you to enlighten me."

"But why didn't you tell me?" Charity demanded, ignoring the last part of his comment, and obviously feeling torn between admiration and annoyance. "And, now I come to think about it, this isn't the first time you haven't told me all you know."

"Yes, I'm very sorry," said Jack hastily, because he didn't want to be side-tracked into an argument. "I won't do it again. But you must admit, I didn't have much opportunity to tell you—besides, it was really only supposition. Until the Earl sent you that letter there was nothing to confirm my suspicions. Now, are you going to tell me why the Duke gave Thomas the pendant?"

Charity looked at him consideringly for a moment, as if debating whether he deserved to be told, but then she glanced back at the letter.

"Well," she said slowly, "according to Lord Ashbourne's interpretation of the diary, the Duke's son was not entirely...sane. He suffered from periods of great melancholy, interspersed with periods of frenzied activity. He must have caused his father great distress and eventually Thomas was the only loyal friend he had left. In the end, there was a fire in which the Duke's son died and, because the Duke's only surviving heir was a nephew he didn't like, he gave the pendant to Thomas instead. Thomas must have told him of the hiding-place he'd devised for it, and the Duke wrote that down in his diary too."

"Very careless," Jack commented. "To write it down, I mean. But I dare say he didn't think anyone would be able to read what he'd written, or that the knowledge of the pendant, would be lost to your family. If the knowledge hadn't been lost, of course, your father would probably have guessed what Lord Ashbourne was trying to do, and none of this would have happened. The only question now is how the Earl came to have possession of the diary, but I dare say that's one thing he'll never tell us."

"No," said Charity slowly. "You know, it's just occurred to me that if it hadn't been for Lord Ashbourne—and Gideon, especially Gideon—we would never have known about the pendant. So at least one good thing has come out of this whole business."

"Only one?" Jack asked, taking her back into his arms.

Charity looked puzzled, and then she laughed.

"Lord Ashbourne didn't have anything to do with you inheriting Riversleigh," she pointed out. "And if you hadn't we would probably never have met."

"True," said Jack. "And that reminds me of something far more important. In less than two weeks' time you are going to owe me ten guineas! I hope you don't intend to renege on our bargain!"

For a moment Charity stared at him in confusion, then realised that he was talking about their wager.

"But I am *betrothed*," she protested half-heartedly.

"Not sufficient. As I recall, the wager was specifically as to whether you would be *married* by the end of February," Jack pointed out.

"Oh, dear." Charity gazed at him helplessly for a moment; then she started to laugh as she remembered something. "I haven't actually got any money," she said. "I was so preoccupied when we left Sussex that I never thought to bring any. Will you take an IOU?"

"If you wish, but are you sure you can't think of a better solution to the problem than that?" Jack asked, wickedly teasing her with his eyes. "I'm sure Lord Ashbourne would be disappointed in you."

"I don't... We couldn't!" Charity gasped as enlightenment suddenly dawned. "We *can't* get married in such a rush. What will everybody say?"

"Congratulations?" Jack suggested. "I'm sure your mother will be delighted. She's been viewing me as a prospective son-in-law ever since we met."

"Mama has?" Charity exclaimed. "She never said anything."

"No, it's a constant source of amazement to me that such a tactful woman could have produced such an outspoken daughter," said Jack, his eyes gleaming humorously as he saw the sudden flare of indignation in hers. "I do not, however, feel this is the moment to discuss your mother."

He smiled down at her and she felt her heart turn over.

"Are you, or are you not going to consent to win ten guineas from me?" he asked.

Charity gazed up at him consideringly for perhaps three seconds, then an answering smile lit her face.

"I would be delighted to do so," she replied.

* * * * *